Th

Mirror Pond
Murders

A Northwest Murder Mystery

Ted Haynes

ISBN 978-0-9646506-8-8
Library of Congress Control Number: 2018915226

Book Design by Jim Bisakowski of BookDesign.ca

The Robleda Company, Publishers
1259 El Camino Real Ste. 2720
Menlo Park, CA 94025

www.robledabooks.com

For Joan

Contents

Chapter 1

Jim

B end, Oregon, is a north-south town. To the west you hit the Cascade Mountains. To the east you run into two hundred miles of sagebrush and rock. The main highway through town, US 97, runs north-south, as does the railroad. The Deschutes River comes from the south and runs north through the city on its long trip to the Columbia. Bend was a lumber town until they cut all the trees there were to cut. Now it's a tourist destination for people escaping the rain in Portland and Seattle. Or skiing on Mount Bachelor in the winter. It has a smattering of tech companies and other businesses and a hospital that serves a hundred-mile radius.

Mirror Pond lies long and narrow near Bend's old downtown. There's Drake Park on the east side and private homes on the west. The pond runs north-south like everything else but with two right-angle turns in the middle of it. The Deschutes River formed Mirror Pond when Bend's first power company dammed the river back in 1910.

The city has been talking about dredging Mirror Pond for years. With all the silt that's built up it's on its way to becoming a mudflat. So in July of 2017 the town hired a company to dredge up samples of the bottom to see what they were dealing with. Could they sell the muck to someone or would they have to pay somebody to get rid of it?

Which is how a skull wound up on my desk at the Bend Police Department in a wet paper bag with two oily rags at the bottom of it. It was dirty but not caked with mud. The workers had probably dunked it in the pond once or twice when they brought it up. It was on the small side I thought.

"The chief told me to give this to you," said the patrolman who brought it in.

"Are they still bringing up stuff from that area or have they stopped?" I asked.

"They stopped," he said. "They moved to the other end of the pond."

Police headquarters was a mile and a half east of Mirror Pond and just south of Pilot Butte, where the city launched fireworks every Fourth of July. The headquarters building was two-story except for a tower in the middle with a third floor that had continuous windows all around it. You could see the whole city from up there, except the part behind the butte. The tower was designed to look something like a fire lookout but many, particularly people who had seen a lot of them, thought it looked like a guard tower in a prison.

It had taken me years to get an office in the top room of the tower. The height, the view, and the light meant a lot to my productivity and my general attitude. I hadn't told that to anyone specifically. I was moderately claustrophobic and I hadn't told anyone about that either except my wife. I could tough it out in small spaces if I had to but I got anxious and my judgment went to hell. People thought I climbed the stairs to my office for my health. I just didn't like taking the windowless elevator. The skull on my desk gave me the willies. Not because it was a skull but because I couldn't help thinking of it lying at the bottom of the pond under all that water. I could swim all right but diving or swimming underwater upset my equilibrium as much as searching through a crawl space with a flashlight.

I assigned a case number and started a file. Just a sentence stating when the skull had been found and the name of the company that found it. I checked in with the dredging company office. The crew would stop work at five p.m. and I could meet the foreman on the shore where they'd parked their truck. I wasn't about to go stand on the bank before then, waving my arms trying to get the crew to stop work before five and come talk to me. They had their job to do and I had mine.

The chief had a bigger office than mine with a bigger window looking toward the mountains, the same view I had. He had a thicker and bluer carpet and three leather visitor chairs to my single wooden one. He didn't really like meetings and he always had papers stacked on the chairs so people couldn't sit down. The upside was, as long as you kept it short, you could usually walk into his office, ask a question, get an answer that he would remember giving you, and walk out to get on with your job. This time I asked him how much effort he wanted to spend investigating the skull. At the moment we didn't know whose it was or how it got in the water. It could have been an accident just as well as a crime. We didn't know how long it had been there. It seemed quite likely we would never figure this out, much less arrest and convict anyone.

"Once the public knows about the skull, they'll want to know what happened," said the chief, "more curiosity than a desire for justice. They've watched *Bones* and *CSI* and think we can figure out anything if we just try hard enough. Do what you can and we'll see where we are in a few days."

"We'll need to bring up the skeleton," I said, "assuming it's there, and whatever goes with it. We'll need divers with forensic experience and a dredge of some kind. That will cost money."

"See if you can get Public Works to take it out of the pond-dredging project. Keep the ball rolling for now but don't make it urgent. Whatever's down there has been there a while. It can wait."

The chief was right. It wasn't as though we had a hot lead we had to follow up. We weren't going to solve this murder, if it was a murder, in forty-eight hours. If we ever solved it at all. But there was a story behind that skull and I couldn't help feeling there was someone out there who knew what that story was.

Before I talked with the dredging crew there was time to see what the county medical examiner could tell me. Bend wasn't big enough to have its own medical examiner so Kristen Valle served all of Deschutes County, from Sisters in the northwest corner to Brothers in the southeast. I called ahead because she was out of the office all the time, going to accidents, suicides, overdoses, and murders— any death that was unusual or suspicious. Kristen had been a nurse before she trained to be a medical examiner. Parts of her current job were gruesome or sad but she had the stomach for it. And parts of her job were plain bureaucracy, as were parts of mine. The secret we shared, as professionals, was that a puzzling murder was a lot more interesting than a car crash or a drug overdose. Murders challenged us, brought us to the top of our game. We didn't tell people this. Murders were not happy events.

Kristen's office was eight minutes away in a county office building behind St. Charles Hospital. I put the bag with the skull in it gently on a metal trolley in her office, the trolley being the only thing there that wouldn't have shown up in dozens of other county offices. It wasn't an examining room. No fresh bodies ever came there. Kristen went to them.

"Tell me what you can," I said. Kristen, a petite redhead with quick movements, put latex gloves on and picked the skull out of the bag like you'd take out a jar of pickles you'd brought home from the market. She put it on her desk and sat down to look at it. After a once-over she picked up a magnifying glass and looked again, specifically at the roof of the mouth. The jaw was missing.

"It's a girl, probably fifteen or sixteen," Kristen said.

"How long has she been down there?"

"At least a year, probably longer," said Kristen. "If she was buried in the mud at the bottom she could have been there a hundred years or more. If she had dental work I would have a better idea, based on the technology they used. But her teeth are untouched."

"Not very helpful," I said, as a comment, not as a complaint.

"One thing, though," said Kristen, "she may very well be Indian. We'll never be sure but she has some traits that suggest it."

"Such as?"

"Individual differences are greater than racial differences. And racial identification from skulls and skeletons is uncertain. But her teeth curve inward at the back of her mouth and that tends to be more common in American Indians and Asians than in Europeans. If we got some DNA out of her we'd know better but I'd say there's a good chance she's an Indian."

"Or Chinese," I said following Kristen's logic. If the girl were American Indian this was going to get more complicated, totally aside from whether she was murdered.

"Could be Asian," said Kristen, "but how many Asians have there ever been in Central Oregon? Not many."

"So with these characteristics, in this area, she's probably Indian, right?" I asked.

"Likely," said Kristen.

"Anything on cause of death?"

"Nothing I can see," she said, "no trauma to the skull. If you want to have a shot at cause of death you need the rest of the skeleton. We'll need to send everything over to Clackamas for a real autopsy." Clackamas, near Portland, was where the state had the staff and facilities the local MEs couldn't afford. All the medical examiners in the state sent their corpses there. It was one hundred and fifty miles from Bend and Kristen's biggest expense was shipping the bodies over the mountains. They hired a local funeral home to do it.

"At least it won't cost much to ship this one," Kristen said. "It's past needing refrigeration and I can put it in with the next corpse."

When I got back to my office there was a voicemail from Fred Karlsen, the chief detective when I joined the force years ago. We'd never worked together but we knew each other.

"I've got an idea about that skull you found," said the gravelly voice on the voicemail. "Call me." Once word got out I'd get lots of calls from people who had ideas about the case. I wasn't going to leap on any of them until we got the autopsy and hopefully made more sense of the detritus we found with the skull. But I wanted to hear what Karlsen had to say. At least he'd be professional about it.

THE MIRROR POND MURDERS

I looked out my window at the snow-capped mountains as we talked. They were twenty-five miles away against a clear blue sky. I'd much rather look at all that space than down at the top of my file-covered desk.

"Before your time," said Karlsen, "there was another girl murdered at Mirror Pond. Never figured out who killed her. But you might want to keep an eye out for a connection."

"I'm not even sure this girl was murdered," I said. "But tell me about the one who was."

"Sharon Forrester. Local Bend girl. High school senior. Elected homecoming princess. Member of the 4-H club and a good rider. Good student but she had a dark side. She took to drinking in bars and hanging out with grifters. She was seventeen and some of the men were a good deal older. This was in 1962 after the Shevlin-Hixon lumber mill closed and Brooks-Scanlon was cutting back as well. It wasn't a good time in Bend. Anyhow, she left her car next to Drake Park one cold February night and walked out over the snow. We think she was meeting someone. Whoever she did meet beat her over the head, looked like it could have been a two-by-four. Then he dragged her, or she dragged herself, over to Mirror Pond and onto the ice by the pedestrian bridge that crosses the middle of the pond. Some kids found her the next day. If the girl you found was in deeper water it might be the same guy and he got smarter."

"Any suspects?"

"Nobody stood out. I put together a list of the people who she hung out with or knew her. But it was sketchy. There were people from her high school that wouldn't hurt a flea and no-goods from bars where all I got was a first name. And then some guys who left town never to be seen again. Nobody knew where they came from in the first place. It was a bad news case from the beginning because a lot of Bend police, state police, and sheriff's deputies knew Sharon from drunk driving, disturbing the peace, and other arrests. Usually it wasn't Sharon who got arrested but the people she was with. The police didn't want to arrest her because they kind of hoped she would turn her life around. She was young and beautiful and people liked her. The police arrested her buddies to protect Sharon as much as anything else. Some guys on the force would pass on arresting her because they thought they were special friends of hers. I think nowadays they call it 'friends with benefits.' I could see these guys had trouble talking with me. They knew their duty and they did want to help find the killer. But they didn't like talking about how well they knew Sharon.

"The funniest thing about the case, though, was the men around town who just happened to be someplace they weren't supposed to be on the night she was killed. Didn't want anyone, especially their wives, asking them where they had been. Really had nothing to do with Sharon. It was hard not to laugh. We heard some mighty tall stories. Most of them straightened out when we told them it was a crime to lie to the police."

"So did you ever catch the perp?" I asked Karlsen.

"We thought we did. Guy named Dowling confessed to everything. Knew a lot about Sharon and the crime scene. Picked it up from the newspapers and bar gossip. Turned out he was in South Dakota at the time of the murder. The judge let him out of jail and put him in a mental institution. We had three other guys who looked likely but we didn't have enough to arrest them. I remember their names were Burrell Johnson, Joe Kuransky, and Gregory Ulen. Johnson died long ago but you might see if you can find what happened to the others."

"Did we get DNA?" I asked.

"Never did," Karlsen answered. "She wasn't raped."

I got to the downstream end of the pond at quarter to five on a beautiful July afternoon. The sun hadn't even begun to think about setting. At first glance Mirror Pond lives up to its name. Flat as glass and you can see the opposite shore reflected in the water. But look closer and you can see current tearing through the middle of the pond. It's more a long wide spot in a fast-flowing river than the still water of a natural pond. The dam at the bottom isn't very high but it is a wide dam and you can see the whole river pouring over it.

The dredgers had two rafts out. A small backhoe with a long arm sat on one of the rafts and a growing pile of mud sat on the other one. Every time the backhoe dumped a scoop on the pile, a worker would take a sample with a trowel, put it in a plastic box, write something on the box, and put it in a plastic bin. The two men wore sunglasses under hard hats with visors. It was bright out there on the pond. They had a rowboat tied to the mud raft and they rowed it to shore when they were done, leaving the two rafts where they were in the pond.

The foreman, Joe Bennett, turned out to be the backhoe operator. He was in his late fifties with gray hair, older than I was, and the only mud on him was on the soles of his boots. The other man had splashes of mud all the way up to the top of his yellow helmet. I told Joe I was surprised a man my age had done such hard work all day in the sun.

"It's my company," he said.

"You find any more skulls?" I asked.

"No skulls," he said. "Mostly mud. At the upstream end the river comes in fast and slows down when it gets to the pond. It drops whatever it's carrying. There's less junk down here at the downstream end."

Joe gave me the GPS coordinates of where they'd found the skull, under eight feet of water and one foot of earth. "The thalweg pretty much goes down the middle of the pond. The skull was just off it to one side."

"The thalweg?"

"The thalweg is a line connecting the deepest parts of the channel, in this case the channel from the upstream end of the pond to the downstream end. It should correspond pretty closely to the course of the river before the pond was created by the dam."

"Any ideas on how the skull got there or when?"

"If it was dumped in the river it's been there a while, with a foot of sediment building up on top of it. Can't say how long. Years. It might've been buried on the bank of the river before the pond existed. Usually people bury a body deeper than a foot but the river may have shifted and washed some of the dirt away."

"Could the body have washed down from upstream?"

"Sure, especially in the spring floods when the snow melts. But you're the detective. If this was a murder and the killer dumped the body in the water then he would have weighted it down and it would still be near where he dumped it. Otherwise it could float for weeks where somebody might see it." I knew all that. But it was good to hear it from a man who knew the underwater world better than I did.

It was important that the girl might be Indian. Kristen and I both knew Oregon state law ORS 97.745 made the difference. It said that anyone disturbing Native American remains had to rebury them in a way that the closest Indian tribe said was okay. Our closest Indians were the Confederated Tribes of Fort Rock. I'd never dealt with them before. They weren't that close to Bend and weren't even in Deschutes County.

The next morning I found a number for the tribal council down in Lake County and gave them a call. A woman answered with country-western music playing in the background. I introduced myself and asked if I could speak to someone about a body we'd found in Bend that we thought was Indian.

"I'll let you speak to Edgar Manning. He's the president. Hold on."

I only waited five seconds.

"Hello, Detective," the man said. "I hear you've found Kennewick Man's long-lost brother." Edgar sounded like a real-world man with a sense of humor. No matter how this came out he might be a good person to deal with.

Edgar knew the law on Indian remains as well as I did. Kennewick Man was an archeological find where there had been a debate about the law. The anthropologists said the man was European. That would be a big deal since the skeleton had been in place long before 1492. The scientists wanted to keep the skeleton while they examined it but the Indians insisted on their rights and they won in court.

"It's a girl," I said, "about fifteen or sixteen. We only have the skull so far and my ME says it looks like she's Indian. They found her at the bottom of Mirror Pond in Bend. We don't know yet how long she's been there or how she got there. It's not even clear that she is Indian but I wanted to notify and keep you informed of our investigation."

"You mean you'd like us to not make this difficult."

"You got it," I said. "We'd like that very much. We don't want this to blow up into something that gets tried in the press or in the courts."

"Sounds reasonable," said Edgar. "What are you planning on?"

"We want to bring up the rest of the skeleton and everything we find nearby. We want to explore the surrounding area underwater to see if this might be a burial ground. We'll get an autopsy on the skeleton, or skeletons if there are more of them, and give you a report on everything we find. If she's Indian, and you're welcome to help us decide that, you can have her to bury."

"What about DNA?"

"We may get to that, I think," I said. "But it can be hard to get enough DNA from the bones. The DNA may have deteriorated too much to be useful. The results of the tests may not be definitive. The analysis takes time and costs money. From what I've seen the state coroner's office will first try to learn as much as they can from the skeleton itself. Then we'll see about DNA. We're looking for you to be patient on this."

"Okay," said Edgar, "but you're not going to destroy the remains or bury them somewhere until we get an answer?"

"Right," I said.

"Fair enough. But I'm going to ask our lawyer to get in touch with you and the state just to make sure."

"I'll tell him the same thing I told you," I said.

"Her," said Edgar. "Her name is Sarah Chatham and she's with Oxton, Rath, and Flynn in Portland."

"I'll be expecting her call."

"And you'll save anything you bring up with the skeleton?"

"For sure," I said. "Evidence of a crime, Indian artifacts, and plain old river-bottom junk. Whatever's down there."

Chapter 2

Sarah

I was on my way to a concert in the big amphitheater in Bend where the old Shevlin-Hixon lumber mill used to be when I got a call from Edgar Manning, the president of the Fort Rock Indians, a long-standing client whom I liked and respected. He could have had a successful career in Portland or any other city but he'd made the decision to stay on the reservation and do what he could to make life better for his fellow Native Americans.

I locked my car and marched briskly while I talked on the phone with Edgar. I pictured him leaning his powerful frame back from a desk at the tribal offices. He'd be dressed in slacks and a golf shirt, a little odd, I always thought, on an Indian reservation in ranching country and nowhere near a golf course.

"They found a skull," Edgar told me, "in Bend, at the bottom of the pond. They say it's an Indian girl. They had to call us."

"Yes, they did," I said. "Who called you?"

"A detective from the Bend police. James Sorenson. Sarah, can you call him for us?"

"Sure," I said, "I'll make sure they do everything they're supposed to do. Who found it?"

"Someone sampling the bottom of the pond. Sorenson knows who they are."

"Edgar," I said, "this sounds like it's not the most important thing in your life."

"Not really," he said. "You know and I know how this is going to turn out. Nobody will know who she is or how she got there. Won't know how long she's been there. Maybe centuries. And for sure they won't know whether she's from one of our tribes or some other. I only care about this because we have to insist on everything we're due."

"Still at war with the white man," I said.

Edgar chuckled. "The battles go on and on," he said. "But at least we've got you to fight this one for us."

"I'll let you know what I learn," I said.

"Not too much," he said. "I won't be waiting by the phone. Do what you have to do." He changed the subject without pausing. "So," he said, "what're you doing in Bend? I called your office in Portland and they told me you'd moved."

"Oxton opened a new office. They've been toying with the idea for years and we have this young associate, Dan Martinez, who's good at getting new clients. The firm needed a senior partner to keep an eye on things and give the office more credibility. I was planning to retire here and I moved earlier than I thought."

"So you're closer to us. That's nice. Come down and see us sometime."

"I may do that, Edgar. On a weekend. Not billable."

"I'll show you around the res. The few times you've been here you've mostly been cooped up inside somebody's house."

"That was before you built the casino. We had a meeting in a nice office there last time."

"The casino's the same," said Edgar. "It's pretty small but it provides jobs for us and makes a little profit. We can pave some roads and send some kids to college." We said goodbye.

Vandevert Brewing, one of Oxton's first clients in the Bend office, had invited me to the concert, along with Dan Martinez, my associate, and his wife, Amy. The brewery was sponsoring a pavilion at the top of the hill at the back of the amphitheater. I followed the crowd until I passed a booth with a Will Call sign. They gave me a ticket and a plastic wristband that showed I was old enough to buy alcohol. At sixty-seven I thought it would be obvious but, as a lawyer, I appreciated the wisdom of rules and standard procedures. I wore a white linen dress and a vest with a swirling blue design on it that I could button when the evening got cooler. Rothy's flats. I thought I looked well put together, a woman who cared what she looked like but didn't take herself too seriously.

I was looking forward to being out in the open air in the midst of a happy crowd. I wanted to reconnect with our Vandevert clients, whom I had only met briefly before. And I wanted to meet some new people. It was funny that I was so comfortable about meeting new people, even happy about it. They had never known Ray or known me when Ray was part of my life for thirty-four years. Ray had died three years ago. Seeing my old friends in Portland was hard. They missed Ray, too, and they felt sorry for me as well. Though they wanted me to be happy, it seemed that my showing any actual happiness was a sign of disloyalty.

I stalked a row of white tents until I found my host's pavilion. It was an area of lawn enclosed by a white picket fence. A tent where they served food and drink covered about a third of the area. Another third was picnic tables and the last third was taken up with white folding chairs facing the stage.

Dan and Amy were hard to miss and I went over to say hello to them. They were an attractive, even striking couple. Dan was tall, easily six four, with dark hair and an erect posture, like a Spanish aristocrat. I could see why our clients had confidence in him and, with his relaxed charm, why they liked him. Amy was five years younger than Dan, still as lively as an undergraduate though a little subdued around me. I didn't mean to intimidate her but I wasn't going to rush to reassure her either. She was taller than me, and moved like the athlete I knew she was. She had beautiful, curly, sandy-blond hair and a brilliant smile.

When the three of us got in line with our paper plates in hand, a fit-looking man about my age got in line behind me.

"Hello," he said, "My name is Bud Russell." He had a nice voice but I wasn't ready to notice things like that. I thought he'd made a point of meeting me and I wasn't ready for that either.

"Sarah Chatham," I said, and trying to steer our conversation toward business as quickly as possible I went on. "And what is your connection to Vandevert Brewing?"

"Hops," he said. "They use my hops in their beer."

"I didn't think you could grow hops in Central Oregon."

"My farm is over in the valley north of Salem. We sell mostly to craft brewers that are looking for something different. We grow hops that not too many other people grow. It keeps it interesting."

"And how did you get into that business?" I asked, not looking at him, as I slid a square of frittata onto my paper plate.

"I like land and I like making the land produce. The beer business was growing so it seemed logical to buy a hop farm."

"My husband and I liked land, too, but we had taller plants."

"Pseudotsuga menziesii?"

"Exactly," I said. "Doug fir. Were you in the timber business?"

"I sold equipment to sawmills—live decks, green chains, conveyors—anything that moved their wood around."

"We must have sold to the same mills," I said, glad to think we could have a good long conversation without getting too personal. We sat at the same table as Dan and Amy but Bud and I were off and running on the people we knew in the lumber business all over Oregon, Washington, and Idaho. Which mills had folded or been bought out. Which were still going. I did learn he was a widower.

"Ray's career was in land and timber," I told him. "We owned small parcels of forest in Oregon and Washington. Ray was very smart about what land to sell and what land to buy," I went on. It was fun to talk about our business with someone who understood it.

Bud and I moved to the chairs facing the stage and listened to the music for long stretches between short bouts of talking. We touched on the happy times we had when our spouses were alive. We had that in common, happy marriages and happy lives, and we didn't get to talk about them as much as we liked. We agreed our friends thought we were living in the past sometimes, that we were covering up for the pain of our losses. They felt they still had to talk about the deaths. They wanted to be assured that if they lost a spouse it would be possible to live through it. Bud and I didn't want to talk about death. We had talked about it enough.

We both recognized, I thought, that we might want to see more of each other. But neither of us was in a hurry. We hadn't counted on a mutual attraction ever happening to us again. If all we had was this pleasant evening together it would be fun in itself. It would be sufficient.

Dan

When I was laid off by Oxton, Rath, and Flynn in Portland and retreated to my parents' house south of Bend, I kept finding people who needed a lawyer and I kept recommending Oxton to them. The Oxton partners saw me in a new light. The freshman walk-on had become the new star wide receiver. They asked me to open the Bend office, find space, and hire an administrative assistant on a temporary basis. They wouldn't hire anyone permanent until they had someone more senior than me running the office.

So I negotiated a lease for eight hundred square feet downtown, on Bond Street. I rented desks, tables, chairs, lamps, PCs, printers, and a copier. I got telephone and internet service and got us listed in the local business directories. Oxton put out a press release that got articles in *The Bulletin, The Oregonian,* and online in *Cascade Business News.* I had to dog the company for stationery. I finally bought some letterhead on my own that was printed with contact information for the new office. I was reprimanded for doing it but at least it got them to add the Bend address to the standard letterhead and send me a ream of it.

My father, who had painted all his life and had taught art in high school, helped me pick out the color scheme for the office—rug, drapes, and wall color—and we got some inexpensive art to hang on the wall. Some of the art was my father's, on loan he said, so we didn't have to pay for it. One of the pieces was an oil painting a former student had given him. She'd gone on to be something of a celebrity in the art world and I thought someday some client or potential client would recognize it in the conference room and be impressed.

In three months I'd added four clients to the scoreboard. I was working hard, being responsive to them while going out in the community hunting up new business. I had some fun doing it. I looked up my high school friends in businesses that might be big enough to need attorneys. I met people while working out at the Bend Athletic Club. I showed up for charitable functions, too—the High Desert Museum, Habitat for Humanity, Deschutes River Conservancy—though I was crippled by how little Oxton was willing to donate.

"Get our name on the list of donors if it doesn't cost too much," my boss said from Portland. "And chat people up at the fund-raisers." I didn't want to blatantly solicit business at what was supposed to be a benefit for a cause that deserved it. So I talked about myself and about the connections I had in Bend from growing up there. I'd wait until they asked me what I was doing now before I ever mentioned Oxton. Sometimes they never asked. I figured at least they would know my name and my face. If I ever had a chance to do business with them it would be a head start.

My problem was I wasn't doing much legal work. I was just the front end, almost an administrative assistant or paralegal for the attorneys and associates in Portland. My boss would praise me whenever I brought in a new account, small as it might have been. Then a week later he'd grumble about my lack of billable hours.

"Make up your mind what you want me to do," I said. That stopped the complaints for a while. But I could tell the managing partner above my boss was still asking why I wasn't pulling in more revenue.

They picked Sarah Chatham to come head up the office and be my new boss. I was afraid she would impose big office procedures on my more improvisational style. But Sarah had a way of getting people to trust her. She had a reputation for making her arguments in court, though they were legally rigorous, sound like so much common sense. Still, I'd gotten used to running things, small fish

THE MIRROR POND MURDERS

in a small pond, I guess. In my egotistical, youthful way, I wished I could build up the office entirely on my own. Would Sarah take over and make me disappear? Or was she about to get all the credit while I did all the work? Would she be so good at getting new business that my contributions would get lost?

Amy, my new wife and the love of my life, was leery of my having a new boss, particularly a woman. Amy knew how much I liked operating on my own and having the freedom to come home early some days when there was no work to do and no functions to show up at. Once I had to answer to Sarah, Amy would have a new competitor for my time and attention. I told Amy that my commitment to our marriage was much more important than my commitment to work and that, as far as loyalty and affection, Amy didn't have much to fear from a woman my mother's age no matter how important she was.

Sarah got the best office. The one with the most light and a view of the Cascades. It was only right. We spent a morning in that office going over the clients I'd brought in and what matters we were working on for each of them. Each client had an attorney assigned to them in the Portland office and we talked about which ones we should try to handle locally.

"Vandevert Brewing is the first client you brought to Oxton, is that right?" asked Sarah.

"Yes," I said. "It was started by two friends of mine and then acquired by another friend of mine. Oxton handled the acquisition."

"And their current issues?"

"Signing contracts with beer distributors. Pretty standard stuff now. And then a brewer on the East Coast is suing them over trademarks."

"Vandevert is such a catchy name," said Sarah.

"Right," I said. "It's hard to remember, hard to spell, and you can't be quite sure you're pronouncing it right. And people think it's Vanderbilt, like Gloria Vanderbilt."

"It's just the thing you want to order in a noisy bar," said Sarah.

"But the company name isn't the problem. They called their first beer 'Bear Hunter' and now two other breweries on the other side of the country brought out beers with the same name."

"Do they sell in the same markets?"

"No," I said, "but they all have dreams of going national and then there'd be a problem. We can demonstrate we were first to use the name. But if one of the others gets acquired by a big brewer we're going to be in bed with a whale. We'd like to get this settled before there's more money at stake."

"So we're negotiating while threatening to litigate?" asked Sarah.

"And each of the parties waxes and wanes in their interest in negotiating. They all have businesses to run and this issue isn't pressing them yet. We're building up our case so we'll be ready to litigate if we have to."

"Have we offered to mediate?"

"No," I said, surprised at the idea. "I didn't think the others would trust our firm to do that."

"It's in our client's interest to resolve this, even if they have to give something up. I think you should try to persuade everyone to sit down together, even if it's a conference call or two, and see if you can hammer out a solution. Ask our own client first."

"I'll give it try," I said. "It's a good idea, I think, and we're not making much progress sending letters back and forth."

"Let me know how it goes," said Sarah.

That went well, I thought, as I sat in my new second-best office. I was probably going to like working with Sarah. But I still didn't know whether she truly wanted to be in Bend. She'd lived in Portland for over forty years. It seemed rude to confront her with the question, especially since her decision must be tied in some way to the death of her husband.

Sarah and Ray were here one weekend and took a walk in Drake Park, between downtown and Mirror Pond. At the south end, where the paved path comes near the street, a teenage driver busy texting on his cell phone left the road and slammed Ray ten feet in the air. The district attorney charged the kid with vehicular manslaughter but they bargained it down to reckless driving and the kid got a suspended sentence. I heard that Sarah spoke in favor of the light sentence. She said she had children of her own and said kids make mistakes. She didn't think it served anyone to ruin another life. The kid wasn't on drugs or drinking and he was working on his family's ranch down in Christmas Valley. I don't think I would have been that forgiving but she set a mark for me to remember if I were ever in a similar situation. I thought if someone killed Amy, no matter how accidental it might have been, I would throw that person down to the ninth circle of hell with all the strength I could summon.

Amy had become my principal reason for living. We met training for an off-road triathlon. I fell in love with her and, with some feminine caution, she fell in love with me. We married two years ago and were building our life together. By this time next year, we hoped to have a house and a baby, or at least be pregnant. Amy had stopped using the pill and we were counting on nature to take its course. We were very much in love.

We were saving for the down payment on a house. The cheap apartment we'd chosen to live in was on the east side of Bend. The place was called the Mirror Pond Apartments, even though it was nowhere near Mirror Pond. All the plumbing and electrical features were cheesy, as though they had about one more month of life in them before they broke.

The apartment was cramped but we didn't have much furniture and, when we weren't working, we were usually out hiking or biking or kayaking or climbing rocks. In the winter we skied, both downhill and cross-country. We told ourselves we would remember this apartment fondly, along with our scrimping and saving for the future. We didn't like to admit, though, that the place was a dump and a grim one at that. It was like the visiting team's locker room.

There were eight buildings in the apartment complex, each with four apartments, two downstairs and two upstairs. We had the downstairs one on the right. We asked the family above us, with two small children, to wear slippers or soft shoes when they walked around. Sometimes they forgot but at least they tried. They said they were glad not to be smelling marijuana coming from our apartment and glad we didn't have loud visitors staying until the wee hours of the morning.

If we didn't have a lot of coming and going, our next-door neighbors did. People came and went at odd hours. The neighbors themselves seemed nice enough when we saw them in the parking lot. They were a couple about five years older than I was, so about thirty-six. Mary Jane favored long, loose-fitting dresses and heavy wood and metal jewelry, kind of a mature hippie look. Brad was clean-shaven with medium-length sandy hair and he usually wore Carhartt work pants. He worked for a roofing company. We all said hello and had short conversations about the weather and sports. But we stayed in the shallow end of each other's lives. Amy and I were better educated and were obviously on our way up and out of there. For Brad and Mary Jane, this might be about as good as they were ever going to do.

"There are some shady people around here," Brad told me. "People who're letting their lives run downhill. They're using drugs. Getting in debt. Not watching their kids." He scanned the parking lot as if to spot someone in particular he could point to. "Mostly they won't bother you," he said. "They've got their own problems. But don't let them in your apartment and don't loan them any money, even a little bit. Don't give them a ride anywhere if they ask you. Once you give them something they'll come back and ask for more." Nobody had asked us for anything so far and Brad sounded a little harsh to me. But I told Amy what he'd said and we agreed to be on our guard.

"You got a gun?" asked Brad. I said I didn't. "Well, I do," he said. "Never used it. Hope I never have to. But I keep it clean and I know how to use it. It's a little margin of safety, just in case."

"You keep it locked up?" I asked.

"I keep it hidden," he said. "But I can get to it in a hurry if I need to."

"Well," I said, "I'm glad you have it." I was being neighborly. But not entirely untruthful. I had adopted my parents' philosophy. They didn't own a gun but they were glad some of their neighbors did. A criminal would have serious second thoughts before barging into any home in Central Oregon. Bend might be a modern, prospering city but people still had a strong dose of rural western tradition in their attitudes.

Nobody I knew left their guns out in the open. Nobody talked about them very much. I was used to knowing there were guns around in the hands of responsible people. Amy was used to it too, growing up near Boulder with a father who had guns for hunting and a pistol for target shooting. He had been a Marine and was proud of his marksmanship.

My attitude changed somewhat when we heard Brad and Mary Jane arguing through our bedroom wall. We tried to ignore it but it was still going strong after fifteen minutes. We tried not to listen. A lot of it didn't make too much sense and we didn't know what had started it. There was a lot of *You just don't care, You never take responsibility, I can't stand this,* and even, *I never should have married you.* What iced it, though, was Mary Jane yelling, *Put that thing down. You're not going to use it anyway.* Maybe it was a piece of paper, maybe something heavy, maybe something else. Or maybe it was a gun. If they fired a gun next door, especially in a fit of anger, a bullet could easily come right through our wall. We moved ourselves quickly to the far corner of the living room. A bullet could even find us there, I knew, but it would be less likely and going through at least two walls would slow it down. I stood in front of Amy, trying to appear relaxed about it, so any bullet would hit me instead of her.

"This is stupid," she said. "We should get out of here." So we walked out the front door in our bare feet and down to the other end of the complex. The office was closed and there was no common area so we started back, hoping Brad and Mary Jane were done. We hadn't even locked our door. There were flashing lights outside Brad and Mary Jane's door. And the police were inside their apartment. We went into our apartment and tried to go to sleep. If I were younger and still by myself I think I might have chalked up the disturbance to another experience in the great adventure of life. I might have gone right to sleep. But after ten minutes with the lights off we were both still wide awake.

"This isn't the place for us," said Amy.

"We've made a mistake," I agreed. We both knew that breaking our lease and finding another place to live, probably more expensive, would set back our dream of buying a house. And houses were getting more expensive all the time.

"Tonight," I said, "we sleep in the living room, you on the couch and me on the floor. Tomorrow we'll figure something else out."

Chapter 4

Sarah

In downtown Bend a three-story building was a high-rise. Oxton took eight hundred square feet on the top floor of one of those few three-story buildings. My new office looked west toward the mountains. I couldn't see Mirror Pond past the roofs of other buildings but I could glimpse the chimney cap on my own house on the far side of the water. When the weather was nice, which was most of the time, I could walk to work over the bridge at the north end, the downstream end, of the pond.

The morning after the concert the first thing on my list was to act on Edgar Manning's request. One of the first cases I'd worked on out of law school was for the Confederated Tribes of Fort Rock. Edgar was too young to be an officer for the tribes back then but he'd gone to college and he was pretty smart. So the reservation leaders brought him with them. That was forty years ago. Now he was president. Or at least he'd been president last I knew. I'd have to ask him. I'd worked with Edgar on and off over my career, mostly on land deals and land disputes between the tribes and the federal government or with their neighbors. And I shepherded them through getting the permits and the contractors they needed to build the Fort Rock Casino.

I called Detective Sorenson. "My name is Sarah Chatham. I'm with the law firm of Oxton, Rath, and Flynn, here in Bend. I'm representing the Confederated Tribes of Fort Rock in the matter of the Native American skull found in Mirror Pond. Can you tell me where the skull is now?"

"It's in the medical examiner's office," he said. "We haven't talked before, have we?"

"No, we haven't," I replied. "I just moved here from Portland to help start the new Oxton office. But as a matter of fact, I grew up here in the fifties and sixties."

"Well," he said, "I've been here a while. What was your family's name?"

"Paulsen," I said, "with an *e*, not an *o*."

"Kurt and Lisa Paulsen? Used to live on Columbia?"

"Those were my parents," I said. "Gone now. Did you know them?"

"I started here as a patrolman in the late eighties. Bend was smaller then. I knew almost everybody. Nice people, your parents. Your father was still driving a 1959 Studebaker in the twenty-first century."

"That was my father," I said. "I'm very glad you knew him." I liked Jim Sorenson already. I would never have had a conversation like this in Portland. And he had me well on the way to trusting him. But that was the mark, I thought, of a very good detective. I wanted to be friendly and I would be friendly. But I would be cautious too.

"So I think the Fort Rocks are going to be pretty reasonable about whatever remains are down there," I said. "But who's paying for the excavation?"

"The City of Bend. This is just a test excavation. To see what they're dealing with before they commit to digging up the whole pond. They're in something of a panic about this skull over at the city, afraid there's a whole Indian burial ground under the pond. You'll want to talk to the city attorney. Her name is Leona Behrendt."

"How did you get involved with this?" I asked. "Any sign of foul play?"

"It's only a skull and it's intact. But if it isn't an Indian burial then it does look like murder. If she had drowned on her own the body would have come up long ago. Somebody had to weigh her down with something."

After I hung up with Jim I called Leona at the city offices. She was eager to get this matter done and over with.

"We've hired the contractor to sample the length of the pond," said Leona, "and now we're telling him there's one part he can't touch. How long do you think it's going to take to get this resolved? What do we need to do?"

"You need to hire an archeologist, preferably one focused on North America and, if you're lucky, one who knows something about sites under water. He or she should give you some direction on how to explore the area."

"Do you know anybody?" she asked.

"I've never had to do this before," I said. "So no, I don't know anyone. But I'd start with the Anthropology Department at Oregon State. You're going to need someone with credentials before the tribe signs off on that person's recommendation."

"Will the tribe help pay for this?"

"I'm afraid not. The law says the responsibility to do right by Indian remains falls on whoever found them. That's the city."

"So be it," said Leona.

"You'll keep me informed on what you're doing?" I asked.

"When we get a final report we will," said Leona. "If you want to know status at any time, you call me."

When I started my legal career I didn't set out to specialize in Native American clients. Or learn how all the treaties and laws—whether broken, abandoned, or still in place—shook out in modern courts. I'd planned to practice business law, make partner, and make money. Business law did turn out to be the majority of what I practiced. I worked on contracts, mergers and acquisitions, initial public offerings, resolution of trade disputes, and so on.

But when I started as a junior associate I worked on whatever the firm needed at the moment. They put me on a case where the Confederated Tribes of Fort Rock Indians thought they should have a hundred more acres than the federal government survey had given them. The Oxton partner on the case reminded me I was lucky to be working on something that would be tried in federal court if it ever went to trial. But we both knew the downside. The treaties, judgments, agreements, and past errors went back more than a century. It would take months and months of work to build a case, present it, and argue it in court. And almost nothing I learned while working on this case would be relevant to business law, or even general real estate law. I was disappointed but what could I do? Other junior associates were getting work they were bored to death with. At least my case was interesting.

The hundred acres in dispute were dry, with no roads, no wells, and no irrigation. The land was lava, sagebrush, and juniper in the middle of nowhere. As well as we could estimate, the land was worth about two hundred and fifty thousand dollars, or twenty-five hundred an acre. The Indians wanted the federal government to stand up to its treaty obligations which were, unfortunately, open to wide interpretation. The ancestral hunting grounds of the three confederated tribes were much larger than the acres they wanted or the hundreds of acres they already had. They had fought other tribes for years before the United States showed up. Now they were fighting with the white man under the white man's laws. But they were as determined as their ancestor warriors had been.

After we won the Fort Rock case, I was marked as the specialist in Native American law, though there was an immense amount I didn't know yet. I was assigned to every case that involved Indians, for them or against them. I became an expert, not just in our firm but in the field. The Fort Rocks, and other Indian tribes, have been our clients ever since. Judges ruled for my clients based on my credibility alone. When the Supreme Court ruled that federally recognized tribes were entitled to have casinos, our business with Indians took off and I became a rainmaker. Native American law is an area where long experience and personal relationships count double. In that, for sure, I could not be replaced by an army of junior associates no matter how many hours they put in.

After years of representing Indian tribes, I came to identify with their problems, their desires, and their grievances. I read a lot of history and it gave me a new perspective. My country, America, won most of the wars it fought, certainly the big ones. And despite a few raids on United States territory, we've never been invaded. American Indians, on the other hand, have lost every war they've fought and almost all their land has been taken from them. It's made many of my Indian clients, like Edgar, eager for heroes, admiring of true warriors. I was enlightened when I heard an Indian speaker mention one of the few Indian victories over the US Army, the Battle of the Little Bighorn, and then, in the space of thirty seconds, mention the courage of Indians fighting for the United States in World War II. Who the enemy had been wasn't his point. What he was saying in both cases was that Indians were brave and valorous fighters. Edgar Manning, in his modern way, was a warrior as well. No matter how this skull incident turned out I would do battle for him and for justice as best I could.

Chapter 5

Richard

I still have temptations. But as an adult, I have never given in to the worst of them. I've never molested anybody. I've been faithful to my wife and a good father, I think, to my two daughters. I've never cheated anybody in business though sometimes I have pressed my advantages as any good businessman would. Cary and I contribute to charities. We've helped some people with "gifts". We go to church every Sunday. What mistakes I have made and whatever injuries I've done, I did when I was young and I've asked the Lord's forgiveness for them. I've led a Christian life since then and I believe the good Lord has washed me of those sins.

My family and neighbors don't know of my youthful mistakes. But other people I've never met have wanted to hold my past failings over my head. Three years ago, soon after my brother died, I got a phone call out of the blue from a young man who said my brother might have found a daughter who belonged to me. He said he had the DNA to prove it. The man didn't explicitly threaten me and I told him I didn't know what he was talking about. But if he wanted to make me angry he succeeded.

The man wasn't making it up. When I was thirty-two, in Prineville, I fell in love with a girl named Vickie Coate. She was eighteen and she was in love with me too. I knew if Vickie told her parents they would end our relationship. When Vickie got pregnant we left town. We went to Denver where I got a job at a car dealership and she got a job as a seamstress where she wouldn't have to stand. We had very little to live on so when Vickie went into labor we went to the emergency room. The hospital was in such a hurry they never took my name, though I was with her. When Vickie died in childbirth I made a quick decision. Much as we had both looked forward to the child, a little girl, I couldn't take care of the baby by myself. I got up and walked out of the hospital. I knew the child would be better off without me. To this day I'm sure I was right. I've never told anyone what happened, not even my wife. I could only guess, when that young man called me three years ago, that Vickie's daughter had surfaced and had made the connection to me. DNA or something. The young man didn't ask for anything and I've never heard from him again. But that phone call still hangs over my head.

I see Vickie's parents around town sometimes and ever since I got that call they look at me funny. They obviously know about the girl, presumably from the same young man who called me, and they know about me. They could tell my family or my friends anytime they wanted. So far, they haven't. Do they think they are being charitable by not saying anything, like good little churchgoers? Or are they afraid of what I might do if they said something? Actually, all I would do is say I don't know what they are talking about. Half the people in town would trust me more than they trust the Coates or what somebody in a lab says about DNA. All the others would shrug and say, "So what?" Most of them have some sort of family secret themselves. And nowadays, with so many people having children out of wedlock, people divorcing, deadbeat dads, family members lost to drug addiction, and people with all kinds of sexual orientations and preferences, who in Prineville would want to attack a church-going family man, a successful man for that matter, who may or may not have made a mistake?

Still, I'd like to make sure that Vickie Coate's parents, the young man who called me, and the woman who claims to be my daughter will never bring up the past as long as I'm alive. Call it insurance. I think I've found a way to do it. I need to hire a lawyer. A specific lawyer. I need to hire the young man who called me. I need to hire Dan Martinez.

Chapter 6

Sarah

After my calling Leona Behrendt, the city attorney, every day for a week, the city finally got the excavation company back to the upstream end of the pond, teamed with two scuba divers who had done archeological dives in the Caribbean. I needed to check that they were actually there. Due diligence. Were they bringing up objects from the pond bottom in a way that looked, at least to a nonexpert like myself, as though they were being thorough and professional? If the tribe and the city somehow got into a battle over whatever was down there, it would help to have a sense of how the men were going about the job.

At lunchtime I walked down to the Galveston Avenue Bridge at the upstream end of the pond, where the Deschutes River came in from the south. It was a beautiful, clear July day, warm but not hot. The trees on the pond's east bank were still in shadow. The houses on the west bank were in bright sunlight.

My house was out of sight at the far end of the pond, the north end, the downstream end. Ray and I had spent weekends and vacations in that house for many years. It had room for guests and we hoped at least one of the two children would want it when we were gone. It was an older house, built for a lumber company manager in the 1920s in one of the prettiest locations in Bend. We looked across the pond at a restaurant that had a porch and a lawn with tables on it.

We enjoyed thinking what a nice time people were having and how much they were paying to look across the water at our house. Yet we were far enough away we couldn't hear them. We had lunch or cocktails on our own porch and watched the paddleboarders head up toward the top of the pond and come back down again.

Ray and I used to walk around the pond clockwise—across the Newport Avenue Bridge at the downstream end, through downtown and along Drake Park, back across the Galveston Avenue Bridge, and home past a park and the residential streets I had grown up on. Ever since Ray died three years ago I walked in the opposite direction, counterclockwise. That way I didn't retrace those last steps we walked together. I still pass the spot where he was hit but I feel like I am going back in time to encounter the moment, not going forward in time, dreading its arrival.

When Ray died, I realized how happy my life had been up to that point, how easy it had been. I had grown accustomed to long-lasting happiness and I had to learn, in my sixties, how to deal with its absence. For a long while, *keep slogging* was the only motto that helped. My two grown children, both married but so far childless and in distant cities, were a consolation. But it hurt me to see the pain in their faces for the loss of their father and their worried looks when they visited me.

Finally I realized how sad Ray, my husband, would have been to see me so unhappy and how disappointed he would have been at my lack of direction. I resolved to build a new life, a new me if necessary, to make the best of the years left for my sake and the sake of other people.

I stood on the pedestrian walk in the middle of the bridge and looked out over the pond. There was a heavy-looking blue raft on the water with a gasoline engine chugging away in the middle of it, a rack with equipment on it—including scuba tanks—and a flat deck at one end. A hose and a black cable ran over the side and into the water. A man on the deck was emptying another hose onto a horizontal screen set on table legs. Muddy water fell from the screen onto the deck. Frequently he would shut a valve on the hose, pick some objects off the screen, and put them in a small plastic box. Then he would let some more water run.

The dry desert air smelled fresh and clean, and the pond looked bright and peaceful, waiting for the hundreds of little round yellow rafts that would float down the river into the pond later in the day, each with one, two, or three people in it who would clumsily paddle over to Drake Park to take their rafts out. The truck with a wire cage on it to take the rafts back upriver was parked almost exactly where the pickup truck had jumped the curb and killed Ray.

Leona had told me the divers would put a grid down over the bottom and suck up mud from one square at a time, then filter the mud to see what was in it. The grid allowed them to keep track of what they found where. The man on the raft was sorting what he picked off the screen into plastic bins according to some system I couldn't comprehend from where I was. I took some pictures of the raft with a telephoto lens in case there was something about it I needed to remember.

That afternoon I spent some time in my office on the firm's plans to recruit big local clients to Oxton. Dan had done well, and his success had led to my being here. But his clients were small. They only called us when they needed us. We only had one client on retainer and the client's monthly fee was smaller than almost any account we had in Portland.

The biggest accounts we could shoot for included the medical center, five or more resort destinations, a tire company, a nationwide trucking company, the local cable company, and a brewer of beer. We already had Vandevert Brewing for a client. Our partners back in Portland would happily resign Vandevert for a larger brewer but we had no advantage in soliciting the larger brewer. So prudence and virtue were aligned in staying loyal to the brewer we had. Besides, Vandevert Brewing was growing and that could only be good.

There were some regional offices of banks, call centers, and retailers. They might handle some local matters with local firms but most would be controlled out of their headquarters elsewhere. Not the most likely prospects. There was also a local airplane manufacturer and the biomedical company that Amy worked for. We had some opportunities and, if Bend continued to grow, we would have more all the time.

Detective Sorenson called at about four o'clock. I could tell the time without checking my watch because the shadow of my window top reached a certain tassel in a tall watercolor of Indian dancing regalia that hung on the wall opposite my desk. "There's no Indian burial ground," said Jim. "The only body down there is the girl. It looks like she was wearing a backpack with an aluminum frame when she went under. If the backpack is hers she's been there less than fifty years."

"So it wouldn't be an Indian burial?" I asked.

"Not with an aluminum backpack," said Jim, "unless the backpack was lying behind her shoulders just by chance."

"Not too likely," I said.

"Not likely at all," said Jim "It's looking more and more like murder, or possibly suicide."

"But she's Indian?" I asked.

"We're still waiting to hear from Clackamas on the autopsy. The state calls it an autopsy even if there's nothing but bones. When we get the report we'll have a better idea whether she's Indian."

I didn't say it but murder or suicide would increase the likelihood that the girl was Indian. Native American women were raped and murdered at much higher rates than women in any other ethnic group in America. White men who raped Indian women on reservations knew they would probably get away with it. They could not be prosecuted under tribal law and federal law enforcement was weak. Indian suicide rates were higher than other groups and many Indian women simply disappeared. If this girl was Indian she was that much more likely to have died a violent death. And if she died a violent death she was that much more likely to be Indian.

Chapter 7

Sarah

Ray and I took our last walk around Mirror Pond together on a Saturday afternoon in June 2014. As we got to the south end of Drake Park, not far from the Galveston Avenue Bridge, a car came up behind us, left the roadway, and overtook us. The car might have killed both of us but Ray heard it coming and pushed me away just before it hit. An ambulance took us both to St. Charles. I rode in the front seat. They rushed Ray into the bright white emergency room with an oxygen mask on him and a paramedic giving him CPR. A doctor put a stethoscope to his chest and listened, for what seemed like forever. They'd taken away the oxygen and nobody was doing CPR. Nobody was doing anything proactive. The doctor stopped listening and shined a light in Ray's eyes. I thought I knew what was coming but resisted, holding on to hope, waiting for the doctor to say, "We'll stitch up the damage, set some broken bones, and he'll be fine." That didn't happen. The doctor pressed his thumb into Ray's right eye. It made me angry. I didn't want him to hurt Ray, especially when Ray was so vulnerable.

"I'm sorry, Sarah," he said, "your husband is dead. There's nothing we can do to save him." He said it slowly and looked me in the eye. There was a suggestion of concern in his voice. But it was more an official notification than a message of sympathy, more like a judge handing down a verdict. The life Ray and I had built together, and our beautiful home on Mirror Pond, had lost the contest to this little room with light blue curtains, a steel bed, so many tubes, wires, metal stands, and strange-looking electrical equipment.

A nurse asked who she could call for me. My children lived far away and I wanted to call them myself. The person who could help me right now was my childhood friend from Bend, Elizabeth Martinez, Dan's mother, whom I had rarely seen over the past fifty years but whom Ray and I had visited a week before. She'd given me her cell phone number and I still had it in the pocket of my slacks. I heard the nurse call and tell Elizabeth what had happened and where I was. Elizabeth and Leon lived half an hour south of town but were already on their way into Bend for dinner. They would come directly to the hospital.

The nurse sat with me, God bless her, after the call. She asked me whether there was anything else I needed to do right away. I said no. I would wait for Elizabeth. Then she asked me if there was a funeral home I preferred.

"Is Niswonger still around?" I asked, a name I remembered from my parents' funerals years earlier.

"Yes," she said.

"That will do," I said.

A policeman came and asked me to identify Ray. I got up, looking forward to seeing Ray again, letting myself imagine for a second that he would be sitting up on the gurney, smiling at me, somehow miraculously recovered, and apologizing for making me worry. At least he still looked like Ray, though his torso was twisted in a way that looked very uncomfortable.

Elizabeth was in the waiting room when I went out. We embraced spontaneously. I cried a bit but I got myself under control.

"Could you drive me home?" I asked.

"Of course," she said. Leon drove while Elizabeth and I sat in the back. They patiently waited in my living room while I called the people I needed to call from the bedroom, starting with my two children. Elizabeth and Leon stayed the night in the guest room. I was immensely grateful to them. It was odd suddenly having my high school friend so close to me, physically and emotionally, on the same day I'd lost my husband. I felt as though I were being yanked back in time, as though someone were starting to erase my entire adult life.

I've had bad spells since then. I will never recover from losing Ray. What do I miss? Having cocktails with Ray at the end of the day, hugs, laughter, watching him happily engrossed in fixing something or tying a fly for our fishing. I miss his doing things I didn't expect but that he knew would delight me. When we sold my parents' house he had my favorite tree, a crabapple, dug up and moved to our house in Portland. I came home one day and saw it in the front lawn. That tree made me happy every time I saw it. It came to remind me more of Ray than of my parents. Who is going to think of things to surprise me with in the future? My children, occasionally, if I'm lucky.

I've gone out on dates but I haven't made it a project to meet men. I only date widowers, only men who have had happy marriages. The men and I have sympathy for each other, a silent bond, even if we recognize in five minutes that our hike or dinner or Trail Blazers game is never going to develop into a relationship. Some of the dates have been fun and some of the men had possibilities. Still have. But I will not marry just to be married. There was no man in Portland who made me have doubts about moving to Bend.

It had been three years since Ray died and I could function almost normally now. I could even laugh again without feeling guilty, go a whole day without feeling depressed. Then, this summer, Ray's death took on a new perspective, a monstrous and enraging new aspect.

It hit me while I was doing the most boring thing in the world, going through old legal files deciding what Oxton should keep and what it should shred. The firm's agreements with its clients said we would keep their case files for ten years after a matter was closed. Then we would give the files to the client or destroy them if the client didn't want them. I went to Portland to make sure the firm didn't throw out any files my past clients might need. That was especially important for my Native American clients. Many of their issues went back over a century and had been adjudicated multiple times. It was not inspiring work. I was in an unused associate's cubicle with stacks of yellowing old file boxes. The files must have had a fine dust on them, or mold, invisible but irritating enough to keep me sneezing. I wore an older beige pantsuit where any dirt I got on it wouldn't be too obvious. It was comfortable but between the retread pantsuit and the sneezing I wasn't feeling my best and most professional self.

The work required paying attention, searching my memory, and making some arbitrary judgments. And it brought in zero revenue. But I'd known for a long time that this task would have to be done.

I was looking, a little sentimentally I admit, at my first case with Edgar and the Fort Rock Indians. I could throw out some of my drafts. But I would demand the firm keep all the correspondence and pleadings. I was about to drop one document into the "keeper" box when something on the front page caught my eye. I didn't know exactly what had stopped me but my shoulder blades squeezed together and the hair at the back of my neck stood up. I scanned the page quickly and saw nothing remarkable. It wasn't an important document. In fact it was almost irrelevant. It was a petition to the court from a group of ranchers who had grazing rights on the federal land that the Indians said was theirs. The ranchers claimed that, even though the grazing rights were renewed annually, the ranchers had leased them for seventy years and had a right to keep on leasing them. Therefore the government, in this case the BLM, Bureau of Land Management, could not give the land to the Confederated Tribes of Fort Rock no matter what the treaty said. It was a very weak argument and I remembered the judge threw it out of court.

I put the petition flat on my desk and read it word for word, wondering what my eyes had seen but my brain hadn't registered. Finally, in the list of ranchers submitting the petition, I recognized a name I knew. The name was Tingley. Stewart and Marilyn Tingley. That name was what had stopped me. I let out a gasp. The associate in the next cubicle came around the partition and looked at me.

"Are you all right?" he asked. I'm sure I didn't look all right. My mouth was still open and I'm sure my eyes reflected my panic.

"I'll be okay," I said, holding a hand over my heart. "Just a surprise in these old papers. Don't worry. I'll sit here a minute and breathe. You go back to what you were doing."

"Let me know if you need anything," he said, pulled back to his office by the relentless pressure of billable hours. I think I looked calm enough for him to leave me in peace. Long years of training in professional decorum.

I looked again at the page in front of me. Tingley. Not a common name. But the young man who had killed my husband and nearly killed me was named Floyd Tingley. He was from Christmas Valley, the same small town that Stewart and Marilyn Tingley were from. I supposed he was their son or cousin or something close to them. The connection was not random. What it meant was that Ray's death had not been an accident after all. Floyd Tingley had wanted to kill me. Ray had saved my life and lost his own.

Floyd wasn't even born when the Fort Rock case was decided. But the family must have nurtured their anger year after year, passing it down like gospel to the next generation. Poor Ray, to die because some people had harbored revenge for decades, like members of some primitive tribe, hating, fearing, and killing the tribe next door for generations. The Hatfields and McCoys. The Tingleys and the Chathams.

I understood the Tingleys' anger, if not their logic. I now embodied that same kind of anger myself. I felt a burning desire for revenge on Floyd Tingley. I wanted to think of the most terrible punishment possible and drop it on that boy's head. Stewart and Marilyn too if they were still alive. Death and pain mixed together. People feeling the way I did were how wars got started. It made me even madder that I had been so understanding about the "accident." A young man had made a mistake, I'd thought. The charitable thing to do, the right thing to do, for his sake, my sake, and the sake of the larger community, was to let it go with a severe warning. Why destroy his life over texting while driving? What a sucker I'd been! What an idiot! How profoundly I had failed to avenge my husband's death.

I sat in the cubicle chair not moving, with a stern look on my face and my arms on the desk like a dictator trying to project authority. I was seething but not moving. I picked up the phone and called the assistant district attorney in Deschutes County who had plea-bargained with Floyd Tingley for reckless driving and a suspended sentence three years ago. Her name was Jocelyn Nelson. Dan had commented she had the perfect personality for a district attorney. She could switch from ice cold one minute to warm and sympathetic the next. Dan said he couldn't figure out which was the real Jocelyn, if either one of them was. From what I'd seen I thought she chose her personality as it fit the circumstance.

"I need to meet with you," I said. "I'll be back in Bend tomorrow."

"Is this about the girl in the pond?" she asked.

"No," I said. "It's about Floyd Tingley, the young man who ran over my husband. I have found good reason to believe that it was intentional, that he was trying to kill me or both of us. It was murder."

"That case is closed," said Jocelyn in her currently ice-cold personality.

"Tingley was never charged with murder," I said, an edge in my voice. "This is a new case with some of the same facts."

"I don't think you're wasting my time," said Jocelyn, shifting her tone at least as far as lukewarm, "but you sound upset. Can we meet the day after tomorrow, at nine thirty in my office?"

"Yes," I said, "I'll be there."

"Don't be embarrassed to cancel if you think twice about this."

I flushed at the suggestion that I wasn't serious. All I said was, "I'll see you then." Anger by itself wasn't going to get me anywhere, I'd learned from long experience—though I may have a genetic predisposition to turn anger into calculation. Nature or nurture, I switched pretty quickly from blind fury to calculating how to bring justice to Floyd Tingley. Or revenge. Or possibly both.

My first calculation was what was the worst that could happen? That Floyd would attempt to kill me again? And near to being the worst, would I have to look over my shoulder forever, wondering whether, where, and when he might make an attempt? Actually, I thought, I was probably safe from Floyd Tingley. He'd be crazy to come after me a second time. Once is an accident. Twice is intentional. Besides, he should realize, if he had any brains at all, that he'd already had his revenge in killing my husband of many years. A more terrible revenge, in many ways, than killing me.

Second in my calculation, what was the best that could happen? That Floyd would be convicted of murdering Ray and spend the rest of his life in jail. Possible but not likely. A district attorney could see the connection and readily believe that Floyd tried to kill me. But to get a conviction the DA would have to convince a jury he knew what was in Floyd's mind. If Floyd told his friends what he planned to do they would probably deny it and, in any case, their testimony might be inadmissible as hearsay.

Thirdly, how much did I care about seeing Floyd go to jail? I cared a lot, somewhat to my surprise. I prided myself on not getting upset, on being even-tempered, on stoically accepting the ups and downs of life, on not wasting my energy on fruitless emotions. But I cared deeply about Tingley's crime. Ray had been what my life was about. If anything else was sacred to me, after Ray and our children, it was a commitment to seeing justice done. So yes, it was fundamentally important to me that Floyd go to jail, that he pay a price. And it seemed to me the only way Floyd was going to jail was if he confessed. As unlikely as that seemed, I'd try to think of a way to make it happen.

Jim

I sent the skull and skeleton for autopsy and kept the objects found near them, including the frame for the backpack. The cloth of the backpack itself was long gone and it would be tricky to sort out what went in the pond with her and what was irrelevant junk. People had been boating and rafting and throwing stuff in that pond for a hundred years. For thirty years in the middle of the last century there was an annual water pageant on the pond. It had decorated floats and a queen of the festival who swept over the pond on a giant swan. Thousands of people came to Bend for the water pageant. They could have dropped all kinds of things down there.

The autopsy could take two weeks. It didn't have the priority a recent death would. In the meantime I asked Sarah if she wanted to look at the objects found near the skeleton. She did. I set up in a conference room near my office at police headquarters. I signed some of the smaller objects we had out of the evidence room and brought photographs of the larger stuff we'd stored offsite.

Sarah was chatting up the female officer at the front desk when I went down to meet her. The officer, and most officers on front-desk duty, are not easy to engage in conversation. They are constantly interrupted, they interact with scores of people every day, and many of the people they talk with are criminals, the criminal's low-life relatives, or people who want some kind of special favor, as though they were longtime customers in a retail business. Sarah and the officer were talking about mountain biking, which the officer did with her family on her days off. Sarah didn't look like a mountain biker. She was in her sixties with dark brown hair. Five foot seven and maybe a hundred and forty pounds. She wore a tailored suit that fit her well and looked on the expensive side. Her shoes—light brown leather, low heels, pointed toe, gold buckle—were what some women in Bend would wear to a party. But most businesswomen would have worn a less formal outfit. Even professionals, like lawyers, wore athletic shoes all the time around here.

Sarah looked me in the eye and said how glad she was to meet me face-to-face. I had expected she would be brisk and businesslike and act like I was just another public official, and not a particularly high-ranking one. But she acted as though she expected us to work together frequently in the future, as though we would become colleagues in a way and even friends. I had doubts about that but I liked her attitude. She accepted coffee, with cream and NutraSweet, in a paper cup. We stood at the conference room table looking over the exhibits.

"The table isn't as big as the survey area but I put all the items roughly where they were found in relation to each other."

"Did the girl have any company down there?" Sarah asked.

"No more bodies," I said. "More bottles than anything else. I didn't bring them out for you because there were so many and they seemed unlikely to have anything to do with the girl. There was also a steel and wood folding chair I didn't bring. I don't know why anyone would throw it in the water but people do strange things. And one thing that was near the girl but isn't on the table, for safekeeping, is about thirty-five pounds of coins, worth four hundred sixteen dollars and twenty-two cents. They may have weighed the girl down. It's all 'maybe' right now but it looks like she was wearing the backpack and it looks like the backpack might have held the coins. The shoulder straps and the belt on the backpack could have held her down long enough for her body to decay. After that it was just bones stuck in the mud and they weren't about to come up again."

"Did she drown?" asked Sarah.

"Don't know," I said. "If she went into the water healthy and not panicked or drugged, she probably could have slipped the backpack off and swum to shore. But she might have been tied up. The skeleton was bent back when the divers found her, like someone with her hands tied behind her to her feet. Of course, the current might have bent her body that way when it left her in the mud."

"Any items that look to be Native American?"

"We found eighty-eight small stone beads, light blue or turquoise in color, that might be from a necklace. They might be Indian but they may just be cheap jewelry. The beads are all the exact same size and shape so they were probably mass-produced."

"Any silver?" asked Sarah.

"Two knives and forks but they're stainless steel," I said, "probably spilled out of a picnic basket. No arrowheads or spear points either."

"Any guns or knives?"

"Not anywhere near the body. They found a revolver near the bridge and we're tracing the serial number. But it wasn't near the girl and doesn't look to have been there very long."

Sarah looked carefully over the table. Some paint cans. Nuts, bolts, screws, and nails. Picture frames of various sizes. A fire extinguisher. Two mufflers. More junk. Every item with a barcode label stuck to it or tied to it. Then she looked at the photos of the bigger things that I hadn't brought from storage—two automobile tires, a fender, other stuff—nothing that looked likely to be associated with the girl or with a crime.

"Where are her shoes?" Sarah asked.

"Didn't find any. Found a pair of hiking boots nearby but I think they're too big to be hers. If she was wearing sandals or canvas shoes they could have rotted and washed away."

"Okay, thanks," she said. "Do you mind if I take photos of the table to show to the tribe? They may recognize something that I don't. And they'll be more confident we've shown them everything there is to see."

"Be my guest," I said. Sarah was methodical. It took her three minutes to snap about twenty photos around the table, high angle and low angle. We were done. I showed Sarah to the door of the station and got out a cart to put all the stuff back in the evidence room. I hoped the Indians could see something in the photos that meant more to them than it did to me.

Chapter 9

Dan

A my and I borrowed a canoe and strapped it onto the roof of my Toyota 4Runner. We drove in two cars, the Toyota and Amy's Subaru, to the takeout on the Deschutes below Lava Butte. Amy left her car there so we could get it at the end of our float. We drove the 4Runner and the canoe up to the put-in near Big River Campground. There wouldn't be any white water on our float but we would do some serious paddling from time to time. Amy and I had both grown up in the outdoors, Bend for me and Colorado for her. We liked being in the wild and challenging ourselves, though today wouldn't be much of a challenge. When we went hiking we found ourselves going faster and faster until we were running. The canoe would be fun because for once we would be pulling together, like the rowing team Amy had been on in college. And I was eager to show Amy a stretch of the Deschutes she had never seen before.

At the end of our float, after we retrieved the cars and loaded the canoe, we would go to my parents' house in Upriver Ranch to freshen up and have dinner. Sarah was going to join us there on her way back from visiting an old client at the Fort Rock Indian Reservation. Amy had only met Sarah a few times. I hoped Amy and I would both get to know Sarah better on a social basis.

We pushed ourselves to enjoy the outdoors because we knew we wouldn't have that kind of freedom much longer. Once we had a child, days like today would be hard to come by.

The river was forest on both sides for the first quarter mile, then lined with vacation homes, old and new, grand and rustic. We made seven sharp turns in the next two miles, with houses on the outside banks of the turns and low marshes on the insides where the river flooded every spring as soon as the snow melted. We talked about which houses we liked and which ones we didn't, keeping our voices low so that none of the owners, if they were around, would hear our comments. We tended to like the small to medium-sized ones that were cute or had something unique in their design. They had to be in good shape or clearly show potential and they had to have a dock. If they didn't have a dock already, the chances of the state letting the owners add a dock were almost nil. There were some very big houses, with four times the frontage as the others and great expanses of thick green lawn. We admitted they were beautiful but we wouldn't want them. Was it because they were too far out of our reach? Because any aspiration to such a house would probably be disappointed? Because we wouldn't want to take care of such a house? There was a man fishing from an inflatable raft at the apex of a wide left hand. He'd found one of the good spots I knew about for trout. The Upper Deschutes looked like a beautiful river for fish but, unfortunately, it wasn't. As soon as the farmers downstream stopped irrigating their fields in October, the irrigation district dropped the level of the river and started storing water upstream, in Wickiup Reservoir, to use for irrigation the following year. In the winter the flow in the Deschutes dropped to a trickle. Fish died by the thousands. When spring came there weren't many fish left.

We'd talked about fishing from the canoe as we went downstream. But the fish were concentrated in a few spots, like where the man we saw was fishing. Without an anchor one of us would have to paddle upstream against the current while the other cast the line over the hole where the fish were. That kind of paddling would be hard work.

"What are you using?" I shouted to the man.

"A caddis with a dropper," he said, with more obligatory politeness than enthusiasm.

"Any luck?"

"A few nibbles," he said.

"Well, they're in there," I said. "Good luck." He didn't answer. I thought he was getting a little discouraged.

"We have to go fishing," said Amy. "Add it to the list of things to do before we have a family."

"We should go to East Lake," I said. "Fish from a rowboat. Catch four species in one day. They even have Atlantic Salmon."

"Add it to the list," she said.

"How old do children have to be before you can take them fishing?" I asked.

"One step at a time," said Amy. "First we have to have children. Before that we need to have one child."

"You want to find a shady spot and work on that?" I asked. I raised my eyebrows and gave Amy a big smile, half mocking my own enthusiasm.

"Calm down, soldier. I don't like bugs and I don't like dirt and I don't like worrying about somebody seeing us."

"You didn't used to mind," I said in a taunting way.

"I'm a married woman now."

"And marriage has made you more beautiful than ever," I said. No reply from the front of the canoe. Amy's sandy-blond hair was cut a little shorter than when I met her. But it still rested on the strong shoulders that were driving the canoe downriver. Not a wasted motion.

We slid the canoe up on a low bank and walked into the shade of some big lodgepoles for lunch. The land belonged to a family who had owned it for years, back when the place was a sheep ranch. My mother knew the people and asked if we could stop there. They said come ahead but hide the canoe and stay back from the river so other people didn't think they could stop there anytime they liked. We had chicken that we'd cooked at home and a plastic container of Caesar salad we'd made as well. It was a big step up from the gorp we used to eat when we first met.

We changed places after lunch. Amy took the stern and I took the bow. It made me impatient to no longer have the responsibility for steering. I dismissed my anxiety as some vestige of male vanity. Amy knew perfectly well how to steer a canoe and I had nothing to worry about. I knew the river here and she did not but it wasn't hard to follow. You could hardly go wrong. We passed the Upriver golf course and some more houses before the river ran through forest for the final four miles of the float. It would be easy to see the takeout and I would point it out as we got near.

Still, my ripples of anxiety increased the farther we went. I began to rattle my feet around on the bottom of the canoe, a sure sign I was getting nervous. When I was a child my father, whose family came from Spain, would play the guitar and I would dance, standing straight up like a flamenco dancer, rapping my heels on the floor. Even as an adult my inept simulation of flamenco dancing restored my confidence and peace of mind. When Amy and I stood at the altar getting married my legs twitched and my feet started to bobble. I didn't want to spoil the ceremony, especially not for Amy, and I tried mightily to control myself. I only partially succeeded. Fortunately Amy and our families, who were sitting in the front row, thought it was funny, or even, as Amy's mother said, charming.

"Okay, Dan," said Amy from the front of the canoe, "time to stop." She wasn't being mean. I'd told her my dancing feet were embarrassing me and I wished I could stop doing it. Her request was a reminder and a help.

What had made me so nervous on this beautiful, smooth river? Ahead of us, downstream, below the place where we would take out, was Benham Falls, a steep, rocky chute where the whole river jumped from rock to rock in massive twisting surges. Taking a canoe down there would surely kill us both.

I knew my fear was irrational. The falls were past the takeout. There were signs warning boats not to go any farther. There was even a cable across the river below the takeout. But as irrational as my fear was, I'd fallen into Benham Falls once and nearly lost my life. Some primitive part of my brain didn't want to go near the place.

Amy beached the canoe effortlessly at the takeout. She looked at me quizzically when I stepped onto dry land and my shoulders relaxed.

"Benham Falls," was all I said. She understood.

We chained the canoe to a tree and drove Amy's Subaru back up to the put-in to get the Toyota. After our day in peace and quiet, away from the world on the river, driving down US 97 seemed sadly mundane. Up at the put-in we agreed we wanted to get back on the river and live the whole float over again.

When we got to Upriver my mother and Sarah were in the kitchen getting dinner ready and remembering teachers they'd had in high school. Dad knew the teachers who were still around when he came to Bend and started teaching art.

Mom said Dad should show Sarah his studio while Mom finished dinner. Amy went to help Mom and my halfhearted offer to help was refused. I loved to watch Dad show off his paintings. He took them very seriously when he was painting but he treated them as little amusements, done to pass the time, when he talked about them. There were paintings on the studio walls, jammed together unlike the ones he'd chosen to hang elsewhere in the house. There were some on the floor leaning together against a wall. And some were in a cupboard with vertical partitions. There were paintings that went back to my childhood and paintings I had never seen before, all mixed together. As I'd seen him do before, he'd pick up one at a time and talk about how he came to paint it, a combination of seeing something that interested him and, coming from the technical side, trying to work out a certain combination of colors or the juxtaposition of recognizable, abstract, and surreal objects. Then he would pick up a painting seemingly at random, though I knew it was a painting he'd just finished or was still working on.

"Now what do you think of this?" he would say. "I can't quite decide about it."

The person, whether a fellow artist or someone who couldn't tell Picasso from Rembrandt, would say something, usually complimentary.

"Hum," my father would say thoughtfully, inspecting the painting again. "I think you may have hit on something there."

Sarah played her part much better than most. She said the painting he held up, of a tall young man my age standing beside a more portly man in his fifties, seemed very powerful, though she couldn't say why. It suggested, she thought, an antagonism between the two men. The older man looked angry or impatient. The young man looked bewildered.

"Father and son?" she asked, "though obviously not the two of you."

"No, no, no," said my father, "but that is a very helpful thought." He gave the painting a good long look before he put it back.

"You should paint the ghostly figure of a woman standing behind them," I said. I was teasing him and he knew it. I was not an artist by any stretch and had no business making suggestions. But he loved me and he had to put up with me.

"So tell us about your trip to the reservation," I asked Sarah after we'd each had a few tapas to start dinner. "None of us here would ever go to the casino and I don't think they really want tourists."

"They'd be happy to have you visit their museum but, no, they aren't fond of people wandering around the reservation poking into their community."

"They'd probably like a fence and a security gate, like Upriver Ranch," I said.

"They might," said Sarah, "and they might actually be able to afford it. But I think better schools, better houses, better roads, better healthcare, and their own police force would be higher priorities."

"With the casino, can they do those things now?" asked my mother.

"It helps but the casino isn't very profitable. It's a very long way from any city and not that many tourists go out there."

"And you have friends there?" Mom asked.

"Clients who have become friends," said Sarah. "I've worked on and off with Edgar Manning for forty years. Today was my first combined business and social visit. He took me out to some beautiful spots. We saw some cattle grazing and he showed me a hayfield where they have a pivot."

"What's a pivot?" asked Amy.

"It's a long pipe on wheels with sprinklers along the pipe for irrigation," said Sarah. "One end of the pipe turns on a pivot and the rest of the pipe rolls over the field in a big circle. When you look down from an airplane and see a big green circle, that green is irrigated with a pivot." That seemed to satisfy Amy. She even looked a little embarrassed. We'd all seen pivots near Redmond and east of Bend. She just didn't know what they were called.

"And of course," said Sarah, "we had to visit the casino. They have four blackjack tables and three hundred slot machines. Edgar almost forced me to play the slots for a few minutes and he put money in the machine next to me. I told him I was glad the casino was doing well but I didn't gamble. I knew the odds were against me and when I got money back I didn't believe for a second that I was lucky or that some god of fortune or something was smiling on me.

"Edgar told me it looks bad when people come in and don't gamble. And it would look terrible if he acted as though he were above it. He tells the members of his tribe, if they come to the casino, they should play a little. But don't play a lot, he tells them, or they will lose everything. He says they are allowed to kick members of the tribe out of the casino if they overdo the gambling They can't kick out the tourists but they try to politely encourage them to leave if they're losing too much. He says the slots give people good odds but, unlike the casinos in Nevada, the Fort Rock casino doesn't give them free drinks."

"So what was the business you went there for," my mother said, "if you don't mind my asking?" My mother had overseen all three branches of a bank in Bend and she still loved stories about businesses.

"Well, it wasn't related to commerce exactly," said Sarah. "You may have read about the skeleton that was found in Mirror Pond. They think it was an Indian girl and they found some things with her that might help identify who she was. I showed Edgar pictures of the whatnot at the bottom of the pond to see if he could identify anything of Indian origin. He said there wasn't anything that looked Indian to him. He said that his tribe at least didn't usually bury anything with the dead anyway, they distributed the deceased's things among the mourners so they could better remember the person."

"Can I see the photos?" my father asked.

"Sure," said Sarah. "The skeleton isn't in the photos so there's nothing grisly about them." Sarah went out to her car and brought the eight-by-ten photos back in a manila envelope. We had moved back to the living room for coffee and we passed the photos around in a circle from hand to hand.

"We're looking for anything that will tell us who this girl is or how she got there," said Sarah.

The photos piled up in my father's hands. He'd look at each one, then put it down and stare off into space for a while.

"Can they tell when the backpack was made?" asked Amy.

"No luck so far," said Sarah. "The police have found some people who sold backpacks thirty or forty years ago but nobody remembers the frames that well and, unless it's some oddball design, it won't help much to know what brand it was."

"It's a mala," said my father, holding two photographs, one in each hand. "These beads and this picture frame went together."

"A mala?" I asked. "What's a mala?

"It's a string of beads, usually one hundred and eight of them. How many did they find?"

"Eighty-eight," said Sarah.

"So some got lost or are still in the mud," said Dad. "A mala is like a rosary for Buddhists or Hindus. They use it to count how many times they say their mantra. Usually there is a hundred and ninth bead called the guru bead that tells them when to turn around and go back the other way. The guru bead often has a tassel hanging from it. But followers of Bhagwan Shree Rajneesh hung a picture of him from their malas instead of a tassel. In a little round picture frame like the one in this photo."

"What's something like that doing in Mirror Pond?" I asked.

"Wasn't Bhagwan the one with all the Rolls Royces?" asked Mom.

"That's the one," said Dad. "Bhagwan Shree Rajneesh founded an enormous colony north of here, out in the middle of nowhere, east of Antelope. Every day he'd drive by all his followers in a different Rolls Royce and wave to them. They called it 'the drive-by' and they loved it."

"Here? In Oregon?" asked Amy.

"He was called 'The Golden Guru.' When he started off in India he was known as 'The Sex Guru' because he recommended sex, as well as meditation, as part of the path to a fuller life. Then he told his disciples that they should draw from the best of the East and the West, the spiritual side from the East and the prosperity and happiness that people in the West were after."

"Having multiple Rolls Royces doesn't sound like my idea of a guru," I said, totally ignored by everyone else.

"So how do you know this mala had anything to do with this particular guru?" asked Amy.

"I am guessing a bit," said Dad, "but most malas don't have a picture frame on them and it looks like this one did, though it's detached now. And you know, Central Oregon has never been a hotbed of Eastern religions, except for Bhagwan. So a mala at the bottom of Mirror Pond with a picture frame on it probably belonged to one of his followers."

"What ever happened to this Bhagwan?" asked Sarah.

"They ran him out of the country for lying on his immigration form. Then he changed his name to Osho and died in India in the early nineties. He wrote a lot of books both before and after Oregon and still has many followers all over the world."

"And the colony near Antelope?" I asked.

"Abandoned, then bought up by a rich man who turned it into a Christian youth camp. The whole Rancho Rajneesh just fell apart."

"When was this?" asked Amy.

"Early eighties," said Dad.

"This should be grist for Detective Sorenson's mill," said Sarah. "He hasn't had much to go on so far."

Dad handed the photos back to Sarah and we said our good-nights. Sarah left ahead of Amy and me.

"I wish we could go back to Bend in one car instead of two," I said to Amy.

"Will you follow me?" asked Amy. "We can talk on the phone."

"Okay," I said.

"I like Sarah," Amy said. "And if your mother likes her that much she must be all right. And she didn't boss you around tonight or act superior. Outside of work maybe she could be a friend."

"She's not going to work forever," I said. "So I think she'll be a nice person to know in the future." As we stood in the dark by our cars the moon, almost full, was rising in the eastern sky. Saturn hovered below the moon, shining brightly in the clear desert air.

Amy brushed the back of her hand across the front of my trousers. "Meet me at the teepee," she said, turning up her face for a kiss. The little soldier in my pants rose quickly to attention and I pulled Amy up toward me with a hand below her buttock. She raised one leg and slid it down mine to encourage me, or to encourage us both.

Upriver Ranch had a teepee set back in the woods, a kind of symbol for the ranch, tied to the past, tied to the wilderness, and evidence of a fanciful extravagance. It had a fire pit in the middle of it and couches made of logs for sitting around the fire. The couches had red vinyl cushions on them, long enough to lie down on. Hardly anyone ever went there, especially not at night.

"Great idea," I said. "I wasn't sure married women liked teepees."

"Wouldn't you like to tell Little Nell she was conceived in a teepee?" asked Amy, gently gripping my privates. Little Nell was the nickname we'd given to the child we were trying to conceive. We were going to have to change the name soon. In the Dickens novel Little Nell dies. I had suggested Cordelia because she was loyal to her father. But we'd have to choose something more reasonable. Cordy sounded like the name of a dog and Delia sounded like a character in a gothic novel.

"Can't wait," I said. "And our Huck will be thrilled to know about the teepee just as much as Little Nell."

Chapter 10

Sarah

I called Detective Sorenson on Monday to tell him about the possible connection to Bhagwan Shree Rajneesh.

"Ah, Rajneeshpuram," he said, "that was a crazy deal. Seventy-five miles north of here the swami and his followers bought this enormous ranch called the Big Muddy and decided to build a city on it. Had plenty of money. People giving all their cash to the guru. Professionals. Hollywood people. They had seven thousand people there before they got run off. Can you imagine that many people plunked down in the middle of nowhere? Thought they were going to build a paradise on earth."

"So you've heard of it?" I said with a laugh.

"You could say."

"Will that help you figure out who the girl in the pond was?"

"Those Rajneeshees are scattered to the wind. Might be hard to find anyone who remembers this girl, even if you're right that's where she came from. We'll have to do some thinking about how to go about this efficiently. But before I get too far down that road I'd like to see what I learn from the autopsy report."

"Fair enough," I said.

Sorenson called me the next week and we met in his office. I sat in his single chair facing him across his desk.

"Shall I leave the door open?" he asked.

"What is the world coming to," I said, "when two experienced professionals, no longer spring chickens, can't trust each other enough to shut the door? I don't think you're going to molest me and I don't think you're worried I'm going to accuse you of molesting me."

"I'd just as soon make sure nothing gets overheard and leaked to the press," said Sorenson. He shut the door. I had to laugh a little and shake my head.

"The girl was five foot two, medium build. Can't tell if she was fat or thin or somewhere in the middle. Nothing on hair or eye color of course. About sixteen years old. They're not so sure she was Indian but she might have been."

"How did that change?" I asked. "I thought the medical examiner said she was Indian."

"The medical examiner hasn't seen a lot of skeletons. Most of what she sees are recent deaths. When she looked at the girl's mouth, the palate was elliptical and that's more typical of Indians. And there's a line across the palate in the back that is generally straight in Indians, curved in blacks, and jagged in whites. The girl's line, the *transverse palatine suture* I'm reading from the report, was straight. But that's all the medical examiner looked at.

"In Clackamas they looked at other factors. The nose aperture in the skull could have been any race. There's a bone in the back of the skull, called the mastoid bone, that looked Indian. But the most important indication was the shape of the front teeth. The girl's incisors, the teeth at the front of her mouth, were concave on the back, not flat. That is much more likely to be Indian than European."

"So can we say the girl was definitely Native American?" I asked. I was thinking an American Indian who wound up at Rajneeshpuram would have to be a very unique individual.

"We're just getting started," said Sorenson. "She might not be Indian at all. The Indian characteristics in this skeleton also apply to Asians. She could be Chinese."

"Why didn't the medical examiner say that in the first place?" I asked.

"We thought the skull was older than it is. Up until the late 1800s the only people here were Indians. Then almost all whites. Even today, only one percent of Deschutes County is Asian. Still, she could be half Asian. Or simply Latino. Most Mexican-Americans are a mix of Spanish and Native American."

"That helps a lot," I said. "Edgar Manning's going to throw up his hands at the whole thing. What do you propose to do with the skeleton?"

"The city attorney says we should explain what we've learned to the tribe and work something out with them. As long as we're making progress on a murder investigation we'll want to keep the bones. If there's a conviction we'll keep the skeleton for years in case there is an appeal. If we don't find out who the girl was and we abandon the investigation, the city doesn't really care what becomes of the remains. The tribe can have them or they can agree to have the city bury them. What Leona wants to avoid is our disposing of them and the tribe suing us."

"I think they'll be pretty reasonable when the time comes," I said. "Did you learn anything else from the autopsy that helps your investigation?"

"The skull was intact and there were no broken bones. So blunt force trauma is unlikely. Same with a bullet or a knife—no marks on the skeleton—though either could have simply missed the bone. Could have been strangled but also somewhat unlikely. Her hyoid bone, up under her chin, would probably be broken if she were strangled but it isn't. So it seems most likely she drowned. Maybe tied up and thrown off the bridge. It would not have been hard. She wasn't that big."

"No other marks that tell you anything?"

"She broke both bones in her left wrist about two years before she died. But the bones were almost certainly set by a doctor. She healed perfectly. There's only the one injury. Looks more like a childhood accident, not child abuse." Sorenson stopped and looked up at me in surprise. "What?" he said.

I, who had trained myself over decades to never look unsettled in court, had put my hands over my mouth and rammed myself back against my chair. I was staring at the photos of old bones arranged into human shape. I'm sure my eyes were wide as silver dollars. There was one person in Bend who knew who that girl was. I knew who that person was. That person was me. I sat there flooded with a mix of emotions to the point I couldn't tell where one ended and the next began—sorrow, guilt, excitement, and even an inkling of relief.

"She's not Latino or Asian," I said. "She is one quarter Cherokee." It was the detective's turn to look surprised.

"Her name is Pamela Paulsen," I said, "and she's my sister." My credibility with Jim was taking a dip.

"How the hell do you know that?" he asked. Then, looking at me with doubt in his eye, "What makes you so confident about who this girl is?"

"My sister was the same age and same size. She left home at sixteen and was never heard from again. She broke her wrist when she was fourteen. And it's natural that her bones would have some Indian characteristics."

"That helps a lot if you're right," said Sorenson, encouraging me even if he suspected I'd gone off my rocker.

Guilt rose to the top of my emotional trash heap. Why hadn't it occurred to me earlier that this might be Pammy? The truth I faced was I'd largely forgotten her. There were nineteen years between us. I was in college when she was born and I was accustomed to being an only child. Pammy clearly wasn't planned and she placed a burden on my parents, then in their forties and fifties, that drained their energy and attention. While I had been an obedient and dutiful daughter Pammy had been more spirited and rebellious. While Mom and Dad were very sad when Pammy disappeared I was secretly relieved for them. No more tantrums, no more arguments, no more defiance, and no more self-recrimination about what they'd done wrong in bringing her up. And I had my mind on other things when Pammy left. I had a career, a new husband, and my first child. Though I attempted to console my parents I didn't have much time to think about Pammy. And I thought of her less and less as years went by.

"She disappeared from home in 1985," I told Jim. "In my parents' things I still have her dental records and probably an x-ray of her wrist. We can compare them."

"And you haven't seen your sister since 1985?"

"She disappeared from home in June of that year." I spoke rapidly. "My parents put out a reward for information about her. There should be a missing-persons report in the police department files."

"Bring in whatever X-rays you have," said Sorenson, "and I'll send them to Clackamas for comparison."

"And you'll open an investigation?" I asked.

"We already have. It's a suspicious death. But I have to warn you I don't know how far we'll get. We haven't even figured out how she died."

"How could this not be a murder?" I asked.

"If she was drunk or stoned or injured in some way and she fell in the water wearing a heavy backpack she could have drowned. That would be an accident. And I'm sorry to say this about a girl who might be your sister, but she could have committed suicide."

"Pammy was a good swimmer and a strong-minded girl. She was less than a mile from our parents' house. Somebody else put her in the pond."

"We'll take all that into account. Once we're sure it's your sister I think the DA will want to get a deposition from you. Probably a long one."

"Good," I said.

Poor Pammy, I thought, driving home a little more calmly, well within the speed limit but getting more impatient than usual at the traffic on Greenwood. My poor parents, now dead and buried in Pilot Butte Cemetery. They had posted flyers all over Bend and took out newspaper ads throughout the Northwest. No one had seen Pammy with a stranger. No one had seen her get into a car. My parents went on the local TV station but, with no indication of kidnapping, the newspapers and TV stations outside of Bend didn't think they had an exciting story to tell. Teenage girls run away all the time.

Mom and Dad worried that Pammy was living on the street somewhere, doing God knows what. Or maybe she had gotten into drugs. Why didn't she come home, or at least call my parents to say where she was?

Pammy exhausted my parents the way a puppy can exhaust an older dog. She skipped second grade and wanted to do what her older classmates were doing, even though she was a year younger than they were. A lot of battles with my parents were over parties and dating. She took up passions for things. Horse riding for a few months, then reading Walt Whitman, then modern dance. One time she was determined to become a Catholic. She went in for the ritual and the stories about saints and martyrs. Our parents grew accustomed to indulging her, though, much to Pammy's disappointment, they declined to finance her decision to visit Rio de Janeiro for Carnival.

I was living in Portland when Pammy disappeared. I spent an afternoon there going around to all the shelters for teenagers and homeless people looking for anyone who had seen her. No one had. I was disappointed for my parents and a bit more ambivalent about Pammy. If she had run off I was angry for the pain she'd caused Mom and Dad. If she had been kidnapped I felt very sorry for her. Once I said to Ray, in a jest I immediately felt terrible about, "God help her kidnapper." She wouldn't be docile and it might get her killed.

I had multiple copies of Pammy's dental X-rays and an X-ray of her wrist. Years ago my parents were prepared to send them to anyone who had found a girl who might be Pammy. I don't know how often that happened. I brought the X-rays to Sorenson that same afternoon.

"Since I saw you this morning," he said, "I spoke to the sheriff's office in Wasco County. He said they've got filing cabinets full of evidence to support the prosecution of Rajneeshpuram leaders for all sorts of crimes. And the county has records of land purchases and sales, building permits, zoning infractions, and all kinds of violations and disputes with the county and the state. What he doesn't have, unfortunately, is a list of all the people who lived there. He has some partial lists but usually the names are ones assigned by the Rajneeshees—Swami this and Ma that. He said we're welcome to look through it all but he doesn't think we'll find your sister's name."

"Thanks for doing that, Jim," I said. I wanted to encourage every effort he put forth, especially given how slight the connection to Rajneeshpuram seemed to be, some beads and a picture frame that might not be Pammy's and might not have anything to do with Bhagwan Shree Rajneesh.

"I learned another thing that could help us," he said. "We may have a good idea when your sister went under."

"Did you find out when the backpack was made?" I asked.

"Better than that," he said. "The most recent coins we found with her were dated 1985. I asked a numismatist, a coin expert, to come in and look at the coins. He estimates they were taken out of circulation about three quarters of the way through the year, or roughly in September."

"I didn't think coins had months on them," I said.

"They don't. But if you have that many coins and they were all recently in circulation you can approximate about how many dimes and nickels, et cetera, you ought to have from this year, last year, and every previous year, depending on how many coins of each type the treasury decided to make in any given year and how many old coins should have disappeared from circulation. So my expert made some calculations. The dimes say August, the nickels say October, and the quarters say September. So best guess is September."

"Time to go back to school. Maybe she was on her way home," I said. "I wish my parents knew at least that much."

"Also," said Sorenson, "September 1985 was when top management left Rancho Rajneesh and the whole place started coming apart." Sorenson was rather pleased with what he'd found out about the coins and I appreciated his initiative. But we were a long way from answering all the questions I had.

"This still doesn't tell us how she got in the pond," I said.

"It helps though," said Sorenson. "The timing tends to bolster the Rajneeshpuram connection. If we can figure out who she was with in September and what she was doing, we'll be a lot closer to getting the full story."

"You're right," I said, "and thank you."

"What you might do," he said, "if you're willing to spend the time, is see if you can dig up some people who were at Rajneeshpuram in 1985 and find out if they remember her. That's a lot of legwork and I have other cases I need to work on. You can probably do it as well as I can. Maybe better. Some people don't like talking to the police."

"I know how much work that is," I said, "from finding people to give testimony in civil cases. Shall we say the time I save you finding these people and talking with them you can use later in the case?" I was bargaining with Sorenson for as much attention as I could get from the Bend Police Department.

"Let's see what you find out first," he said. He cared about what I wanted but he wasn't going to bullshit me about what he was going to do and what he wasn't.

I owed it to Pammy and to my parents to find out how my sister died. I owed it to my commitment to justice. I owed it to my own self-respect, especially after neglecting Pammy and her memory for so many years.

My parents and the Bend police had exhaustively questioned all of Pammy's school friends after she disappeared. They had learned nothing back then and hunting those classmates down now would be fruitless. The best place to start would be Pammy's possible connection to Rajneeshpuram. I didn't know anyone who had ever been there, or even anyone who was likely to know someone who had been there. The people I knew were lawyers and business types from Portland.

And what was worse, even if I found followers of Bhagwan Shree Rajneesh I wouldn't be good at cajoling information out of them. I was good at examining witnesses who were in court under oath. I didn't intimidate them. I was polite and considerate. But I followed the facts wherever they led, clearly and logically, until the judge and

THE MIRROR POND MURDERS

the jury, if there were a jury, could read the testimony like a book. But I couldn't be sly or duplicitous. I couldn't seduce people into telling me things they really wanted to keep hidden.

The person who had a network of friends and acquaintances, I realized, and the person who could win people's trust and get them to reveal their secrets much better than I could, was Dan Martinez. Would he be willing to do this? I thought he would. Not only would he be better at it than I was, he might actually enjoy it. He'd be sympathetic enough, I thought, to undertake the task for my sake. But I would have to pay him. It would only be fair. I'd pay the same net amount per hour that he made working for Oxton. But I wouldn't cycle it through Oxton. I'd pay him directly. I could afford it.

It was a good idea to recruit Dan for this investigation. Even brilliant. What I overlooked was how valuable Amy was going to be.

Chapter 11

Amy

The most important thing I learned in college I didn't learn in class. I learned it rowing on Lake Cachuma with my UC Santa Barbara teammates. I learned the value of teamwork. As hard as each of us might pull, as dedicated as each of us might be, if we didn't stroke in sync, in perfect harmony, we couldn't win. So when I moved to Bend out of college to take a job with Greenwood Biomedical, I began my search for good teammates, not for rowing but for life. I would help them and they would help me. We would succeed together.

My first teammate was my boss at Greenwood, Grace Wray, and she was a principal reason I took the job. She said the greatest satisfaction she could get out of her job was seeing me succeed and I believed her. She taught me everything she could possibly teach me and gave me clear direction when she thought I could do something better. I, in turn, worked hard to make her and the company successful too. Within a year of my arrival we both got big raises and I got a promotion.

But the best recruit to my team, and he recruited me as much as I recruited him, was Dan Martinez. We became co-captains for life. I married him. Training for a race, which brought us together, can be a team effort even though the race itself was not. We were motivated to show up for training sessions and to push ourselves because we knew the other guy would be there. It became more and more motivating as we fell in love.

Dan coached my swimming and I coached him in downhill trail biking, which I'd done all my life in Colorado. Dan learned racing techniques methodically and I profited from that. I taught him to be a little more reckless and I know it helped. I always pushed myself to go fast, in biking and skiing. Going fast forced me to learn control. Unfortunately my love for speed has cost me two tickets on US 97.

I wanted Sarah Chatham, Dan's boss, to be on my team as well. Not in a big way. She was my mother's generation and I couldn't see that much we could do for each other except keep Dan happy. But we could also be friendly when we saw each other and keep an eye out for opportunities to do one another a favor. I didn't overtly volunteer it but I saw such an opportunity when Sarah was looking for people who might have seen her sister at this Rajneeshpuram place. I had another teammate who probably had some sort of connection to it.

When I first moved to Bend I had two roommates. We all got along but the one who supervised a goat farm in Tumalo was pretty much a loner and we lost track of each other when she moved to Nevada. I didn't think I'd have much in common, at first, with the other, a yoga instructor. Her name was Shanti Sargent. She was a well-balanced and responsible person, older than me, and just the sort of roommate your parents would hope you'd have when you moved to a new community. She had a calming aura about her and something I decided was a sort of unspoken emotional wisdom. She never gave me any advice I could remember but somehow I felt more on top of things after I talked with her. I went to some of her yoga classes at the fitness center. Shanti was a good teacher but I didn't stick with it. If I was going to do something physical I wanted it to be higher energy.

It was a good thing Shanti was a calm and capable person because her life had a level of difficulty built into it that many lives, including mine, did not. Her father was African-American and her mother was Australian. She was coffee-with-cream color with features that could have come from either parent. When she straightened her hair and wore an Indian print some people asked her what part of India she was from. What could be more natural for a yoga instructor named Shanti? She didn't dress like that very often.

"It's hard enough establishing who I am," she had said, "without complicating it further." She'd grown up in Bend, which I think must have been a little hard in an almost entirely white community, but she said it helped that she had friends who had known her since kindergarten. Some of them had been very unkind to her at one time or another but they were nice to her now, hoping she'd forgotten what they had said or done. She said she didn't let it bother her. "People grow up," she had said. She was friendly to them now if they were friendly to her.

Shanti came to our wedding and we saw each other every month or so. She'd gotten married herself, to a software engineer from Finland who had convinced her to take up skiing. They had a sauna in their house and she had a large room there where she ran her own small yoga studio, bringing in other instructors to teach a wider variety of yoga practices.

It occurred to me, given Shanti's connection to yoga and meditation, that she might know someone who was at Rajneeshpuram, the place where the mala might have come from. I met Shanti for a cup of tea in her breakfast room after one of her morning classes.

"I was born there," said Shanti. "I don't remember it at all but my father does. You've met him. I'm sure he'd tell you what he could." I had only met Shanti's father twice when he'd come by our apartment. He was a wiry, serious man, polite and even friendly. But he didn't have time for chitchat.

"What about your mother?" I asked. I'd never met her and I half remembered she lived far away. Shanti had never said much about her.

"I'd rather not ask her," said Shanti. "We haven't spoken in years. She and Dad got a divorce when I was five and she moved back to Australia where she was from originally. She has a whole other family. To the extent she could remember Rajneeshpuram, I think she would rather not. Frankly, I think she'd also like to forget I ever happened."

"That's harsh," I said.

"I went to visit her once in Australia. I went out of curiosity more than from any hope of resurrecting our relationship. My presence embarrassed her. Her new children wanted no part of me. The only person who was decent to me was her husband and, after a while, she didn't like that at all. And Australians thought I must be mixed-race aborigine. It was not a happy trip."

So I called Shanti's father, Bruce Sargent, and arranged to meet him at a jobsite where he was working. Dan gave me a photo of Pammy, Sarah's sister, that Sarah had given him and offered to go with me.

"No, thanks," I said, "I think I can handle this." It would be great if I could do a favor for Sarah, help her find out what happened to her sister. We'd be better friends.

Bruce Sargent had a company that put up the framing for new houses. I met him at the house he was working on in Upriver Ranch, not far from Leon and Elizabeth's house. Bruce shifted a watchful eye between me and the jobsite he was responsible for, even though his crew was taking a break for lunch and there was nothing going on. I sensed he was eager to get back to work. I also sensed he wouldn't call people on whatever bullshit they told him but he would know it was bullshit the moment he heard it. He'd just take that into consideration when he gave them a reply. I'd want to be straightforward with him.

The concrete foundation for the house sat in the middle of a two-acre lot that had recently been a forest of lodgepole pines. The crew had put in a wooden subfloor and added the frame of one wall with a big window space in it. A table saw sat on the concrete floor of what looked like it would become the garage. Lumber and pallets of reddish-gray rock were stacked around the outside of the house. I sat next to Sargent on the subfloor with our feet hanging down toward crushed rock in the trench around the outside of the house.

We looked out toward mounds of willows on either side of the Little Deschutes.

Mr. Sargent, who asked me to call him Bruce, had two sandwiches and an apple. I had the tuna salad I'd brought in a plastic container. I showed him the picture of Pammy that Sarah had given to Dan. It showed a dark-haired girl with two braids hanging down below her shoulders, widely separated so you could see both braids from the front. She had a stern but composed look on her face, reinforced by strong dark eyebrows. This was a girl who wanted to be unique and wanted to be taken seriously.

"Don't recognize her," said Bruce, "but she could have been there. We had over two thousand people at Rancho Rajneesh all the time and thousands more at the summer festival. I worked construction all day and, aside from Shanti, I didn't spend much time with children, especially not ones the age of this girl."

"If she had been there," I asked, "what would life have been like for her, sixteen years old, without her parents?"

"Well, she was bound to be in love with Bhagwan. Everybody was. People used to turn out every day at two o'clock to see him drive by in one of his Rolls Royces and wave to them. Everybody believed he was leading us to a better life, to be better and happier people. And that was what he was doing, as long as it lasted.

"This girl," Bruce said, "probably worked in the communal kitchen or something like that. Worked long hours but not too hard. Everybody was helping to build the community. They used to say, 'Our work is our play.' There were PhDs building roads and loving it. And we all liked to party. No drugs and not too much liquor but lots of dancing. And I suppose you've heard, a lot of sex. People liked that."

"But Pammy would have been underage, a minor."

Bruce ducked his head and cast his eyes up at me. "She wouldn't have been coerced into it. Nobody would have forced her or threatened her," he said, "and of course, I didn't know her specifically. But there was sex all around her, some of it with girls younger than she was."

"Is that what got you interested in the Bhagwan?" I asked. Bruce gave me a sideways look that said a lot. The look said it was presumptuous of me to ask the question. That the question was too personal and I was out of line. That he'd given me the benefit of the doubt and I had gone too far. That he didn't trust me, or even like me, as much as he had previously. But possibly remembering that I was his daughter's friend, he answered my question.

"I wasn't like most of the other sannyasins," he said. "That's what Bhagwan called his followers." Bruce pronounced it *san-YA-sins*. "My connection to Bhagwan started because I liked to work. Not that I ever thought work was play. Before the Rajneeshees ever came to Oregon they had a meditation center in New Jersey, where I grew up. I knocked on their door when I was in high school and offered to mow their lawn. They'd been neglecting it and I not only mowed it, I pulled up weeds and trimmed the borders. Then I offered to paint the house and they hired me to do that too. There were about fifteen of them in the house. They all wore orange clothes and they seemed to make a point of being happy and being kind to each other. I never heard them arguing.

"But sometimes I sure heard them yelling and screaming something awful. It was worse than a dog fight with a dozen dogs at once. They each shouted the most terrible things about what they had done in the past and what they wanted to do, now and in the future. All of them talking, crying, and laughing at the same time. After ten minutes of that they would all start shouting 'Who am I?' in unison. After ten minutes of that they'd go silent. When I peeked in one time they were each sitting with their legs crossed and their eyes closed just breathing in and out. The whole thing had started with ten minutes of heavy breathing and was called Dynamic Meditation.

"Craziest people I'd ever seen. But I kept coming back to mow the lawn and do odd jobs for them. Then one of them, a woman, sat me down and started to tell me about Bhagwan Shree Rajneesh and all the Rajneeshees around the world. I started doing the meditation with them and eventually I moved in with them. My parents didn't like it. But they had to admit I was happy. I had work and the people

I was hanging out with didn't look like they were headed to jail. I went to see my parents less and less though, and they were even more unhappy when the Rajneeshees asked me to move to Oregon to help build Rancho Rajneesh.

"The ranch was a long way from New Jersey. We were forty miles from the nearest town and it wasn't much of a town. Called Antelope. Country like I'd never seen before. Dust, grass, and sagebrush, that was about it. Here and there a scraggly tree. Bhagwan's people thought they could build whatever they wanted there, to do whatever they wanted, and the government would leave them alone. I liked building things and all these people who had more education than I did were in love with Bhagwan. We built a big pavilion for Bhagwan to teach in, a dining hall, a shopping center, dormitories, and even houses. They were simple buildings but they were solid. We had water and sewer, electricity, and our own generating plant. We built roads and we even built a lake. I was happy. People liked me and, I don't mind telling you, I got all the sex a young man could want. There weren't many black people there and I stood out."

"How did you meet Shanti's mother?"

"It was an arranged marriage," he said, looking at me for my reaction. I could tell he enjoyed the surprised look on my face.

"Bhagwan arranged it. She was Australian. She was at Bhagwan's place in India and she wanted to come to Oregon. Lots of sannyasins did. The only way she could immigrate was to marry an American. So they matched us up. The Rajneesh Foundation flew me to India to get married and bring her back. Flew me to Bombay. Now they call it Mumbai. I've seen poverty in the United States but nothing like that. At the taxi stand at the airport there were beggars, women and children, who came and licked my luggage, hoping I'd give them something. Never seen anybody so desperate, not even a junkie. Right outside the airport, bang, we were in an Indian village. People drawing water out of a well in buckets. Cows and pigs and chickens wandering around on the street. The taxi I took was so beat up that water splashed up through the floorboards when we went through a puddle. On the road to Poona, where the ashram was, we passed rows and rows of shacks with whole families living in them. People squatted right next to the road to do their business. And then the funniest thing. Little kids walking to school in clean shorts and bright white ironed shirts, carrying their books. Well, I knew I wasn't in the USA anymore.

"So I married Margaret, that was my wife's name, in Poona, and we came back to the United States together. We got along all right and we were both in love with making Bhagwan's dream real. We all wanted to make Rancho Rajneesh a Buddhafield as he called it, an energy field that emanated from Bhagwan himself. Bhagwan said if we got it right then we could build Buddhafields all over the world. We would eventually bring peace and love to everybody. Margaret and I decided to have a baby, partly to strengthen our claim to a real marriage so immigration couldn't deport Margaret and partly because we just wanted to. We wanted a child to share with us the joy of following Bhagwan. So we had Shanti. It turned out Shanti became more important in my life than Margaret. Or, for that matter, Bhagwan.

"When Rajneeshpuram fell apart we moved to Bend and I started working construction. But outside of the Rajneesh community our marriage didn't last. We'd shared a commitment to Bhagwan. We'd never built much of a commitment to each other. Margaret moved back to Australia and Shanti stayed with me. I met my second wife and we've been together ever since. She raised Shanti and our two other children."

I didn't want to ask if his second wife was white or black. It seemed impolite, like it shouldn't matter. And for what I wanted to know about Rajneeshpuram, it certainly didn't matter. Still, I knew there were hardly any Afro-Americans in Bend and it must have taken some serious calculation for Bruce to raise black or biracial children there. But he stuck it out. Whatever he wanted from living in Bend, it looked like he got it.

Bruce said he didn't keep in touch with any former Rajneeshees except, from a distance, his former wife. But he knew of two who lived in Bend somewhere. One was a woman named Roberta Avery.

He'd seen her once at St. Charles Hospital where she was a nurse. The other was Eva Keefer. She was a sort of spiritual advisor, he said. He hadn't seen her since Rajneeshpuram but she was listed in the yellow pages.

"Calls herself Pranalika. She's sort of a life coach who can talk to the dead," he said, casting his eyes upward as if the dead were up there, fair enough, but not very interesting. "You have to watch out for Eva. When the mucky-mucks at the ranch wanted to make some visiting county officials sick, it was Eva who brought them glasses of water on a tray. She was only a teenager at Rancho Rajneesh, maybe eighteen, very innocent looking. Maybe she didn't know what was in the glasses and maybe she did. One guy was sick in bed for days. Anyway, Eva was about the same age as the girl you're looking for so, if that girl was there, she more than likely knew Eva."

When I called Sarah to tell her about my conversation with Bruce Sargent she said she wished I had talked with her first. "I'm sure there was more he could've told you. And what he did tell you isn't as definitive as it could've been."

"He doesn't remember Pammy. That's kind of a dead end, isn't it? And I think he gave me the names of all the people he knows who might know anything."

"All the local people," said Sarah. "New Jersey is only a phone call away. As are India and Australia for that matter. Does he remember any other teenagers who might remember Pammy? What might have led Pammy to leave Rajneeshpuram? How and with whom? Did you get his okay for me to call him and ask him more?"

"No, I didn't," I said. I was embarrassed to not have thought of the questions Sarah was asking me. But I wasn't happy to be reprimanded either. "We're further ahead than we were," I said. "Do you want me to call him again?"

"No," she said. "I'll do that. Thank you for finding him though, and for getting the names of the other two. I'll call them. And probably go see them."

"Okay," I said. "I want to help. Let me know if I can."

At home that night I told Dan about Bruce and about my conversation with Sarah.

"Sarah is a kind person, generally," he said, "but finding out what happened to her sister is important to her. And when she puts her lawyer hat on, she can be confrontational with the best of them."

"Unlike my husband," I said.

"Unlike your husband who is a prince one hundred percent of the time."

"Oh, that husband. Sometimes I get him mixed up with the husband who only thinks he's a prince."

Chapter 12

Sarah

I took a call from a man in Prineville who wanted to set up a trust. He wanted to leave some undeveloped land to his children. I told him Oxton was well equipped to help him and, if he would give me his contact information, I would have our attorney in Portland who handled wills, estates, and trusts give him a call. Her name was Patsy Weil.

"I want to deal with someone local," he said, "someone I can sit across the table from and look in the eye."

"We can do that," I said. "We can work out the arrangements you want here but I'll want to pull in Patsy to write the final trust document. And she may know of approaches that will make the trust more advantageous to you and your heirs."

"Sounds good to me," he said. "I'll be in Bend two days from now. Can we meet then?"

I asked him to bring his current will and a description of the property.

My moving to Bend was the right decision. I didn't miss the big Portland office. I liked the people there but my interactions with them were almost entirely taken up discussing clients we were working on. The other partners had their outside lives. The associates were grinding away, hoping for a better future but not very happy in the present. Dan and I, by contrast, were breaking new ground, finding new clients, getting to know them and their issues, learning the ins and outs of the courts in eastern Oregon. What were the idiosyncrasies of each judge and district attorney? What procedures did each court follow and which procedures that had seemed standard in Portland or Salem did they dispense with altogether? The partners back in Portland didn't expect us to fill our days with billable hours at this point. I even had time to gaze out my office window at the mountains in the distance and a sliver of trees on the far side of Mirror Pond.

And I liked Bend. You could get from one end of town to the other in fifteen minutes, even with the traffic that was increasing as the town grew. People were friendly, partly because the whole economy depended on the tourist industry and everybody knew it, even the salespeople at the hardware store who rarely saw a tourist. The locals wanted everyone else, neighbors and tourists, to be happy. And partly, I think, the friendliness was due to Bend's isolation. Except for Redmond, all the towns for hundreds of miles around Bend were small. Bend wasn't like the suburbs of Portland or any other big city. We didn't have towns that blended into one another where you couldn't tell what town you were in. If you were in Bend you were in Bend and nowhere else. We all had that in common. We wanted the city to prosper, to be a great place to live. We were all in this together.

Every day Bend felt more and more like my true home. Even the deaths of Ray and Pammy, which logically might have made me loathe and fear the town, drew me to it. I lived in the house on Mirror Pond that Ray and I had chosen together, where we had spent many happy days, and where we had planned to live the rest of our lives. Aside from her sojourn to Rajneeshpuram, Bend was the only town Pammy had ever known. I wasn't sentimental about my childhood in Bend and the city had changed a lot since then. Yet I felt good about rekindling my friendship with Elizabeth Martinez and I found a quiet satisfaction in the things that hadn't changed— the mountains, Pilot Butte, the old buildings downtown, and even some of the less-than-elegant motels and restaurants on Third Street.

When Richard Winterpol, the man who wanted the trust, came to the office two days later, it seemed he felt that same way I did about Central Oregon in general. Prineville, a smaller town about thirty-five miles from Bend, was having a boom of its own. Though the two hundred acres he wanted to put in a trust was hilly sagebrush and juniper now, it might be worth something in the future. The land was adjacent to good, flat, irrigated farmland near the main road that he and his wife had lived on for years. His wife, Cary Winterpol, had inherited that land and according to their prenuptial agreement she was still the owner. But Richard was the sole owner of the two hundred acres he wanted to put in the trust.

Though heavyset, he looked like a strong man, once athletic, who had put on more weight than he should have. He was fifty-nine years old, he told me, and in good health with no expectation of dying anytime soon.

"We could raise cattle on that land," he said, "but I really bought the land to protect what we already have." He raised hay and cattle on his wife's land and, he said, that land would go to his two daughters. I took him through all the relevant questions about the trust he wanted and said I would give all the answers to Patsy to draw up the draft of the trust document. Basically Richard would be the sole trustee of the unused acres until he died and then his children would own them equally. He thought the land was worth about six hundred thousand but might be worth a lot more by the time they inherited it.

The trust seemed like the most straightforward thing in the world. He could almost download a sample trust document off the web and fill it in, though that would entail the risk there was some wrinkle the standard document didn't cover and Richard hadn't thought about. The trust was simple except for one strange thing Winterpol balked at. I asked for the names of his children and their current addresses.

"Just write *my children*," he said. I explained that *my children* would legally suffice but it was a good idea to be specific so that the successor trustee, who would take over the trust and dissolve it when he died, knew exactly who the children were and where to find them. He insisted on *my children*.

"You realize if you leave it that way some person or persons could claim to be your child and tie the trust up in legal fees?"

"DNA can clear that up," he said.

"On that basis your two daughters might have to submit to DNA testing."

Richard paused to think about it.

"They won't like that, I suppose, and neither will my wife. But they are my daughters, sure as shootin', and DNA will prove it."

I told him we'd have a draft trust agreement to him in two weeks and he said that was fine. He wasn't in a hurry.

Well, I thought, *I've brought a new client to Oxton, even if it was a walk-in and a very small matter.* I still had game. And I didn't think I had any special advantages in getting Mr. Winterpol's business.

I'd had a special advantage when I was hired by Oxton and I'd felt awkward about it for years afterward. The most sought-after job for me and many of my classmates, when we got out of law school at Lewis and Clark, was a junior associate position at Oxton, Rath, and Flynn. We prepped each other for days ahead of our interviews. I bought my first business suit.

I was qualified. They might have hired me anyway. The partner who interviewed me for the job seemed to like me. He was giving me encouraging signals. Then he mentioned the firm had a diversity objective in hiring and asked if I could contribute anything to that goal, aside from being a woman. I'm sure he expected a no. My unmarried name was Sarah Paulsen and, true to my name, I looked about as Northern European as anybody could get.

I considered my answer for eight years or for five seconds, depending on how you count it, before making the decision that changed my entire law career. I really wanted the job.

"I'm one quarter Cherokee," I said. They hired me. Well, why not? I was as good as any other candidate. And I proved they made a good decision by, in good time, becoming a partner. And I had given the man the truth.

When my father was fourteen his parents told him his mother was actually his stepmother. His real mother was Native American. My father's father married his first wife in Oklahoma and she died soon after my father was born. The grandmother I knew was my grandfather's second wife. My parents waited until I was sixteen to tell me about my biological grandmother. They hadn't told me earlier because they didn't want my friends to know.

"Some people aren't very nice to Indians," they said, "and we thought your friends might tease you."

Later that day I looked at myself carefully in the mirror. I'd always thought I looked like my mother—short nose, fullish lips, and kind of bold eyebrows. My brown hair and hazel eyes could have come from either side of the family. But my high cheekbones obviously came from my father. I had flattered myself that I looked a little like Katherine Hepburn. I wondered if anyone had ever thought I looked Indian and had chosen not to mention it. As dispassionate as I could be, even at age sixteen, I couldn't see how anyone would think I had a drop of Indian blood unless I told them.

I hadn't put my Indian ancestry on my college applications and I still got into the University of Oregon. I didn't tell anyone about it. It just wasn't who I was. More than the plusses and minuses I could see to being Indian, or part Indian, it was just so complicated. I didn't want any of it. Saying I was part Indian would make me slightly exotic, would make me seem like a more interesting person. And I knew, vaguely, that people, universities, and all kinds of government agencies would want to help me out in ways I had no concept of. But I didn't know any more about Indians than what I had learned in high school. I knew what a wickiup was. I couldn't pretend to any Indian culture. I would be faking it. And I certainly didn't deserve any special help.

How much the diversity I brought them influenced Oxton's decision to hire me I still don't know. If being relatively good-looking influenced their decision I couldn't help that either. I tried to look like a professional attorney rather than some sort of conceited glamour puss. But I didn't hide my light under a bushel.

When I was first introduced to the three Fort Rock tribal representatives, including Edgar Manning, the supervising partner from Oxton announced that I was Cherokee.

"I'm not enrolled," I said quickly, embarrassed and trying to hide my anger. "A grandmother I never met was Cherokee, from Oklahoma." The Indians nodded their heads and looked back at the partner to see what was next. As I came to understand later, Edgar and the others were used to people whose status as Indians, and their desire to identify as Indians, covered a range as wide as the Great American Desert.

"What does *enrolled* mean?" asked the partner when the meeting was over.

"It means I'm not listed as a member of the tribe. The Cherokee don't even know I exist. I'm Cherokee by blood only."

"Can you prove it?"

"Yes. But I really don't want to make a big deal of it. I didn't know my grandmother was Cherokee until I was sixteen. I wasn't brought up as an Indian. Claiming to have anything in common with the Fort Rocks would be deceptive."

"It isn't a lie," he said, "and it helps the relationship."

"Well," I said, "I have Neanderthal blood too. If we have any Neanderthal prospects, I'm your gal." I walked away, twitching with anger and fear at the same time. It wasn't a smart thing for a junior associate to say.

Yet after twenty years, I enrolled with the Cherokee Nation. I became, officially, an Indian. I felt this was something I could do. I would not be pretending to be something I was not—partly because of something that was unique to the Cherokees. The Cherokee called themselves a nation, not a tribe. Their nation had a constitution that said they could grant membership to anyone they wanted, with or without Indian blood. My long career of advocating for Indians, though I was paid for it, made them happy to accept me, they said, even if I didn't have Cherokee blood. I became a citizen of the Cherokee Nation.

Ray asked me whether I felt any different.

"Yes," I said. "Honored. Proud. I've accepted them as part of who I am and they have accepted me."

"Are you going to act any differently?"

"I hope you like fry bread," I said, though I didn't know how to make fry bread. I did learn though. Ray liked it with honey.

Chapter 13

Sarah

My children and I found a time the three of us could talk together on the phone. I told them it was important but nothing to worry abo ut. Kurt wrote me three emails before we spoke and
he copied his sister.

"We're adopted after all," said the first email. "Our real parents
were much nicer."

"You're hopelessly in love with an orangutan that smokes cigars,"
said the second, "and you've written us out of your will."

And the third, "You're coming to live with us and bringing a neti
pot."

I wrote back, "The orangutan is bringing his own neti pot."

"Well, Mother, what is it?" asked Kurt when we were on the
phone. "You've put us in great suspense." His humor hid his worries.
I'd never set up a call like this before.

"I discovered something recently that I thought you should know.
Your father's death was not an accident. He was murdered. It was
intentional."

"I thought that was all settled," said Kate, "with a trial and everything. You even asked the court to show leniency to the boy who
hit him."

"It turns out the boy is the son of some people who lost a court
case I was involved in years ago, before I even met your father. I had

forgotten all about them but they clearly harbored a grudge all these years. They passed it on to their son, who wasn't even born when the case was settled. It was me, not your father, that the son wanted to kill. And it would have been me if Ray hadn't pushed me out of the way."

"Has the boy been arrested?" asked Kate.

"Not yet," I said. "The evidence isn't strong enough yet. I only came across the old case recently and recognized the name. We're working on it—me, my associate, Dan Martinez, whom I've told you about, the police, and the district attorney. But we're just at the beginning."

"Do you think he still wants to hurt you?" asked Kate.

"I don't think he'd dare. He came close to going to prison once. If anything happens to me the police will be all over him. Besides, I helped get his charges reduced. He owes me."

"Logic doesn't help if he's crazy," said Kurt.

"I don't think he's crazy. He honored his family's festering revenge wish and look where it got him, a suspended sentence and the threat of much worse. Unless he's much more deeply warped than he appeared in court he's not going down that road again. And for my own part, I can't live my life worrying about him."

"How are you holding up with this, Mom," asked Kate, "knowing it wasn't an accident?"

"I'm having some revenge fantasies of my own," I said. "I have to keep them in check. They are not healthy. I remind myself I want justice, not vengeance. I owe myself that much. Justice for Ray, for our family, and for society as a whole. I try not to feel guilty either. Floyd Tingley was out to get me, not Ray, because the Tingleys imagined I'd wronged them many years ago. But nobody wronged them, least of all me. The government wasn't required to renew the Tingleys' grazing rights and it didn't. I didn't represent the government. I had no involvement with the Tingleys. Your father's death was the result of a fantasy they concocted on their own."

"Someday you'll have to take me through all that," said Kurt. "It's a bit much right now."

"Will do," I said.

"Are you depressed?" asked Kate.

"No," I said, "I miss your father and sometimes I'm sad. But work is going well. The house is holding together and I'm loving being in Bend."

I didn't tell them about Pammy. One revelation at a time was enough. Kurt never knew Pammy and Kate wouldn't remember her. To my children, Pammy was a small collection of photographs and an old family story, like their Cherokee great-grandmother. I'd tell them about Pammy if and when I'd learned more about what happened to her.

My next step on Pammy was talking with Roberta Avery, the nurse that Bruce Sargent said had been at Rajneeshpuram while he was there. I phoned her, at work, at St. Charles Hospital. I felt I could interview Roberta myself. I wouldn't need sweet-talking or guile to get answers from her. She was a nurse, I thought, a person who wanted to help people. She would give me straight answers. We met in the hospital cafeteria at the end of her workday, three p.m. on a Wednesday afternoon. It was a big, clean, open space with hardly anyone in it. Still in her nurse's uniform, Roberta was a white-haired woman of about sixty. She spoke with a Boston accent. I sensed she wanted to give me the information I wanted. But aiming to ease my mind might be more important to her than aiding my quest for the truth.

"I don't remember this girl," she said when I showed her Pammy's photograph. "When was she at Rajneeshpuram?"

"She would have arrived the summer of 1985. I don't know how long she stayed."

"Oh, dear," said Roberta, "I was gone by then."

I was deflated. It looked like Roberta was disappointed too. But we had gotten together and we tried to salvage something of our conversation.

"What can you tell me about the ranch as you saw it?"

"The ranch was a very happy place for most people that year. They were busy building for the future and everyone was devoted to Bhagwan. They were working hard, meditating, dancing at night, and lining up at noon for the drive-by. That's how excited they were and how much they loved Bhagwan. The ranch welcomed guests, especially for their worldwide festival in July, but if your sister, Pammy, stayed there all summer, Devya would have had to approve it. Everyone had to have a job of some kind. You couldn't just show up and live there. Many of Bhagwan's disciples wanted to come. But he said he couldn't start with meditators. He had to start with people who knew how to build a city. So he asked for the disciples who were city planners or knew about construction, or water and sewer systems, electrical grids, roads, and everything else they would need. They worked long hours and they did it for no pay."

"Who is Devya?" I asked.

"Devya worked directly for Bhagwan and she ran everything. She consulted with Bhagwan every day, alone, just the two of them. Then she'd tell her assistants and the whole community what Bhagwan wanted. Looking back, you know, it's kind of a hard place to understand. People were thinking peace and love and making the world better. People worked very hard at what they were assigned to do and they were happy doing it. But it was kind of like a dictatorship where we all loved the dictator. Have you seen any videos of Bhagwan or read any of his books?"

"No," I said, "I haven't."

"Even if you did, I don't think you'd truly get what he meant to people. His smile, his welcoming arms. He created an energy field. You felt it was a physical necessity to be near him. He didn't preach a religion. He said very little about what people should think and not think. He simply said he wanted people to be conscious. He said he'd been asleep and now he was awake. Other people could be awake and he wanted to help them."

"I can see how a sixteen-year-old girl might have gone for that."

"There were Rajneesh meditation centers all over the world," said Roberta. "There still are. After Oregon he changed his name to Osho. People read his books everywhere, even though he died in 1990. He's more popular than ever."

THE MIRROR POND MURDERS

"Do you read his books today?" I asked.

"Yes, I do," said Roberta. "On a personal level his writings inspire me even though I know Bhagwan's dream of a community didn't work out."

"How did you come to be at Rajneeshpuram?" I asked.

"I got my nursing degree back East and started working at Mass General. A friend introduced me to Bhagwan's teachings and I became a member of the meditation center in Boston."

"And Rancho Rajneesh needed nurses?" I asked.

"Exactly," said Roberta. "I worked in the medical center at the ranch. The center was three trailers in the middle of the city. We had doctors, modern equipment, and a pharmacy. The construction and farming people got injured regularly and we had to patch them up. And we had a lot of venereal disease. Bhagwan believed people should enjoy sex with whomever they liked. He said that marriage interfered with an individual's ability to grow. So we had everything—syphilis, gonorrhea, chlamydia. If people had HIV, though, or had had contact with anyone who had HIV, we didn't treat them there. We got them off the ranch as quick as possible. The community finally had to forbid sex, even kissing. That disappointed a lot of people and quite a few didn't obey."

I wondered how far Roberta had gone into the sexual free-for-all. She was much younger then, and sold on Bhagwan, but all the diseases she saw might have made her cautious.

"And why did you leave when you did?" I asked. "That was months before the organization collapsed. Did you see something coming?"

"Not precisely," said Roberta. "I only vaguely knew the county, the state, and the federal government were all out to put a stop to Rajneeshpuram. I had no idea how close they were to winning and how close we were to losing. I didn't know that Devya and the others were fighting them so desperately, both legally and illegally. And I didn't know that Devya had hidden microphones and cameras all over the city and that she was spying on hundreds of people. Like most others, I believed that Bhagwan was in charge and that, with a few bumps, everything would get better and better."

"But there was something that bothered you enough to make you leave?" I asked.

"There was a part of the medical clinic I wasn't allowed to go into," she said. "One of the ranch higher-ups, Shakti, spent a lot of time in there. No patients ever went into that space. The people who worked there sometimes emerged with rubber gloves on and they were very disciplined about washing their hands. In the common area their conversation kept to topics outside the medical center altogether. But every once in a while they would say something to one another about *batches* or *sterilizing* or *potency*. I thought after a while it sounded like they might be cultivating a germ. It took me much longer to realize that it was salmonella and it was related to the sudden illness of over seven hundred people in The Dalles. That was a famous incident. It made all the papers. It took years before they made the connection to the Rajneeshees. Do you know about this?"

"Fill me in," I urged.

"The Dalles was the largest city in Wasco County, the county Rajneeshpuram was in. And someone had the idea that if enough people in The Dalles were sick on election day—this was the election in November 1984—we Rajneeshees could elect our own commissioners to the county board and stop the county from harassing us. That was what the whole Share-A-Home program was about, where Devya brought in thousands of homeless people so they could be registered as voters and vote for Rajneeshee candidates. But a few months before the election, the county decided they simply wouldn't register any new voters. I didn't think they could do that. Voting rights and all that. But apparently they could.

"After that I kept more of an eye on the lab in the back," said Roberta. "They were branching out. I discovered they were trying to cultivate typhoid fever. That would be mass murder. As much as I loved Bhagwan, and as much as I loved living at Rajneeshpuram, I had become a nurse to help people, not to kill them. I thought about telling the top people at the ranch, like Devya, but it seemed to me they must know about it already. I saw the whole community in a new light. We had become so intent on defending ourselves we had lost sight of what we were trying to build in the first place.

"So I left," said Roberta. "I didn't tell anyone the real reason. I told them my mother was sick and I needed to take care of her. I didn't go to the authorities in Oregon and tell them what I knew. I couldn't prove anything. And I had come to understand how ruthless Devya and the other leaders could be. I wanted to get away and hide. I went back to Massachusetts and worked as a nurse there for a while. But some of my happiest moments were spent at Rajneeshpuram and something in me clicked with the high desert. So I came back to Bend and married an Oregonian. We have a little ranch out toward Millican. It's about as far into the desert as I can live and get to work in Bend."

"Do you think Pammy would have been aware of what was going on in the lab when she was there?"

"Hardly anyone knew about the lab and those who did worked hard to keep it a secret. I think everything looked rosy until the law started closing in and Devya left with some of the other top people in September. Where is Pammy now?"

"Did you read about the skeleton that was found in Mirror Pond?" I asked. Roberta nodded. "That was Pammy. She may have been at Rajneeshpuram and been murdered shortly after she left. She never made it home to our parents' house."

Roberta's face slackened. "I'm so sorry. And you think her death might be connected to something that happened at Rajneeshpuram?"

"I'm trying to find anyone who has a clue what happened."

"If it happened at the ranch Devya would know all about it or be able to find out. But if it was after your sister left the ranch I don't know what you can do. You know the Rajneeshees never actually killed anyone, even with all the people they poisoned and the talk about killing a district attorney. I just can't see them killing a sixteen-year-old girl."

"I understand. But right now the connection to Rajneeshpuram is the only lead I've got."

Roberta looked at me sympathetically. "Bhagwan did a lot of damage," she said. "He didn't mean to but he didn't live up to his responsibilities. He led people into the desert and told them it was the Promised Land, or that it would be. Everyone's hopes were dashed. Anything might have been going on with your sister."

"But you left before it all collapsed," I said.

"I felt bad for not staying and helping people. And for not trying to stop what was going on in the back room. But I was afraid. I was surrounded by people who were committed to the path they were on. So I got out. I still haven't decided about Bhagwan, whether he approved the backroom work or Devya kept it from him. In any case, he denied knowing about it."

"So you have no idea what might have happened to my sister?"

"Well, after Devya fled the country the whole thing pretty much collapsed. If your sister was there in the fall she had almost certainly left by Christmas."

"Next on my list to talk to is another Rajneeshee named Eva Keefer. Are you in touch with her?"

"I ran into her once at Costco years ago but we didn't have much of a conversation. She was always a little secretive, didn't want you to know too much about what she was doing. I never got to know her at Rajneeshpuram. She was a teenager then. I was a trained nurse and I don't think she had graduated from high school. All we'd had in common was Bhagwan and he led us all into a mass delusion. So I think we were embarrassed when we saw each other."

"Do you think Eva can help me?"

"She was closer to your sister's age and she might have been there when your sister was. So maybe she can help you more than I can. But I never felt Eva was a truthful person, even when I first knew her. People said she spied for Devya on other sannyasins. Now she makes her living as a psychological counselor. I don't think she has any education for it. She just makes it up. I wouldn't be surprised if she's trying to copy Bhagwan's charisma, to make money from people. I'd worry that she's lying to you, even if she has nothing to gain by it. It's just the way she is. Or at least the way she was."

Roberta hitched herself up a little straighter in her chair. "Now I'm being negative and I shouldn't be. I hope Eva can tell you what you need to know. By all means go see her and talk with her."

Chapter 14

Dan

On a hike with Amy on the trail beside Little Tyee Creek in the Cascades I brought up the issue that had been troubling me and that I knew would trouble, if not infuriate, Amy. Sarah had taken on a new client for the firm, Richard Winterpol, who wanted to leave some land he had in Prineville to his children in a trust. Sarah wanted me to take over interfacing with Winterpol locally while Patsy Weil in Portland drafted the trust document. I knew who Richard Winterpol was and I had serious reservations about discussing anything with him.

"Which children are the beneficiaries?" I had asked Sarah.

"Funny you should ask that," said Sarah. "He very specifically wanted the trust to go to his children but he didn't want to put their names in it."

"I'm not sure it would be appropriate for me to handle this client or this matter," I said.

"What's the problem?"

"I don't think I can tell you right now," I said. "I may be able to tell you more in a day or two."

I had spoken to Richard Winterpol only once in my life. It was brief and it was over the phone. In that phone call I had warned him to keep his distance from Amy. Now he had found a way to involve himself with me and with her. Richard Winterpol, though he had tried to escape any connection to her until now, was Amy's biological father. He had gotten Amy's mother pregnant, whisked her away to Colorado, and abandoned both the mother and Amy when the mother died in childbirth. It was largely by accident that Amy discovered who her father was. She had met Richard's estranged sister and both women noticed how similar they looked. DNA testing showed the sister was Amy's biological aunt and Richard's dead brother, Ken Winterpol, was her uncle. Richard had to be her father. After Amy learned how he had abandoned her as a baby and walked away after seducing her mother, she never wanted to have anything to do with him. I believed Amy would feel the same way about him regardless of how much land or money he left her. And she would not want me to have anything to do with him either.

"You have to stop him," said Amy when I told her about Richard. We were sitting on a bed of pine needles beside Tyee Creek. "I don't want any part of it."

"You can simply not claim your share of the trust. It's called a disclaimer. And if he doesn't tell anyone you're his daughter it's likely the trustee won't ever know you have a claim. They won't come knocking on your door."

"Not good enough," said Amy. "I don't want to have to decide anything or do something or even not do something. I don't want that man to think for a moment that he's doing anything for me. That he's making up, even a little bit, for what he did to my mother or to me."

"I know," I said. "But there's no way to stop him from setting up the trust the way he wants. He can make anyone a beneficiary—from Charles Manson to Angela Merkel."

"I don't want to owe that man anything," said Amy. "The least you can do is not help him."

"I won't help him," I said. "That's final. You can count on that. But if we don't want Sarah to help him I'll have to tell her why. Is that okay?"

"No, it's not okay. You know what he's trying to do. He wants to leave me money to make up for disappearing the day I was born. He's trying to salve his conscience. Well, I don't want any part of it. He ruined my mother's life and he has no right to interfere with mine. Furthermore, once he's set this up he'll probably want to meet me and he'll think he has a hold on me because I'll want this lousy inheritance, which I don't."

"I think you're better off if I ask Sarah to resign the account and explain to her why. I'm going to be working with her for years and I don't think she'd want to be part of something you'd resent."

"Then he'll just go get another lawyer to make the trust. It won't accomplish anything."

"At least the lawyer won't be someone you know and who is part of our lives, like Sarah is. And what if Winterpol brings more business to the firm? There could be constant pressure to have me work on his account and more and more pressure on the firm to keep the account. Now is the time to cut it off and I'm sure Sarah will agree if I tell her why."

"I want to be done with this," said Amy. "So tell Sarah if you have to. Keep that man away from me."

So that is what I did. I asked Sarah to resign the Richard Winterpol account and I told her about Amy's connection to him. Sarah said she understood. But she was a negotiator. She said she needed someone to talk to Eva Keefer, the woman who might have known her sister, Pammy, if and when Pammy was at Rajneeshpuram.

"The thing is," said Sarah, "I don't think I'll be very good at talking to a spiritualist. I can't get over the idea that they're lying from the moment they open their mouths. On her web page she calls herself Pranalika and says she's a medium, which means, I imagine, that she puts people in touch with the dead. I have no idea how to talk to a person like that. I want to be rational and nail down the facts. We need someone who can be devious but that we can rely on."

"I'm not sure I know anyone like that," I said, "but I'll think about it." And I did think about it. My father came to mind. He was an artist. He loved poetry and music. He definitely wasn't spiritual but was definitely in touch with the emotional and nonrational side of human nature. And he'd been a teacher. He'd taught high school art for many years. So he had a good sense of people, albeit younger people, but that good sense might extend to a woman in her fifties who worked in a field that required creativity. If she talked with the dead, I thought, she had to make stuff up all the time.

But my father was not sly. He had too much empathy with people to fool them into telling him things that, if they had time to think about it, they would not want to tell him. He could not pull anyone into a con.

What made me suddenly think of Amy, who was never devious, was that in a college production of *Blithe Spirit*, she'd told me she'd played Madame Arcati, an enthusiastic medium and clairvoyant. Acting itself required pretending to be what you were not. Amy looked eminently young, forthright, and innocent. Even sweet. But Amy was smart and she loved a challenge. I hoped deceiving "Pranalika," for a good reason, might capture her imagination.

Chapter 15

Sarah

T he portable phone rang while I was out on my deck before dinner reading a book of short stories set in Central Oregon. It was
Bud Russell.

"I'm going to be back in Bend in about two weeks," said Bud. "I
was hoping I could take you to dinner."

"That would be fun," I said.

"This is a date," he said.

"I haven't had a lot of recent experience with dates, but I'm game
if you are."

"I haven't had much recent experience either," said Bud, "and
what experience I've had hasn't gone particularly well. I have high
hopes for this one though."

"That's the first mistake," I said. "Let's keep our expectations in
check."

"I was sure you'd be dating glamorous and charming men all the
time."

"Some old friends have taken me to parties but dates like a real
date have been few and far between. The good men my age get
snapped up by younger women. I had one slightly younger man ask
me out but he had money on the brain. His first question at dinner
was whether I had a plane. I told him I flew Greyhound. It was a
short dinner."

"I've met some ladies who had planes," said Bud. "They're not so special." I remembered how much I had enjoyed our conversation at the outdoor concert. I thought I would be happy to talk on the phone as long as he wanted.

"What was your worst date?" I asked. "I mean now, not when you were young."

"I'll tell you," said Bud, "if you promise not to think of me as a cad. The wife of a friend of mine, whom I liked and thought had good judgment, told me there was a woman I absolutely had to meet. The woman was a widow, very sociable, and an excellent cook. Dressed well and very attractive. My friend's wife said I would just love her. So I called the woman up to ask her out and she asked me to come to her house for dinner, a small dinner with some of her friends, including a local film critic whose name I recognized. It sounded like a generous offer. I thought this would be a great time even if romance did not come calling.

"'Why don't you come early so we can get better acquainted?' she asked. Of course I said yes. I was looking forward to being better acquainted. Well, getting better acquainted turns out to mean I'm going to help her cook dinner. I don't really like to cook but I'm determined to be a good sport about it. I cut up some vegetables and she's unhappy with the result. 'I suppose they'll just have to do,' she says. Then I toast some almonds. I watch them carefully but I've never done it before and I burn them. She gets upset about that, can hardly contain herself, but she has more almonds stashed away and I get them right the second time. Then she goes to get dressed and asks me to greet her guests if they come before she returns.

"So I answer the door for people I don't know, hang up their coats, and scramble around to find things for them to drink. They all know each other and I have no time to talk with them anyhow. I'm essentially a butler. I finally get them set and I start a pretty good conversation with a guy whose hobby is the history of Oregon. I know enough to ask some questions and he's eager to answer. Then our hostess reemerges and reintroduces me to the people I've already met. In a grand and supposedly witty manner she says I'm her sous-chef and I'm still in training. She apologizes if they can smell burnt almonds, though the smell is pretty well gone by then, and explains that I had a little error in the kitchen.

"The film critic, unfortunately, cannot come after all and, after helping to serve the meal, I find myself seated between two of the dullest women I have ever met. The woman on my left has nothing to say whatsoever. When I ask if she has children she says yes and looks absent-mindedly across the table. The woman on my right can talk as long as the subject is her dogs. After I explore the life history of Ruffy and Scruffy, and when and where they've pooped that day, the expression *dog years* takes on a whole new meaning.

"When we're done with the main course the hostess clinks her wineglass with her knife. 'Do you know,' she says, 'that Bud once taught in a one-room schoolhouse? I think that is so interesting. Bud, can you tell us all about that?' So I'm now to provide some general entertainment. She hadn't told me she was going to ask me but this is my moment, nonetheless, to adorn her dinner party. Though I'd gone on to teach high school in Bend, built up a successful business from scratch, raised a family, and once been mayor of a suburb of Portland, this 'one-room schoolhouse' was what I was assigned to talk about.

"'It was a small high school,' I said. 'There were thirty-six students in grades seven through twelve. This was in Jordan Valley, in southeastern Oregon a long way from anywhere. I taught English and history in tenth grade through twelfth. The special thing about it was that all the teachers knew all the students in the school, knew their families, knew what their lives outside the school were like.' I am warming to my subject, searching my memory for an interesting anecdote, but already losing my audience. Their own more engaging conversations have been interrupted by this talk on a totally unrelated subject, narrated by a man they've just met, who seems to be a performing seal for the hostess. Nobody asks me any questions when I pause and my hostess looks annoyed that I haven't made it into a one-room schoolhouse with a bell to summon the children, no electricity, no running water, and a wood-burning iron stove for heat in the winter.

"Well, a few minutes after my unsatisfactory performance and with a brief mumble to the dog woman on my right, I go to check on something in the kitchen. It's a quick jog from there to the front door and I leave. I simply and quietly walk away.

"I did write a proper thank-you note, though, without a hint of sarcasm. My friend's wife, who had set this up, called me to say my hostess was miffed that I hadn't stayed to bond with her over washing the dishes. But, she said, the woman was open to reconciliation if I called her. I seem to have lost the lady's number."

"How was the food?" I asked Bud.

"It was actually very good," he said. "And I hear she has a boyfriend now that the dog woman introduced her to. He can't cook but he's very good on a leash."

"You said you taught high school in Bend. When was that?"

"Fall of '83 to Spring of '85," he said. "I taught English. Then I moved to Portland and went into the mill equipment business."

"Do you remember a student named Pammy Paulsen? She would have been a freshman and a sophomore in those years. Short with dark hair, smart, and loved English. But probably not the most cooperative student. She was my sister." There was a pause on the line.

"Sorry, I don't remember her. I had at least a hundred students over those two years and it was a long time ago."

"I know what you mean," I said. "I have classmates I don't remember from high school, college, and law school." I didn't say I did remember most of them.

If Bud had been Pammy's English teacher he might have had a powerful influence on her. He didn't seem the type to take advantage of such an influence, if he even had it. I didn't want to spoil my ripening relationship with Bud with some farfetched suspicion. But I needed to know if they had crossed paths and what had been the result of that encounter.

Chapter 16

Amy

Dan talked me into going to see Eva Keefer. He said I was good at persuading people. I think he means I'm good at persuading him. My jobs at Greenwood Biomedical have all involved talking people into things, at first talking individuals into being test subjects for our company's products and more recently talking big corporations into including our product inside their own. Our product is a very tiny chip that goes inside a pill. When the patient takes the pill, the chip sends a signal to a cell phone so the patient and the patient's doctor will know that the patient is staying on their prescribed medication. But just because I talk people into things doesn't mean I'm sneaky. I don't lie to people. But I was going to lie to Eva Keefer. It was for a good cause.

Eva claimed to talk with the dead. That made me feel less guilty about lying to her but it made me more concerned about her catching me. And there was a very fundamental problem at the heart of my asking Eva for information. Pammy pretty clearly died in 1985 and I wasn't even born until 1991. We decided my first lie would be that Pammy had lived well into the 1990s, that she had been my aunt, and that I missed her very much. I would have to watch carefully to see if Eva recognized Pammy's name or her picture and if she acted as though she knew Pammy was dead. If she believed that Pammy was still alive, Eva should be more open about what she knew.

The part that required acting was pretending I was foolish and gullible enough to believe Eva could help me, could even put me in touch with Pammy's spirit. I made an appointment to see her.

Eva lives on Geneva Street in Bend. The first things I notice are the hooded eyes painted on her chimney, like the eyes looking out from a stupa in Nepal. Her front porch has ten or more mobiles hanging down from the soffit—big bells, little bells, chains of crosses, stars, crescent moons, wands, swords, pentacles, infinity symbols, squares of stretched yarn, stones, and little chunks of driftwood. Her doorframe and door are painted with nested rectangles in bright colors. Instead of a doorbell there is a *pull handle* message hand painted neatly on the doorframe. The handle looks like it's from an aluminum watering can. The handle is tied to a yellow nylon rope that goes into a hole in the wall. When I pull the handle I hear nothing but feel a heavy weight on the other end of the rope. I slide the handle back into the wall and pull harder. A deep gong resounds inside the house.

A full thirty seconds later the door is opened by a woman with long, braided gray hair. The tip of her braid is streaked in teal and the layer of hair closest to her head is cobalt. She is wearing hoop earrings and a loose light blue dress that hits the tops of her plain leather moccasins. She regards me with a steady eye as though I have come to sell her something she doesn't need.

"Yes?" she says.

"Oh, I hope I have the right house," I say, backing away from the door. "I'm so sorry to disturb you." My eyes widen in simulated fear.

"Who are you looking for?" she asks sternly.

"Pranalika," I say. "Do you know her?"

"Well, then, come in," she says. I take quick, small steps into her front hall and stop, looking down at a beige rug with zodiacal symbols on it.

"I made an appointment."

"I only help certain people," she says.

"Oh, I didn't know," I say.

"Who told you about me?" she asks. I manage to blush.

"I saw you on the Internet. I need to find someone."

"You should ask the police. They do missing persons."

"But I think," I say, "she may have…she may have…passed over. I haven't heard from her in so long."

"Come and sit down." She walks ahead of me into a side room with partly drawn drapes and old-fashioned wall-mounted lamps. The lamps are set to dim. She gestures for me to sit in a deep upholstered chair and she sits next to me in another upholstered chair, a little higher and a little bigger.

"When did you last hear from this person?"

"Twenty years ago today," I say. "I've never lost hope."

"That would be August eighteenth, 1997, a Monday," says Pranalika. I thought she must be guessing at the day of the week. Hardly anyone could do that computation that quickly.

"I guess it was a Monday," I say. "I don't remember."

"And you got a letter?"

"No, I saw her. I was six years old and she was babysitting me. She was my aunt but she was more like a big sister. The next day she was gone and no one knew where she went. Some people said later that she'd had a boyfriend and they went to Alaska together. But I don't know if that's true. We were such close friends and I miss her so much. Especially now because I'm all alone."

"Sometimes I can help people like you," says Pranalika, gazing off toward the far corner of the room. "I can't be sure. I can't guarantee anything. But sometimes there is a way. It's very difficult for me, you understand, and I take some risks when I help people. I do it because I can. People need me. But I need to ask for payment. Are you prepared for that?"

"Oh, yes," I say. I dive in my purse and bring out a short stack of bills. "I brought three hundred dollars with me. Will that be enough?"

"For today, of course," she says. "But I don't want to take money you need. Will that leave you short for the month?" So considerate of her.

"Not really," I say, "my parents left me money and Edward Jones sends me a check every month. That's my investment advisor. It's a

company, not a man." I say this with a hint of pride and even condescension. I hand her the three hundred dollars Sarah gave me. We
thought it would be enough to get Eva's attention. I'm neither as rich
nor as ditsy as I pretend to be.

I think she might offer me tea. You'd think for three hundred
dollars you'd get a cup of tea. Maybe a cookie. But there is no time
for that.

"Do you have a photograph?" she asks. I dive into my purse again
and bring out the snapshot that Dan got from Sarah. It's a color
photo of a pretty but somewhat sad-looking girl with black hair. I
hand it to Pranalika with a hopeful look in my eye.

"I'll need to study the photo," she says. "Sometimes I can pick
up something." She holds the photo facedown in front of her and
closes her eyes. She raises her free hand above her forehead, her
palm facing her, then lowers the hand slowly in front of her face,
continuing steadily down past her lips and her throat until she rests
the hand over her heart. She brings the photo up to face her and
gazes at it. She is starting to study it. Her head flinches very slightly.

"Starlight," she whispers. She is about to turn to me but catches
herself and goes back to studying the picture. She doesn't want me
to see that she recognizes Sarah's sister.

"Do you see something?" I ask anxiously. She looks at me hard
now. She half suspects she is being conned. I hope she still sees me
the way she did thirty seconds earlier.

"What was her name?" asks Pranalika, maintaining the tone of a
counselor trying to help. She has her doubts about me but she doesn't
want to give the game away if I truly am the pigeon she thinks I am.

"I called her Alice, after *Alice in Wonderland*. That was my pet
name for her." If Pranalika insisted on learning Pammy's real name
then she really was suspicious.

"And tell me again when you last saw her."

"August eighteenth, 1997. I remember the date very clearly."

"And how long had you known her before she disappeared?"

"All my life, I guess. I was only six. She disappeared sometimes
before but she always came back." This seemed to strike a chord

with Pranalika. She let out a quiet sigh and her whole body relaxed. Whatever I'd said had been the right thing. Or close enough. Time to turn the tables a little.

I ask, "Why do you think she came back before but not the last time?" It was a stupid question but I hoped Pranalika would reveal something about Pammy's leaving Rajneeshpuram.

"Fate goes ever as it must," says Pranalika. "Some mysteries are uncovered and many are not."

"Can I communicate with her? I mean, if she has crossed over?"

"I would need to know much more about her. Can you bring me things that belonged to her or things she touched? Also more photographs, high school yearbooks, anything like that."

"I'll bring you what I can find. There may be things of hers in with the stuff I kept from my parents." In truth, of course, I have no idea what Sarah might have. "When should I come back?"

"As soon as you're ready," says Pranalika, "but we should set a time. How about next Thursday at two? Will that give you enough time?"

I sigh. "I haven't wanted to go through all those old things. But I will do it for Alice's sake. I will see you next Thursday." I give Pranalika a soul-searching look of desperation mixed with hope as she ushers me out the door. I've played my part well, I think. She believes me.

I'm still at maybe but I've learned one big thing. It looks like Eva knew Pammy as Starlight at one time, presumably at Rajneeshpuram. But if Eva doesn't know that Pammy died way back in 1985, she may not be much help with how Pammy died and who was responsible for her death. I doubt I'm going to get much more out of Miss Pranalika the following Thursday, though I would like to see how she gets in touch with the dead. It would be interesting to see what she does to manifest a ghost. Of course, I don't believe that's really going to happen.

And then, thirty seconds after Pranalika closes her door, a ghost appears. I've been focusing on maintaining my timid demeanor as I leave her property and start down the sidewalk. I'm just beginning to look for where I left my car when I see the apparition. He is sitting in a Chevy Suburban. It is Ken Winterpol. He was my land-lord when I first moved to Bend. He died three years ago. He looks very much alive now, just older. He's wearing a heavy plaid shirt with a leather vest that looks more rustic than what he wore when I saw him alive. He sees me but he doesn't react. He doesn't recognize me. Doesn't even notice that I've stopped in my tracks to stare at him. I collect myself and walk on, as naturally as I can manage. It cannot be the ghost of Ken Winterpol, I tell myself. But I do know who it is. He is a man I've never met before. It's Ken's older brother, Richard Winterpol. He is my father.

Is he following me? No. He doesn't even recognize me. He's never seen me before so how could he recognize me? He lives in Prineville. I know that. So why is he sitting in a car on a side street in Bend going nowhere? I get in my car and drive away. He doesn't follow.

I call Dan from my car to tell him what I've seen. He wants me to talk to Sarah.

"No," I say into my dashboard, "I want to talk to you." I tell him with a note of triumph that Eva bought my story. "She recognized Pammy, I could tell. But I haven't learned anything really, only that she might have known Pammy by another name. She whispered *Starlight* when she saw the photo. That sounded hippy-trippy enough for a spiritual commune. I'm going to meet her again but I have to bring more photos of Pammy and things that belonged to her.

"And I have other news," I say. "Guess who was sitting in a car on the street outside Eva's house? Just sitting there. Maybe he was waiting for an appointment of his own with her. Or maybe it was coincidence. Richard Winterpol. I thought it was Ken's ghost come back to haunt me. Don't you think that's weird?"

Dan doesn't answer right away. "It sure is weird," he finally says.

Yes, I think, that is very weird.

Chapter 17

Richard

With all the talk of men harassing women, I'd like to hear some talk about the eighty to ninety percent of men who have never harassed a woman. All the men who consistently treat women with respect. All the men who are one hundred percent loyal to their wives. You might say some of the men who respect women don't do it out of virtue. They are afraid of embarrassing themselves or even getting arrested. But the bottom line is they don't harass anybody.

If you are like most men you are attracted to women—women you know and perfect strangers. You like looking at them, trying not to be obvious about it. You sometimes imagine having sex with them. Right? But you don't go touching them. You don't say rude or suggestive things to them. If you're trying to be a grown-up you don't even make remarks about them to other men. You impose discipline on yourself. It's self-respect, and it's your contribution to a Christian society.

It's like U.S. Grant and his drinking problem. Sometimes he drank too much. But never when he was commanding troops or planning a battle. And he went for months at a time without drinking. He had restraint. The fact that his restraint wasn't perfect shows that he had it.

I, too, have shown restraint. And with a better track record than Grant. And on top of just plain being attracted to women, I have a preference that many people would frown on. In this day and age, when it's okay to be gay or lesbian or bisexual or whatever, God wired up my brain and my body to test me. I'm on the outer edge of normal. Yielding to what attracts me could damage other people. It would be sinful. So I restrain myself.

Ephebophilia. That's the name of it. It's a sexual preference for teenagers, in my case girls. Not really kinky. But frowned upon. And it could be bad for the girls. But not always and not as bad as some people imagine. You've got to be considerate and know what you're dealing with.

Rajneeshpuram brought it out for me. I'd left home and was living in Portland, picking up work here and there. Sometimes I'd rent a room and sometimes I'd live on the streets. The Rajneeshees came and said they wanted people to move to their ranch way out in the middle of nowhere. They'd give us a place to live, plenty to eat, and work if we wanted it. Share-A-Home, they called it. We couldn't figure out what the catch was. They kept saying there was no catch. And they were pretty smart people, college degrees and well-paid jobs before they joined the Rajneehees. They had this leader named Bhagwan that they were crazy about and they promised we'd love him too. He drove by them every day in a Rolls Royce.

Street people said the catch was they were going to experiment on us and we could all end up like zombies. Or they had a religious cult they wanted us to join, like the churches that gave us meals if we would listen to them preach and sing. Except out in the wilderness we wouldn't be able to escape. Some said Rajneeshee religion required human sacrifice and that was what we were going there for.

There was a catch but it was none of those things. They wanted us to vote some officials out of office that were giving them a hard time. And they wanted to change some laws they didn't like. There weren't that many people in Wasco County, where the ranch was, and if they could get enough of us to register in Wasco they could win the election. That sounded crazy to me. But the only way to get away with being that crazy is to have a lot of money. And knowing they had money persuaded me to go with them.

Free love sounded pretty good to me too. That was part of it. This Bhagwan was known as the Sex Guru and thought everybody should have a lot of sex. He said marriage was bad because it was like ownership. It seemed like the *Playboy* philosophy had gone to India and come back wearing beads. Everybody was supposed to wear orange clothes too. Okay by me. I thought the free love angle was a lie to get us to come. But it turned out to be true. All of a sudden sex every night. A different woman the next night? No harm, no foul. And that's when I gravitated to teenagers. There were dozens of teenage girls there, wild about Bhagwan, excited to be part of the community, and as enthusiastic as they could be about having sex. It was part of the experience. Some of them had run away and some had told their parents it was a sort of religious or artistic summer camp. Some, if you can believe it, were at the ranch with their parents. The adults thought the sex part was fine. Why shouldn't the girls have sex with older men? Everybody should be liberated.

The age of consent in Oregon was eighteen but at Rancho Rajneesh that was ridiculous. In Washington and Canada it was sixteen. In France today it's fifteen. That shows how arbitrary and hypocritical the whole idea was. I was in my twenties and reckless about the law anyway. I rationalized that if men my age and older were having sex with teenage girls all around me, how could the State of Oregon single me out? And the state didn't seem to have the teeth to do anything about all the other problems it had with Rancho Rajneesh.

The compound had an extensive mechanic's shop for all the cars and trucks on the ranch and, of course, for Bhagwan's Rolls Royces. The Rolls Royces in particular attracted me and I went to work in the shop. I'd worked with cars and trucks before in Burns, where I grew up. None of us were paid. The idea was we were building this very special community. A Buddhafield, they called it. It was a funny situation. The work was serious and the hours were long. But everybody was friendly. Nobody hounded us or criticized us. We could work at a reasonable pace. After all, if they fired you then you still got to live there and eat their food for free. And the sex. The sex kept me there if nothing else did.

Sex and money. Though we were all living simple lives and bragging about it, there was obviously a lot of money around. The Rajneeshees had their own plane and an airport. New buildings were going up all the time. They owned a hotel in Portland. Bhagwan had over eighty Rolls Royces with more coming every month. It seemed to me that if I hung around long enough and kept my eyes open, some of that money might come my way.

Did I damage any of the girls I had back then? I don't know. At the time, it certainly didn't seem so. I never bullied a girl into it. And after me they went and had sex with a dozen other guys. If they regretted what happened they would have to blame it on the environment they were in. No one single guy gave them a trauma.

Anyway, that's all way in the past. I have a wife and two daughters. I've been faithful to my wife our entire married life. I've never done anything to embarrass her. I try not to look at other women and I avoid being near teenage girls as much as possible. I won't even look at pictures of them. When Briana, my oldest, started subscribing to *Seventeen*, I told her to keep it in her bedroom. I don't think Cary, my wife, even suspects I have an appetite for teenage girls.

Not that it's been easy. Briana is twenty now, just done with being a teenager. Teenage years are hard on parents already and these years have been especially tough on me. All her friends were teenage girls. All her sports, all her parties, all the concerts she wanted to go to were full of teenage girls. Some I avoided. Some I gritted my teeth. Closed my eyes when I could. My younger daughter, Julie, is fourteen and I'm going to have to go through the whole thing again. But I made it through safely once and can do it again.

Being disciplined has cost me. I don't mean in denying my unacceptable tastes. I mean in denying myself the normal expressions of interest and affection that a father usually shows to his daughters. This hit me hard this summer when Briana came back from college. She came into my office, which is a room off the garage, and asked if we could have a discussion. I sat at my desk and she sat in a visitor's chair so we faced each other.

"Daddy, do you love me?" she asked.

"Yes, of course," I said, "and I want you to be happy. How can you not know that?"

"I don't know that you don't love me," she said. "You've never been mean or acted like you wish I weren't around. But I don't see a lot of signs that you do love me."

"I do love you, Briana, and I always have," I said. "I may not have been very demonstrative, is all. I haven't hugged you since you were a little girl. I didn't think it was appropriate."

"But you're my father," she said. "And there were times when things went wrong I could have used a hug. But I never got one." She was thinking of the time she wrote such a good paper her eighth-grade teacher accused her of cheating. Or when her first boyfriend, in tenth grade, dumped her in the cafeteria in front of all her friends. Or she broke her foot in soccer practice just before the senior prom and her favorite boy asked another girl. I felt deeply for her those times but I didn't touch her.

"I've always listened to whatever you wanted to tell me or ask me," I said. "I've helped you with your homework and encouraged you to get good grades. Your mother and I promised to pay for any college you wanted to go to. We came to all your school functions."

"As long as they were local. You made Mom drive me to anything that required an overnight stay." *Right*, I thought, *the last thing I needed was to spend three hours in a car with four or five teenage girls, one of them probably squeezed next to me. Then get them to sleep for the night in a hotel. It would be hell for me and, if I ever slipped, if I ever wrapped my arm around a girl or tried to kiss her my whole life could come unraveled.*

"I had to watch the ranch and your mother wanted to go. You and she had good times together."

"I'm not really complaining, Daddy," she said, "I'm trying to understand. You don't act like other fathers."

And I hope you never do understand, I thought, *though I'm afraid someday you will figure out that I loved you more than I should and in ways I should not. And I hope that you won't be disgusted by your old man. And that you'll appreciate what he did to protect you. From himself more than anyone.*

"I hope you'll hug Julie more than you hugged me. You need to show her that you love her."

"I'll give it a try," I said, fear in my heart, hoping that hugging did not become an ongoing issue. "But let's not mention it to Julie."

"Well, okay," said Briana. Our discussion was over. We didn't hug. I thought I could probably hug her in the future. She was in her twenties now.

Chapter 18

Amy

D an and I took the morning off to watch a solar eclipse that would be visible from Central Oregon, possibly the only solar eclipse we would see in our lives. We talked about driving forty-five miles north where the eclipse would be total, as opposed to 99.4 percent in Bend. We didn't think the drive was worth it for another half a percent. The roads weren't built for the thousands of visitors who were expected. The traffic would be backed up for miles. St. Charles Hospital chartered sixteen helicopters for the day because ambulances would be stuck in traffic. Besides, the entire eclipse might be a bust because of the smoke. The whole Northwest was having a bad fire season. It started with fires up in British Columbia and now there was a big fire less than twenty miles away near Sisters. Depending on how the winds blew on eclipse day the sky could be clear, dim, or completely overcast. For two weeks we hadn't had a bright, sunny day. We could see smoke filling up the air around us. We could feel it in our throats. Running, swimming, or any serious biking was pretty much out of the question. On eclipse day, though, the sky was clearer than it had been in a week. We were lucky. The eclipse would begin at 9:06 a.m. in Bend and the maximum eclipse would be at 10:20.

We were going to watch the eclipse together at the house of our friends, Sean and Grace Wray. The house was perched on the steep south side of Awbrey Butte and had a commanding view of down-town Bend. You could see the Cascade Mountains around to the right and Lava Butte in the distance to the south.

The Wrays were good friends of ours in spite of Grace being my boss at Greenwood Biomedical and their having a lot more money than we did. Sean Wray had joined Facebook early on and made a fortune from stock options. He had been the student manager of Dan's basketball team at Bend High School and, in addition to work-ing at the Facebook data center in Prineville, he'd bought most of Vandevert Brewing.

Dan and I always looked forward to visiting the Wrays, not only because we liked them and admired the view and the spacious house, but because Grace had first introduced Dan and me at their house during a July Fourth party. As with the view of the fireworks at that party, we would have a great view of the eclipse.

We walked briskly up the driveway, feeling how odd it was to be going to a party at 8:30 in the morning on a weekday. Sean waved us in the door.

"Come get a hat," he said. A cabinet in the front hall was piled with baseball caps in multiple colors. On the front of each was an image of the yellow sun partly obscured by a brown disk. "And look at this," he said, turning one of the hats around for us.

ECLIPSE of the WRAYS August 21, 2017 was lettered across the back of the hat.

"You get it, right?" he asked, beaming like a boy. "Rays as in sunrays. I had them custom made in Springfield—company called Richardson Sports." I took a green hat and Dan took a tan one. "We have lots of glasses for watching the eclipse," said Sean, "three pair for every man, woman, child, and dog in the house. You can take a pair now or wait until it starts." He pointed to a paper bucket next to the hats. The glasses were cardboard with dark reddish-brown plastic rectangles for eyepieces. When I tried on a pair I couldn't see anything through them at all.

"Wow," I said, "These are a lot more than sunglasses."

"Wait till you look at the sun," said Sean. "You can look right at it."
I folded the glasses and put them in the pocket of my slacks. People
were coming in the door behind us and we stepped away into the
house and onto the deck. There was a keg of beer, of course, but we
weren't planning to make a day of it. We got coffee.

There was an auburn-haired woman at the far end of the deck that
I hadn't seen for almost three years. She wasn't a woman I trusted.
She was never going to be on my team. As for Candy Winterpol herself, I doubted she ever had a team. What she had was money, good
looks, and talent. She was an artist. A popular and successful artist
in Portland. But her real money came from her deceased husband,
Ken Winterpol, Richard Winterpol's estranged brother, and the man,
or ghost, I thought I had seen in front of Eva Keefer's house.

For reasons of her own, Candy had once given me some good
advice. I first met her when I barely knew Dan. Out of the blue she
told me to marry him. When I did marry him it was my own decision. Candy had no influence on me whatsoever. But I could not
forget that she had been right. Her advice had been perfect—as
though she could see things that other people, especially less artistic
people like myself, could not. But what I wanted from Candy today
was very practical.

She was standing in the corner of the deck railing, looking beautiful in a lightweight multicolor jacket, talking to two of Sean's friends.
Men, of course. She could have been speaking Malay with bad breath
and they would have hung on her every word. She'd just come from
the "Symbiosis Gathering" in a clearing deep in the Ochoco Forest
out beyond Prineville. Thousands of people. "People came from all
over the world for it," Candy was telling the men and beginning to
include me. "Germany, Brazil, Japan, Australia. There were a lot of
Australians. It was a celebration of art and music, the environment,
and personal growth. It's something like Burning Man in California
except it moves around from year to year."

"And you were there for the art part?" asked one of the men.

"The art is pretty terrible. It hasn't progressed much from hippy
art in the sixties. But here and there are a few original things, or the

beginnings of them. And there is such a diversity of people from around the world. I think I got a few ideas."

"But you didn't stay for the eclipse?" asked one of the men. "I thought that was why they held it there."

"I have to be in Portland for a gallery opening tonight," said Candy. "Besides I'd seen the art and met a few interesting people. I left the gathering last night. I thought I'd stop in Bend and see people here."

"The symbiosis sounds like Rajneeshpuram on wheels," I said.

"Totally different," said Candy. "There's no central guru and the symbiosis is more outward, more about people expressing themselves than about meditating."

I turned to the two men. "Would you mind if I had a word with Candy? It should only take a minute and then you can get back to your conversation."

"Sure," said one of them and they headed over to the keg.

"I'm sorry to interrupt, Candy, but do you remember me? Amy Martinez? Dan's wife?"

"Of course," said Candy. "Actually you rescued me. I was backed into this corner and they didn't have a shred of wit between them."

"Do you know if Richard Winterpol was ever at Rajneeshpuram?" I asked.

"Not the faintest," said Candy. "I never met him. Ken wouldn't talk to his brother, wouldn't have anything to do with him."

"Do you have any photos of Richard when he was in his twenties? Or photos of Ken at that age?"

"Why do you ask?"

"I have a friend whose sister was at Rajneeshpuram before she disappeared. We think Richard was there, too, and might know something about her disappearance."

"Why don't you go ask him?" said Candy, "he lives in Prineville."

"He might have had a role in the sister's vanishing. My friend wants to make sure he was there before she talks to him. We know someone who might recognize him from a picture, even a picture of Ken. I understand they looked alike." I was glad Candy didn't ask me how I knew they looked similar.

"I don't have any pictures of Richard," said Candy. "But there are some of Ken at that age."

"Could you send them to me? The man I know might be able to remember Richard if he saw a picture. They all took different names at Rajneeshpuram and the man might not recognize the name Richard Winterpol."

"I can scan some photos and email them to you," said Candy. "I'll need your email." I had business cards in my pocket and I gave one to Candy.

"Thanks very much," I said. "This will help a lot." I hoped she wouldn't forget. She seemed sincere about doing this for me. Dan and I had talked about this. To Candy, we thought, most people were expendable. Dan's family and, by extension, I seemed to be the exceptions.

The two men were back, beer cups in hand.

"I think you're going to have trouble getting to Portland tonight. The roads will be jammed with people who came here for the eclipse."

"Even if you made a reservation to fly out," said the other man, "you won't be able to get to the Redmond airport in all the traffic."

"I'll be all right," said Candy.

"If you go around the long way through Eugene there'll be traffic there too," said the first man.

"I'll keep that in mind," said Candy. "Now I do have to say hello to Grace before the eclipse starts. Nice chatting with you." She left me with the two men.

"How do you know her?" asked one of the men.

"She's my aunt," I said to avoid a lengthier explanation. In a distant, convoluted way, she was. I didn't explain. Neither did I tell them I had a good idea how Candy was getting to Portland in spite of all the obstacles. Private jet from the general aviation airport in Bend. Some people lead different lives from the rest of us.

"It's starting," someone said behind me. I put on the glasses I'd stuffed in my pocket and looked up. There was a dark crescent cutting off a smidgen of the sun on its upper right edge. Dan came over and stood beside me. The moon had not been visible in the bright sky and the shadow on the sun seemed to come out of nowhere. I could imagine how it would have looked to our primitive ancestors, as though the sun were disappearing, being eaten away by something mysterious. They could easily believe it was the end of the world.

I couldn't see the shadow move but I could tell, from minute to minute, that it had moved from where I had seen it before. None of us said it but I couldn't help thinking there wasn't much to see—just a dark disk slowly covering a light disk. It was the sense of occasion that brought us here, a rare event arranged by nature, rather than man, that millions of people were sharing. We began taking our glasses off and looking around. There was still a party going on. Here was a once-in-a-lifetime experience and people were still getting coffee and smearing cream cheese on bagels. They were looking at each other instead of the sun. Conversation picked up again while people put their glasses on from time to time to check the progress of the shadow.

Dan recognized a man that he knew from high school. He said hello and introduced me to him. We went briefly through the story of how I'd come to Bend and met Dan and what we were doing now. I listened with feigned enthusiasm to the man's story but nothing caught my interest. If we were going to see him again Dan would fill me in. I'm sure the man forgot my entire history as well. But we were pleasant to each other, maintaining the feeling of being present together at an exceptional moment. We looked around us, waiting for the landscape below us to get darker. The light didn't change much and we decided it was because our eyes were adjusting to the change as quickly as it was happening. But as the eclipse proceeded, the land took on the soft light of late afternoon or early evening. The only thing missing was the long shadows. It was different and a little eerie. I glanced at the sun quickly when it was down to a sliver. It still hurt my eyes. Even the light from that sliver was strong.

The crescent of light at the lower left almost disappeared before a new crescent appeared at the upper right. It was a sight we would never see again without a special trip. Some people left without waiting for the eclipse to be over, for the sun to regain its full shape. But Dan and Sean were wrapped up in an animated conversation.

"I want you to try this," said Sean, "just taste it. It's a Russian Imperial stout from Canada." Dan smelled the beer in the glass and then took a sip.

"It tastes like you could make a meal out of it," said Dan. "It's good but I can't see drinking very much of it."

"I got it because of the name, Singularity." I want to license the name in the United States and the owners of the Canadian brewery are open to it."

"You don't want to license the formula for the beer itself?" Dan asked.

"The beer is good but the name is better. The beer is twelve percent alcohol. You drink one bottle and you shouldn't be driving."

"So what's the attraction in the name?" Dan asked.

"It'll be a hit with techies. The word *singularity* means a place where all the mathematical or physical laws you've been following break down and a whole new set of laws take over. The Canadian company is building on the idea of gravitational singularity, like in a black hole. A heavy black beer is perfect for that. But I want to build on the idea of technological singularity. That's when artificial intelligence gets so powerful it can improve itself. Once AI can make itself smarter it can accelerate very rapidly, maybe advance further in an hour than humans could in a decade. In months or even weeks, computers could go way past human intelligence, even the intelligence of all the humans on the planet put together. And they could keep getting smarter and smarter. Technological singularity is a very exciting concept if you're into computers."

"And when is this supposed to happen?" I asked.

"Thirty or forty years," said Sean.

"I'm not sure I want computers to be smarter than humans," said Dan.

"In some ways," said Sean, "they already are."

"When they're smarter than we are," I asked Sean, "will they still be working for us or will we be working for them? Will they want

THE MIRROR POND MURDERS

what is good for humans or will they decide we're just a means to an end?"

"Or even an obstacle," said Sean.

"Or suppose they malfunction," Dan asked, "or go crazy in some indecipherable digital way?"

"A lot of very smart people have said they're worried about that," said Sean. "Bill Gates, Elon Musk, Stephen Hawking. But the benefits of artificial intelligence between now and whenever singularity happens are so great that everyone's rushing toward it. So, in the meantime, I think we can make quite a splash with Singularity Beer."

"Make hay, or money, or beer, while the sun shines," said Dan.

"What are you going to call the beer if the Canadian company won't let you use Singularity?" I asked.

"I don't know," said Sean. "Maybe Slouching toward Bethlehem."

"Or Sloucher," I said. Sean seemed to like that.

As Dan and I walked down the driveway the sun was still half-hidden. We were on our way to work. I wondered what Eva was doing at this moment. Something mystical. Holding a séance and charging a fortune for it. Or maybe she'd gone to the Ochocos for the symbiosis.

And what was Bruce Sargent doing? I'd bet he didn't take the morning off. He'd look up from his work from time to time to check on the progress of the eclipse. He'd probably give his crew three minutes off to look at it. I wondered what he would say when I showed him Candy's photos.

Sarah

A my, God bless her diligent little heart, gave me some photos of Richard Winterpol's brother, Ken, when he was in his early twenties. She'd gotten the photos, along with one of Richard himself when he was a teenager, from Ken Winterpol's widow. Armed with these new photos and a few more of Pammy that Amy had not had when she visited Bruce Sargent, I called up Bruce and said I wanted to meet with him.

"I've got work to do," said Bruce when I called him. "I told your friend that I didn't know your sister and I don't know what happened to her."

"I have photos of a man you may know, who may have been at Rajneeshpuram. I would very much appreciate your help with this."

"Well, we're working on a house in Terrebonne. I could meet with you at lunchtime."

"Do you live in Bend? Could we meet in the evening at our office or at your home?"

"No," he said. "I'm doing you a favor. I don't have time to come to your office and I don't want you worrying my wife. If it's as important to you as you say, you'd drive all the way to Paulina to see me. Terrebonne won't kill you."

"Okay then," I said, "how about tomorrow?" Sargent agreed and gave me the address of the building site.

Terrebonne was thirty minutes away and the building site was another ten minutes out of town. I didn't really want to drive up there—part of my long experience in the law, not wanting to spend non-billable time. I had to remind myself that my trip was my personal mission. I wouldn't bill anybody for any of it.

The building site was on an enormous spread of land that looked, over Crooked River Canyon, toward Smith Rock, one of the most famous vistas in Oregon. The rock, or actually a whole range of bare rocks rose steeply from the valley floor in different forms—towers, walls, blocks of stone, gullies, and overhanging cliffs. The stone was reddish and was said to glow when the sun set on it, though I'd never been there at sunset.

The house Bruce was framing was on the edge of a cliff overlooking the river and looking up at the rock formations on the other side. There were two African-American men nailing together the frame for a wall that was lying flat on the unfinished wooden floor of the house and two white men working on another wall on the other end of the house. The dry desert air smelled of sagebrush and sawdust. The sun was mercilessly bright and everyone was wearing a hat except me. I approached the two black men and said I was looking for Bruce Sargent.

"We'll just get this wall up and stop for lunch," said the older of the two men. "Go take a look at the river," he said, "and I'll be with you. Watch your step." I'd worn my Redwing heavy leather boots, knowing the footing around a construction site could be treacherous, and I set off toward the cliff, carefully eyeing the ground in front of me. Was I looking for nails, construction debris, rocks, loose dirt, or rattlesnakes? I didn't know but kept my eye out for all of them. The river came around the corner from the right, around a high peak of rock, and passed through a deep channel before it flowed into a wider valley with acres of corn growing beside the water.

The four men tilted the one frame up and secured it, temporarily, by nailing planks into some of the studs and bracing the other ends of the planks with short two-by-fours nailed to the floor. Then they quit for lunch, reaching into coolers they'd left in a pocket of shade by a short and scrubby juniper tree. Bruce came over to me and we shook hands before settling on a pile of lumber in the bright sun. The lumber was more comfortable to sit on than the ground, but the sun was hot. I wondered if Bruce had chosen our lunch spot to prevent me from overstaying my welcome. He had his hat on and I had only my long hair to protect me. I would have to talk fast.

Bruce had a sandwich and a small salad with sliced carrots in a plastic box. I had cottage cheese with peaches. We had each brought a bottle of water.

"Thank you for your help with this," I said. "The girl I'm trying to find out about was my younger sister."

"Your friend, Amy, showed me a picture of her but, I'm sorry, I don't recognize her."

"I have other pictures to show you of a man who may have been there." I opened the manila folder I'd brought and began to show Bruce the photos. "This is his brother at a young age. Not the same man but apparently they look similar."

"Samirama," said Bruce, recognizing the photo immediately. "That was his sannyasin name. Came to the ranch with the so-called Share-A-Home program, maybe from Portland. He wasn't crazy, like so many of the people they brought in off the streets. And he was willing to work. He started with the cattle but then went to Bhagwan's cars, the Rolls Royces. He washed them and waxed them and he was studying to become a mechanic. They didn't need a lot of mechanics because the cars hardly went any distance at all. But Bhagwan kept buying more of them. I don't remember Samirama's legal name, if I ever knew it, but we lived in the same building." Bruce took another bite of his sandwich.

I stopped with my forkful of cottage cheese poised in front of my mouth. "Do you remember anything else about him?"

"He always seemed to have something on his mind that he didn't share with anyone. He had his eye out for what was going on around him, especially what Bhagwan and the people who were running the place for Bhagwan—Devya and her gang—were up to. Then at the end he got on the Peace Force, the guys with guns who were

THE MIRROR POND MURDERS

supposed to protect us from outsiders. Actually, of course, they were keeping an eye on all of us.

"You had to laugh," Bruce went on. "Here was Bhagwan, talking about compassion and understanding and trying to build a community founded on love, and he had these guys with guns walking beside his car on the drive-by and standing at the front of the room when he gave his talks."

"What else?"

"Samirama liked younger girls, teenagers. I'd grown up with two younger sisters back in New Jersey and I didn't think girls that age knew what they were doing well enough for that, though the girls at Rancho Rajneesh thought they were part of some brave new world and sex was part of it. No ill effects as far as I could tell. I keep wondering what happened to those girls later in life and what they thought about Rancho Rajneesh when they looked back on it. I'd think they'd decide they'd been taken advantage of and that nobody had stood up for them. I'd think they'd be unhappy or angry. But maybe not. Maybe they'd think they made their own choices at the time and that was all part of life. I'll tell you, though, I have a daughter in her twenties now, ten years younger than Shanti, who was my first. And there was no way my two daughters were hanging out with older men when they were teenagers. And they weren't having sex if I could help it. They turned out fine. Both went to college. Shanti has a job and a husband who respects her." Bruce gazed over at the worksite, either thinking about his daughters or thinking about getting back to work.

"Well," he said, "where was I going with all that? Anyhow, Samirama wasn't really a bad guy, at least people didn't think so. If he liked young girls there were plenty of guys who liked a whole range of women and girls."

"What became of him, this Samirama?" I asked.

"He skedaddled that September when everything was starting to break up. Matter of fact it was the day that Devya left or the day after. She and her cronies knew they were about to be arrested and they left the country. Later on Devya got extradited back to the US and

128

went to jail. Samirama wasn't part of the inner circle. Nobody was coming to arrest him. But he got out anyway. There was a rumor that he took a lot of money with him, cash that Devya had just left in the office. He left with a movie producer from Los Angeles. One of those rich guys who adored Bhagwan but didn't want to stay in a dorm or an A-frame like the rest of us. Built a house high up on a ridge above the compound. This guy had his own Bentley. Nobody was allowed to have a Rolls Royce but Bhagwan. Anyhow, this big movie mogul, Henry Walters, you may have heard of him, probably saw the ranch wasn't going to last much longer. He may have had some run-ins with Devya himself. So he left. Samirama knew him because he'd worked on the guy's car and Walters took him with him, along with some other people."

"So Bruce," I said, "I'd like to show you a few more photos of the girl I'm looking for. I know you didn't recognize her before but I'm hoping you might take another look."

"Okay," he said, as though humoring me in a senseless task. I handed him three photos of Pammy and he looked through the first two, studying each one for a few seconds. He stopped on the third and looked at it a while longer. It was a picture of Pammy at least a year before she left. She was standing next to a horse with a riding helmet on her head, smiling and squinting into the sun a little.

"Blond hair," said Bruce. "She had blond hair when I saw her. In the pictures here she has dark hair. She was called Starlight. Teenagers didn't have sannyasin names. They had hippie-type names. When I knew her she was called Starlight."

I wanted to hug the man and kiss him on the cheek. He'd given me independent confirmation, directly spoken to me by a rational adult, that Pammy was at Rajneeshpuram. Bruce must have seen me getting ready to leap because he gave me a puzzled sort of look. I went back to trying to be a dispassionate investigator.

"Did she and Samirama know each other?" I asked.

"Yes, they did," he said without going into detail. Neither of us wanted to picture my little sister having sex with an older Richard Winterpol, or Samirama, or whoever.

"Did they leave Rajneeshpuram together?"

"They might have. Samirama wasn't a close friend of mine. Henry Walters certainly wasn't a close friend. And I barely knew who Starlight was."

"Do you know where they were going?"

"Henry Walters was driving to Los Angeles. He was from there. Maybe they went there with him."

"And when did you leave?"

"Not until the next March. Most people left before I did but the ranch was still a going operation. There was work and there was food, water, and propane for heat. But Bhagwan was gone and the whole thing looked pointless. A guy who owned property in Portland, and had come to the ranch for a couple of weeks a year, asked me to look after two buildings he owned in Bend. Free place to live and I'd actually get paid. Been here ever since."

I was so happy with the progress on Pammy and, prompted by curiosity, I asked Bruce a question that I wasn't sure he'd appreciate. "Weren't you about the only black man in Bend in 1985?"

"Aren't very many now," he said. "And it took some persuasion to get my wife to move here. I met her in San Francisco. But I like it here. It's handsome country and it's sunny most of the time. People are friendly, even if some of them do a double-take when they see me. Why should white people have all the beautiful places to themselves? And Bend keeps growing. Business is good. They don't have enough houses but they sure have plenty of space to build them."

"How do your daughters like it?" I asked.

"They like it fine. They have lots of friends and they can ski like the wind. You can imagine they get some looks on the slopes. They say daughters are more worrisome but I'm glad I don't have to sit them down for The Talk. You know about The Talk?"

"I do," I said. "Is that really necessary here?"

"Damn straight. With all my years here and my business sign on my truck I get stopped two or three times a year for DWB—Driving While Black."

I wanted to tell Bruce that people sometimes treated me differently when I told them I was one-quarter Indian. But it wasn't really the same thing at all. When the police pulled me over, which hardly ever happened, I knew it was for a legitimate reason. I'd done something I shouldn't. It didn't ever occur to me they might shoot me.

"Did you know a woman named Eva Keefer at Rajneeshpuram? Also known as Pranalika?"

"Yeah," said Bruce cautiously. "She was older than Starlight."

"Was she a friend of Starlight?"

"Kind of. I think," said Bruce. "You know Bhagwan was big on community. He didn't talk down friendship but you got the sense that bunching up into groups, even groups of two people, was a distraction from building the Buddhafield. I don't know how close those two girls were. I wasn't that close to either of them."

"Did they leave Rancho Rajneesh together?" I asked, "maybe with Samirama and Henry Walters?" Bruce rubbed his forehead with his hand while he thought about this.

"Could have," he said. "They all disappeared about that same time. But then, a lot of people did."

An electric saw started up at the far end of the house. Bruce's crew was getting back to work. I didn't envy them working through the afternoon with the sun getting hotter and hotter.

"Well," I said getting up, "I think you've told me about all I can think to ask you. I appreciate your help. You've moved me way ahead of where I was."

Richard

M y cell phone rang while I was still sitting in the car and the call was from Oxton, Rath, and Flynn in Bend. Sarah had sent me a draft of the trust agreement and I thought she must be calling to see if it had looked right to me, which it had. Since I was already in Bend, I thought I might swing by their offices and sign a final copy.

"Hello, Richard," said Sarah, "I'm sorry to make this call but Oxton cannot continue to support you as a client. It turns out we have a conflict of interest that prohibits it. Of course we will cancel all our billing for your account—for my consultation with you, for drafting the trust agreement, and for any and all expenses. I'm sorry. Could you return the draft trust agreement document we sent you?"

I didn't like hearing this one little bit. The trust was important to me and it was particularly important to me that Oxton create it. "It's a trust, not a contract or a lawsuit," I said. "What conflict of interest can there be?"

"That's what I thought when we took the project on," said Sarah. "But it turns out there is a conflict after all."

"What is the conflict?"

"I'm sorry I can't say. The conflict is such that I can't reveal the other party or the nature of the issue."

"Look," I said, "I made an agreement with you for your services specifically for this trust. You can't back out of it now."

"The contract says that if we discover a preexisting conflict we can resign your account."

"Ah," I said, "the fine print."

"The clause is in the same typeface as the rest of the contract." God, she was being literal. And a royal pain in the neck.

"Along with a letter formally resigning your account, I'll send you my notes on the discussion we had. And as I said, we won't bill you for our time or any expenses. You'll have to find another law firm if you want to pursue this."

"I don't want another law firm," I said. "I want you."

"I'm sorry, Mr. Winterpol," she said in a tone that started sympathetic and swerved sharply colder, "we can't represent you."

"Well," I said, "I don't think you'll be representing anyone else in Prineville once I tell people how you've treated me."

We said goodbye in what an eavesdropper might have thought was a cordial and businesslike manner. But I was ticked. I wanted very much to have my daughter and her husband know that I was going to do something for them. When I died, Briana and Julie would be surprised to learn they had another sister. But they, and their mother, would not know about Amy until after I was gone.

Chapter 21

Sarah

D an hand delivered an invoice to me in my office for the time
Amy spent interviewing Bruce Sargent and Eva Keefer. It was
just before noon but we had all the overhead lights on because the
smoke from the fires made it seem as dark as a winter afternoon. He
sat down while I wrote Amy a check and a short note of thanks. Dan
and I had agreed, and Amy in absentia, on an hourly rate that was
twenty percent above what Greenwood Biomedical paid her, including benefits.

"Amy says she's on your team and she hopes you are on hers," said
Dan.

"I am," I said.

"We thought I would be helping you with what happened to
Pammy. Amy got out ahead of me."

"And she did great," I said, "but we have a long way to go, I think,
and I don't know what it's going to take from you, me, Amy, Jim
Sorensen, or who knows who else to find out what actually happened. I'm going to go see Eva Keefer myself next and see what I
can shake out of her." I moved a file from one side of my desk to the
other to signal I wanted to move on to a different subject. "Have you
thought of a way to get a confession out of Floyd Tingley? It's the
only way we're going to charge him or convict on Ray's death."

"I think I can try something," said Dan, "which may or may not work."

"What is it?" I asked.

"I think I better not tell you, in case it backfires."

I was a little surprised at this, though I thought I knew what Dan meant. He was going to do something that might be legally or ethically questionable. He didn't want to pull me with him into whatever it was. That was considerate of him. For his own sake, if something went wrong, he didn't want me to testify in court that he'd had a plan, that whatever he did was carefully considered in advance.

"Don't take too much on yourself," I said. "You need to be here for the long haul."

"Don't worry," he said. "I'll handle it."

I dearly wished I could have Eva Keefer in court under oath. That wasn't going to happen. I thought of making up a story to inveigle the truth from her. But Amy hadn't gotten much hard information with that approach and I knew I didn't have much experience with making stuff up. I was too straightforward.

The tack I decided to take was adapted from a documentary I saw about the British turning German spies into British collaborators during World War II. The British had been lucky enough to capture one of the first who parachuted into England. From him, they learned a lot about the spies who were yet to come—who they were, where they would be dropped, and what their objectives were. Each time they captured one they would pretend to the spy that his capture had happened by chance. They would ask the spy what he knew and listen patiently to the spy's well-rehearsed cover story. Then the British would correct the story with what they knew about the spy already and the spy would spin a modified story. They'd correct that story and subsequent stories until they revealed they knew a great deal about the spy already and the spy was worn out. This would all happen in a day or two so the spy could send a radio message back to the Germans saying his mission was going well. The British never tortured any of the spies but they got what they wanted.

So I would ask Eva questions, let her spin answers, and then correct her in the hopes she would decide I knew everything I needed to know already and she might as well tell the truth. It might work and it might not. Any new information I got out of her would help.

One fiction I knew I had to use, because Amy had discovered that Eva believed it was true, was that Pammy had lived for years after Eva last saw her and might even be alive today. That belief, I thought, would make Eva more willing to tell me what happened than if she thought Pammy had died shortly after they parted company—a few days, hours, or even minutes.

I made an appointment to see Pranalika, repeating briefly what her website said about counseling and spiritual guidance. I told her I thought I would need at least two hours of her time in the first session and she told me her fee. My tone was relaxed, modeled on the conversation I had with a new hairdresser in Bend when I called to make my first appointment. I didn't pretend to Eva that I was desperate for sympathy.

My costume was sharply creased tan pants with a blouse that had a floral pattern on it, not too loud. It was what I would have worn to a gathering that called for business casual. It was meant to show confidence and competence—more authority than I had projected on the phone. Eva's mouth dropped just a little when she saw me. I smiled and said I was glad to meet her. I handed her a check to pay for two hours in advance. We sat in the same darkened living room in the same two upholstered chairs that Amy had told me about. I told her that I'd heard about Pranalika from Amy and that Amy and I were looking for the same person, my sister, Pammy Paulsen, whom Amy had called Aunt Alice and who was known as Starlight at Rajneeshpuram. I said, in a matter-of-fact way, that I wasn't looking for emotional support. I was looking for facts.

Pammy had lived at home for a while after leaving Rajneeshpuram, I said, and then she disappeared again. It wasn't true but Eva didn't know it wasn't true. I said my family had hoped for years that Pammy would get in touch with them but she never did. Now I wanted to see if she had gotten in touch with any of the people Eva knew from

Rancho Rajneesh. Pammy remembered her time on the ranch as a wonderful and exciting part of her life. She talked of going to India. She could be anywhere in the world.

Had Pammy, by chance, gotten in touch with Eva or had Eva heard anything about her?

"No, never heard a word."

"Do you remember who her friends were on the ranch and who she was with when she left?"

"I didn't know her that well," said Eva.

"But you did leave the ranch together?"

"I don't remember that."

"You both left the day Devya left, in Henry Walters' Bentley." I wasn't sure of this but even a denial would be useful information. Eva straightened up in her chair and gave me a hard look.

"I only want to know what happened to Pammy," I said. "I'm not looking to cause you any trouble." This wasn't necessarily true either. "Tell me and I'll get out of your hair." She didn't answer, weighing her options.

"Who was Samirama?" I asked.

"Some guy," she said. "Starlight's boyfriend. Or at least he wanted to be. He was older."

"What was his real name?"

"I don't know."

"His real name was Richard Winterpol. He lives in Prineville now." Eva now had a look of real concern on her face. I was getting to her. I followed up quickly.

"So you all got in Henry Walters' car and then some of you got out in Bend. What happened there?"

"Starlight was going to walk to her parents' house. Henry wouldn't take time to get off the main route down Third Street. Samirama got out and went with her."

"What were they carrying?"

"They both had backpacks."

"Did they have any injuries? Were they both feeling well?"

"As well as I remember. Starlight was relieved, even happy to be going home."

"Was there any friction between her and Richard?"

"You're not recording this, are you?" Eva asked me with stern face.

"No, I'm not," I said. "Whatever you tell me is between you and me."

"In any case, I don't know why you're asking these questions," she said. "What difference does it make at this point?" Eva was almost pleading with me to ease up on the interrogation.

"Let me level with you about Pammy and why I'm here," I said. "Pammy never made it home after she left you. She didn't live into adulthood and then disappear. Did you read about the skeleton they found in Mirror Pond over a month ago? That was Pammy." Eva snapped her head back. Very unprofessional, I thought, for a mystic. "I want to find out how she got there and who is responsible. From what you're saying, Samirama, also known as Richard Winterpol, would know a lot about the answers."

"I didn't know," said Eva, mouth open and staring out the window with a stunned look. "I never dreamed…" I could see she was scrambling through her memory of that night, trying to make sense of it. I wished I could read her mind, her memories, her thoughts, her guesses, whatever might help me sharpen the picture. I wanted her to think long enough to remember what she could. But not long enough to make up a story. She surprised me.

"I have something I should give you," she said. "Starlight left it in the car. I thought one day I would see her again and give it back. We were friends, you know." Eva got up and went down a hall toward the back of the house. She returned after a minute and gave me a small book with a padded cover and a photograph of Bhagwan on the front. "This is a diary that Starlight kept while she was at Rajneeshpuram. I read it once years ago but I don't remember what she said. Maybe something in it will help you." It was my turn to be stunned and speechless. I'd been nibbling at crumbs trying to understand what happened to Pammy and here, apparently, was a feast of information.

It might lead me straight to Mirror Pond and it might not. But surely it would be an enormous step forward in the case.

Eva held the book out to me and I took it by pinching the top of the spine between my finger and thumb. I didn't want to mess up fingerprints on the diary that could tell us something. I put the diary in my purse. It was a gift, a valuable and unexpected one. Now that I had it I could study it later, read it over and over. But Eva was in front of me now and apparently willing to talk. She might not be so willing later on.

"Thank you," I said, "What made you keep the diary all these years?"

"I save things," said Eva. "I have every Valentine's Day card I ever got, going back to kindergarten. Every time I thought about throwing this out I thought Pammy might want it. And you see," Eva said with a toss of her head, "it's good that I kept it. I was only a little off on who would want it. And here you are. I hope it helps you find peace."

"Have you communicated with Richard Winterpol since you last saw Pammy with him?" I asked.

"You mean Samirama? No, I never heard anything more about him. I had no idea he was living in Prineville. Have you talked with him?"

"I will," I said, which was, strictly speaking, true. I didn't mention he'd sat in a chair in my office and he was, or had been, my client.

"Were you and your sister close?" Eva asked.

"Not really," I said. "We were nineteen years apart. But I loved my parents and my parents loved Pammy. We spent our Thanksgivings and Christmases together as a family. You could say Pammy and I loved one another, though we were not a big part of each other's lives."

"Starlight was my friend," said Eva, "but we were united in our love for Bhagwan and our commitment to Rajneeshpuram. And after she moved to a different compound within the ranch we didn't see as much of each other."

"And where did you go after you last saw her?" I asked.

"Henry Walters was taking me to Los Angeles. That was the plan. He said I could have a chance at the movies and he would help me get a start. Said I could be another Molly Ringwald. That was the peak of my Hollywood career. That conversation and one night of sex in a motel in Weed. I woke up sick as a dog the next morning. He paid for two more days at the motel and gave me five hundred dollars. Then he drove off in his Bentley and I've never seen him since."

"And then?"

"I went back home to Florida. Twenty years later I came to Bend."

"Why Bend?"

"I liked the climate and the mountains. People I knew said Bend was growing. A lot more than Miccosukee. I had regular jobs here for years—cashier, waitress, bookkeeper. But I knew I could help people. I could give them hope. So I became a counselor. I've done a lot for many people. And they are very, very grateful." Eva said this with some pride. I supposed she believed it. From another perspective, closer to my own point of view, she was defrauding people. But I didn't say that.

"I'm sorry about your sister," said Eva. "She was a sweet girl."

Chapter 22

Pammy's Diary

I drove straight to the office to make copies of the diary and took it out of my purse using brand-new dishwashing gloves from under the coffee bar.

Though the rings in the binder had partially rusted they snapped open easily and I ran the double-sided pages through the feeder on the copy machine. I caught sight of youthful handwriting in a succession of colorful inks. The dates matched the summer that Pammy disappeared. She didn't put her name at the beginning but the diary started with a girl leaving home and going to Rajneeshpuram. I could check the handwriting against Pammy's old school papers that my parents had kept but the diary appeared to be genuine.

I put the original and one copy in a manila envelope to take to Jim and put two copies in a locked fireproof filing cabinet. I would give one of those copies to Dan because he and Amy were helping me with my investigation. But I couldn't stand the thought of anyone reading the diary before I did.

I sat down at my desk to read the copy I'd made for myself, realizing immediately I didn't want to read it there. It was too precious. It was not business as usual. It was personal. It was my family. It was Pammy speaking to me after all these years. I wanted to savor the time I had with her as I read her diary. I could dissect it later for clues. And who knew what tears or anger her words might call up?

Happy or sad or bewildered I wanted to read Pammy's words in my own house.

Jim met me in the lobby of police headquarters and I gave him the original to put into evidence and the copy for him to read. I told him I would read it carefully and write him a summary of what I thought was most relevant to her death. He thanked me in advance and said at some point, as the case progressed, he would read every word of it himself.

Jim also told me he had new information about the Sharon Forrester murder in 1962. A woman had come in to tell him that she believed her older brother, who had gone to high school with Sharon, had lured her to the park and clubbed her over the head when she spurned his advances. The woman had been stirred out of her guilty secret by reading the news about the skull in Mirror Pond, Pammy's skull. Jim said the woman sounded credible and he had independently confirmed that the brother was killed in Vietnam. So, as we had suspected all along, the only connection between the two murders was Mirror Pond itself. Three murders if you counted Ray's death nearby.

"If you don't find anything useful in the diary," said Jim, "and don't think it's worth writing up, let me know and I'll read it anyway. I may find something. I've been a detective a long time." I thanked Jim and headed home.

Between the armrests of Ray's stuffed leather chair I felt a remnant of his comforting strength preparing me for whatever I would discover. On a sunny summer afternoon I would normally read in a chaise on the deck under the shade of an umbrella. This afternoon I felt exposed out there. I rationalized that a sudden breeze might blow Pammy's pages away. Would Pammy say she resented her parents and couldn't wait to get away from them? Would she fault me for not paying enough attention to her or injuring her in some other way? Was she intimidated by the Rajneeshees, maybe even enslaved in some way? Would I wish that our parents could have read this diary or would I be grateful that they had never known what was in it? I dreaded finding, at the end of Pammy's diary, that she was distraught and that her death was self-inflicted.

July 5, 1985 – Wait until they ask me what I did on my summer vacation. I'm going to the Rajneesh World Festival! Beautiful people are coming from all over the world to celebrate and meditate with Bhagwan. He's shown so many people how to live a richer life. Like he says, people worry too much about death. The important thing is to be fully alive before you die.

I haven't told anyone where I'm going. I left a note in the kitchen saying not to worry and I would be back.

This year I read Bhagwan's book, Zorba the Buddha, *over and over for months. He is just so wise. I thought* Zorba the Buddha *would be like* Zorba the Greek *and I could get extra credit for reading it. We read* Zorba the Greek *in school, for Mr. Russell. But* Zorba the Buddha *is totally different. Bhagwan says you have to know your passions and weaknesses and all the ups and downs of life, like Zorba, to really get what meditation is all about.*

So I'm going to learn, learn, learn. There will be classes in meditation and then there will be darshans where Bhagwan gives lessons to all his disciples at once. I want to learn dynamic meditation. And if they let me, I will help build the Buddhafield, which is what Bhagwan wants his place to become.

In the evening there is dancing and parties. But no drugs. People are so happy they don't need them.

July 8, 1985 – I went to my first darshan! Eva and I went early so we could sit near the front but even so we were five rows back. There were thousands of people in Buddha Hall so we were lucky to be where we were. Everybody was wearing orange or red. I wore a simple orange shift that I bought in the shopping center. They have everything here. It really is a small city. Eva is from Florida and eighteen years old. She and I were assigned to the same house with some other women. It's an A-frame on the side of a hill. She read Zorba the Buddha, too, and she wants to stay at Rajneeshpuram after the festival is over. To do that, she says, she has to find a job that she can do for the community.

They played music while we waited for Bhagwan. Some of it was Indian music and some of it was popular music—"I Want to Know What Love Is," "Everybody Wants to Rule the World," "Easy Lover," "We Built This City"—and an old song by John Denver called "Looking for Space." Before Bhagwan came in I was surprised when all these people with guns showed up at the front of the room and faced the crowd. They looked so serious. It seemed very strange when everybody was feeling nothing but love for each other. I asked Eva if they were part of a show, like a music video. She said they were there to protect Bhagwan. She said he has enemies. Last year, she said, they tried to blow up the Hotel Rajneesh in Portland.

And then Bhagwan came in dressed in a long bluish-gray robe, kind of like a poncho with sleeves. He had a hat with no brim that fit over his head made out of material that looked like the curly wool on a sheep. He sat on a chair on a stage above the crowd so we could all see him. I looked as hard as I could into his eyes. I wanted him to know how happy I was to see him, how much I had studied his book, and how closely I was paying attention in the classes I was taking at the festival. For just a moment I knew Bhagwan saw me, just me alone, that he knew what I was thinking, and he was happy for me. Knowing my thoughts had made him happy too.

I was so caught up in just being there I don't remember everything Bhagwan said. He did tell us to live a full life, to not think about ourselves too much but focus on the consciousness of the community. Life will always have its challenges. There will always be pleasure and pain, happiness and unhappiness. You have to learn to balance between the *two extremes. Don't worry about sin or guilt. Don't force things. Life should be about letting go. That's all I remember. His talk was videotaped and I can listen to it again. Many of his talks are taped but I will get a tape of this one because it was the first time I ever heard Bhagwan live and in person. When I watch it I will always know that I was in the audience.*

July 10, 1985 – Eva and I went to see Shakti, a woman who lives at Rajneeshpuram and is in charge of work assignments. We said we wanted to stay at Rancho Rajneesh after the festival and we knew, to do that, we had to have jobs. She reminded us that there would be no pay, aside from free room and board, and the hours would be long. And she asked whether our commitment to Bhagwan and building the community was strong enough for us to keep doing the best job we could do in everything we did. We both said yes. She said she would see what might be possible.

The very next day Shakti sent for us and said the ranch needed people to work in the kitchen for the communal dining hall. We would help prepare the food and clean up afterwards. So we are both going to be able to stay! I'm so excited. Bhagwan says we should balance the good and the bad but right now everything is good. I'm practicing meditation two hours a day. Every day my mind is more tranquil and yet, at the same time, my mind expands in its understanding of the world and of myself. I am growing and learning faster than ever before.

July 18, 1985 – I am a sannyasin! Shakti told me she thought I was ready and that she would ask Bhagwan. So at darshan today, five of us sat right on the floor in front of Bhagwan with our legs crossed in the lotus pose while Bhagwan spoke to the crowd. Then he spoke to each of us individually. The first was a man in his thirties or forties. He said he had read all of Bhagwan's books. He had quit his job and left his family to come learn from Bhagwan. Bhagwan asked the man two or three questions and the man answered very seriously. Then Bhagwan stared at the man for ten seconds or more. He said, "You are not ready." He stopped looking at the man and focused on the next person. The man Bhagwan had rejected started shaking while he sat there. I thought he might be angry but after a while he just bowed his head. He must have been very unhappy.

When Bhagwan got to me he looked at me very hard, as though he could see I wasn't ready and was angry that Shakti had asked him to consider me. I looked back into his eyes, letting him see me as I really was, without trying to pretend anything. He looked at me in a way no one had ever looked at me before. I could tell he was wiser than anyone else I'd ever met. He saw me more clearly than anyone had ever seen me. I decided I should trust him to make the right decision for me. Any pleading or promising or justifying would not have any effect on what he decided. I could only hope that what he saw in me was worthy. Then I suddenly felt this incredible love and compassion coming from him and he asked me a question. He asked me if I had a boyfriend. It was a small question compared to all he could ask me about—what I felt for Bhagwan, all I had learned from his teachings, and all I hoped for. And yet, in some way I didn't understand, answering that simple question, and the way I answered, told Bhagwan everything he still needed to know. I told him no, I didn't. He didn't react. He kept looking at me. Then he smiled at me and nodded. "You are ready," he said. He turned to an assistant and picked up a mala, the string of one hundred and eight beads with his picture attached to it, the symbol that would show I was his sannyasin. He beckoned me to come forward and bow, which I did. And he placed the mala over my head and onto my shoulders.

"Your sannyasin name will be Nakshatra," he said. I raised my head to face him. I'd never been so close to Bhagwan before. In front of those thousands of people it felt as though he and I were the only people in the universe. Then he nodded to me and I understood it was time for me to return to my place. I wanted to stay with him, right where I was, forever. But I was his disciple now and I would do as he directed.

I wasn't sure I even remembered my sannyasin name correctly. Shakti told me again it was Nakshatra and it meant Starlight. It meant hope and purity of purpose, she said, and not just for myself, but being a beacon of hope and purity for others.

So Eva had been more than Pammy's acquaintance. She'd been her friend, at least at one time. They had been allies of a sort, negotiating their way into this new world together. Eva could tell me more about Pammy, I was sure. And as soon as I'd read the whole diary carefully and collected my thoughts I would draw up a well-planned list of questions to ask Eva.

I remembered the note that Pammy left at home. My parents kept it for years. I came across it again after they died. It was written on the top sheet of the pad in the kitchen for grocery lists. It said, *Don't worry. I'll be back. Pam.* That's all. Not even *Dear Mom and Dad.* My parents showed it to me and looked hopefully at my face, imagining I might divine something from it that they could not. Where had she gone? Who was she with? When did she mean to be back? As the days turned into weeks, months, and years, the meaning they gave to *I'll be back* kept changing.

I put down the diary. I was furious at Pammy. The self-centered little brat. After all the love my parents had given her she went off after this guru who had thousands of followers. She was no more special to him than a chipmunk. Nakshatra my ass! Rajneeshpuram sounded like Jonestown to me. Pammy would have heard of Jonestown. It happened in 1978, seven years before Pammy went to Rajneeshpuram. This cult leader, Jim Jones, a devotee of communism, led his followers into a remote corner of Guyana, near Brazil. When things didn't work out he got nine hundred men, women, and children to commit "revolutionary suicide" by drinking Kool-Aid laced with cyanide. Total baloney.

I had to go out for a walk to steady myself. Walking the pond, as Ray and I used to call it, always had a calming effect on me, even after he died and I had to pass the place where it happened. The afternoon I started reading Pammy's diary, though, the far end of

the pond was more than I could take. I couldn't pass both places—
the sidewalk where Ray was killed and the Galveston Avenue Bridge
where Pammy last stood on the earth.

Ray had been dead for three years and I'd decided years ago that
Pammy must be dead or that I'd certainly never know anything
more about her. This summer I was forced to see both deaths from
new perspectives. It made their deaths fresh in my mind, as though
they had just happened.

I would walk south along the west shore as far as the pedestrian
bridge over the pond, cross over to Drake Park, and come home. At
least, I thought as I stepped onto the wood of the bridge, Pammy
hadn't left home because she blamed my parents for anything. She
didn't vent, in her diary, about how horrible her life was. She left
home with hope. Misguided hope but hope nonetheless. It was
almost worse, in a way, that she barely mentioned our parents, as
though she'd dismissed them like childhood toys. And of course,
there was no mention of me at all.

What was I to Pammy and what was she to me? When my mother
announced she was pregnant I was eighteen, about to leave for college and begin charting my own life. I was a loving and considerate
daughter, outwardly supporting my parents' excitement. Inwardly I
felt my parents' devotion to me, their only child, slipping away. If my
parents didn't tell Pammy she was unplanned, she must have figured
it out. Clearly, if my parents had wanted a second child they could
have had it long before. I never asked Mom whether they had considered abortion. It was still illegal in Oregon in 1968 but they could
have gotten a legal abortion in Japan if that was what they wanted.
My parents were not timid people.

I stopped in the middle of the bridge to look back at the pretty
houses on the west shore. There was a big white clapboard that I
loved with oversize black-and-white-striped awnings over the sec-
ond-floor windows, black shutters, and a long covered porch overlooking a jam-packed flower bed and a generous lawn. One could
imagine a large family there in the summertime with children of all
ages running in and out. Grandparents would be drinking lemonade

on the porch. In the house's earlier days someone would be listening to the baseball game on the radio. If my kids would hurry up and have grandchildren my house might be something like that.

The very bridge I was standing on was associated with another death, though not one that concerned me directly. Sharon Forrestor had died beneath this bridge. I walked over the spot as I neared the east shore. Now that Jim knew who had killed her, I'd asked him what, if anything, he was going to do about her murder.

"The man who did it is dead," he said. "I suggested to the sister that she tell the *Bulletin* for the sake of those who remember Sharon. But the woman is ashamed of her brother and I don't think she'll do it. It's not my place to tell the public if she doesn't want to. I can't prove anything."

I recognized Jim's dilemma was something like my situation with Floyd Tingley. I knew that Floyd had murdered Ray and that many people would believe me if I told them. But without a confession from Tingley there was no way to send the man to jail.

Pammy and Sharon had made bad choices. Both had died. Did it matter, I wondered, that Pammy was aspiring to some sort of enlightenment, to expanding her understanding and her capabilities? Did it make a difference that Sharon was opting for lower forms of excitement and easy pleasures? But Sharon didn't leave town. Where were her parents? Where were her teachers? Did they do the best they could? For that matter, did I do the best I could for Pammy? I acknowledged that I could have done more.

I did care about my little sister and I tried to show it, though being a good sister or even a good babysitter did not come naturally to me. My mind was set on college, law school, and my job at Oxton. Once my career was underway my greatest joy and top priority became living my life with Ray. My maternal instincts did not kick in until I had my own children.

My mother said that Pammy admired me and even wanted to be like me. But I think she also resented me and the challenge I had unknowingly set up for her. I had been the good girl. My life appeared to step from success to success. From the distance of nineteen years she didn't see how I'd struggled and failed along the way—the friends I didn't have, the parties I wasn't asked to, the ski team I wasn't quite good enough for, the D in chemistry I got in spite of the extreme effort I made to understand the subject. She didn't see the funks I'd gotten into as a teenager or how many things my parents told me, both important and trivial, that had evaporated into a gossamer mist as soon as they hit my brain.

Pammy was a better athlete than I was and not as diligent a student. She took more risks. She would climb over the chain-link fence to get into a park rather than walk around to the gate. She sassed one teacher so much she got detention for a week. She came home drunk one afternoon when she was twelve. God knows what drugs she might have taken or how much experience she had with sex. Whatever she did I'm sure she wasn't intimidated into it. One boy tried to go further than she wanted and she broke his finger.

Taking off for Rajneeshpuram was bold, even for Pammy. Her diary made it sound as though she'd gone by herself. It didn't appear to be Bud Russell's idea and I was cautiously relieved to see that.

When I got back to the house it was almost cocktail time. I fixed myself a vodka tonic and sat down to read more of Pammy's diary.

Chapter 23

Dan

I was going to get Floyd Tingley to confess to his crime, if I could, and record it with his full knowledge and consent. It was going to take some trickery to do that, some misrepresentation. It would border on the unethical, though it wasn't illegal. It would be like setting up to slam a tennis ball to the back of the court and then dinking it over the net. And it would, I was sure, serve the larger cause of justice.

The police are allowed to lie to get a confession but it's murkier if an attorney, a detective, or a private citizen does it. So even if I got a recorded confession it wasn't a sure thing that a judge would admit it as evidence. I found the Tingley phone number in Christmas Valley and I called it on my cell phone. I made sure it was Floyd I was talking to. "Hello, Mr. Tingley. My name is Daniel Martinez and I'm an attorney in Bend. I've been looking at old cases involving grazing rights and I believe the federal government took some rights away from your family way back in 1975. Is that right?"

"Yes," said Floyd more slowly and tentatively than I would have liked.

"Well, the courts are starting to reconsider cases like your family's and they may be deciding the government got it wrong. Have you heard of a man named Cliven Bundy?"

"Government took his grazing rights too," said Floyd.

"There's a trial coming up about that and people think Mr. Bundy stands a good chance of winning. I think you have a case too, and I'm calling because I'd like to be your lawyer. I'd like to represent you in getting fair compensation for the grazing rights your family lost. Would you be interested in that?"

"You'd get our grazing rights back?"

"Maybe. Maybe not. More likely the court would make the government pay you money instead."

"How much are we talking about here?"

"We can't know what the court will decide. But I think we can make a case for at least half a million dollars. If we can get compensation for all the years you should have had those rights and didn't have them it could be a lot more."

Floyd thought about this for a moment or two. "How much is this going to cost us? If we hire you to do this?"

"Nothing," I said, "unless we win. My offer is to go after this strictly on contingency. If we win the case I get a percentage of whatever you get from the government. If we don't win then you pay me nothing." I waited for Floyd's next question and it didn't seem like one was coming. "If you think you want to do this, we should get together and talk some more. You need to tell me everything you know about what happened and what the impact on your ranch and your family has been. And show me any documents you still have about your grazing rights back then and how the government took them away. Are you coming to Bend anytime soon?"

"Not planning on it," said Floyd.

"Well, if you're serious about this," I said, "I'll drive down to Christmas Valley to meet with you. And I'll bring a copier for the documents. I could make it, let's see, day after tomorrow. Get there about ten o'clock. Will you be at the ranch that day?"

"Yup."

"And do you think you want to pursue this?" I asked. "I don't want to drive all the way down there and have you tell me you've decided you're not interested."

"We're interested," he said firmly and in a louder voice. "The BLM stole that land from my daddy. I'll fight to get it back any way I can. And teach them a lesson at the same time."

"Great," I said. "See you then."

The Bureau of Land Management, the government agency that everybody called the BLM, controlled billions of acres across the country. The BLM hadn't taken the family's land as Floyd was throwing the term around. The BLM had only declined to renew the family's grazing rights on land the government owned. But Floyd was getting motivated and I didn't want to remind him his family had never owned the land itself.

It would take me about two hours to get to the Tingley ranch, taking the well-traveled road past Upriver Ranch where my parents lived, then the still familiar road to La Pine, and then east toward Fort Rock. Christmas Valley and the ranch were another twenty miles. I'd only been to Christmas Valley twice before in my life. People said the town only appeared on maps because there was nothing else near it and plenty of blank space to print the name. In the 1960s a developer began to promote Christmas Valley to retirees and would-be ranchers and farmers. People bought land but hardly any of them moved there. The developer went bankrupt. In valuing the place, a judge said, "The land is arid, dusty, windy, isolated, and subject to temperature extremes." Some people said the development was a mistake and some said it was a scam to begin with. The Tingley family, however, had bought their land back in the 1950s, before the development had ever happened. They should have sold out in the years when Christmas Valley was hot property.

If Floyd's interest flagged I was ready to do a mini pep rally on the Bundy family again. Cliven Bundy stopped paying to graze his cattle on federal land in Nevada, administered by BLM, but he kept grazing his cattle there anyway. He claimed the federal government was illegitimate and the land belonged to the state of Nevada, of which he was a citizen, and the federal government had no authority over him. When the feds came to evict his cattle, he and his friends, with rifles and shotguns, stood their ground. The feds backed off that day but then they went after him in court. Bundy was arrested in 2016 on his way to join his son in another standoff against the federal government at the Malheur National Wildlife Refuge in Oregon, about three hours east of Bend. He said he believed in the "sovereign citizen" where each citizen should decide for himself what the law was and shouldn't be subject to the federal government at all.

As a lawyer, I saw Cliven Bundy as a crackpot. I could imagine, however, how a man sitting on his horse in some great expanse of the West might decide he could get along fine if the government would just leave him alone. But with three hundred million people in the United States the "sovereign citizen" idea was insane.

At the end of a quarter-mile dirt driveway, running through acres of hayfields, the Tingley house sat on a lush green lawn in its own little grove of poplars and cottonwoods. The house was a white clapboard one-story rectangular building, overdue for its next paint job. A plain brown metal building, bigger than the house, stood a hundred feet away and I thought it must be the hay barn. Two horses were standing under a wooden roof, supported on poles, that leaned up against the metal building and was surrounded by a log corral. In front of the house were a four-door Chevy pickup, about ten years old, and a very old Dodge truck with no license plates. I wondered if the Chevy was the same pickup that had killed Sarah's husband and nearly killed her.

"Hello, I'm Daniel Martinez," I said to the young man who answered the door. "Are you Floyd?"

"Yes, I am," he said and turned his head back into the house. "Mom, the lawyer's here. The one I told you about." Then back to me, "Come in." I couldn't tell if he was looking forward to our meeting or was on his guard. He treated me as though I'd come to fix a broken washing machine.

The house was clean and neat inside. The couch and chairs in the living room looked like they'd been there a while but they looked comfortable. The two biggest chairs had armrests shaped like segments of wagon wheels. A woman who looked to be in her sixties, in jeans and a loose top came into the room. She smiled a big smile.

"How do you do?" she said and crossed the room to shake hands. "Would you like some coffee?"

"Yes," I said, "that would be great."

"Have a seat," she said, gesturing toward the couch. I sat down where she pointed. She sat in one of the chairs and Floyd sat in the other. I wondered about the coffee which she didn't leave to get underway. I didn't really need the coffee. I was just trying to be sociable. Neither she nor Floyd said anything further so I introduced myself again and asked the woman if she was Mrs. Tingley and she said she was, Marilyn Tingley. She was Floyd's mother. His father, Warren, had died.

I went over again how they might be able to get compensation for the grazing rights they had lost. Sitting in the homey living room, facing a boy and his mother who looked like the salt of the earth, I had an uneasy feeling about deceiving them. My misgivings began to rise like a bubble from the depths of my consciousness. I felt sorry for Marilyn Tingley if Floyd did go to jail. But then, if he was a murderer, she raised him to be what he was. Floyd's parents lost their grazing rights before he was even born. They must have built resentment of that fact through his entire childhood, along with enough anger and hate for him to attempt to murder Sarah.

"I need to understand what happened when the government took your rights. Do you mind if I record our conversation so I can make sure I get all the facts straight?"

"Go ahead," said Floyd. Mrs. Tingley deferred to him more than I thought a woman who had helped run a ranch ought to defer to her twenty-one-year-old son. But she was going to need him to work the ranch, especially as she got older, and I imagined she wanted him to feel as responsible for it as possible. Invested in it. What was going to happen when he tried to find a wife? I placed my iPhone on the coffee table in front of me, started recording, and spoke at the machine.

"This is a recording of a conversation between myself, Daniel Martinez, attorney, Mr. Floyd Tingley, and his mother, Mrs. Warren Tingley, at their home in Christmas Valley." I gave the date. "Floyd, could you state your name and say you give your permission for me to record our conversation?"

"Floyd Lee Tingley. I give permission." I asked Mrs. Tingley to do the same and she did.

"How did you first learn about the government not renewing your grazing rights?" I asked.

"We just got a notice in the mail," said Marilyn. "Nobody came out to talk to us. Nobody asked what we thought about it. We'd been grazing cattle on that land for over twenty years. Took good care of the land too. Put in fences and watering troughs. They never paid us for any of that."

We went on for thirty minutes about the notices they got, the people they talked to at BLM, and about having to go to federal court in Portland. The way Floyd and his mother told it, there were hundreds of people in the federal government who were either out to get them or just didn't care about them one way or the other. I scribbled notes, asked questions, and tried to show as much interest and seriousness as possible. It was all pretty much irrelevant even if we were serious about the grazing rights. What would matter would be the court documents that I could look up without ever coming to Christmas Valley. But we were on a roll.

"And they haven't stopped," said Marilyn. "What they really want is to run us off our own land. Land that we own outright. It's got to as where rural people like us don't have the power to stand up against the government that's coming up against them. These days they're more interested in bunnies and butterflies and the endangered whatnot. They say the cattle are bad for the snowy plover up in the air and the fish in the creek. But you go out there. There's wild animals all over the place and the cattle don't bother them. It's a peaceable kingdom except for coyote. Now they want to bring wolves in. That's the craziest idea I've ever heard."

"The people in the cities and suburbs just don't get it," said Floyd. "We're feeding them and they're trying to destroy us. We had a neighbor, Earl Westegaard. The stress of dealing with lawyers killed him." He paused to do a calculation in his head. "No offense."

"None taken," I replied.

"We might have had a chance back then," Marilyn said, "if it hadn't been for those Indians."

"It was cowboys and Indians," said Floyd, "and the cowboys lost." I sensed this was a phrase Floyd had been hearing since before he could talk.

"And their lawyer," said Marilyn. "Warren said she was the worst. She kept driving and driving the court to take our rights away. She wouldn't let up. Turned out later she was part Indian too!"

"That might be prejudicial," I said. "What was her name?"

"Sarah Paulsen," said Floyd. "My father said she was the whole reason we lost. She loved those Indians and she didn't care about us."

"There'd be times," said Marilyn, "Warren would sit in this house, in that same chair that Floyd's in now, and he would hit his fist into his hand. And every time I would ask what was wrong he would just say, 'Sarah Paulsen.' But he never swore. He wasn't a swearing man. The way he said her name, though, it sounded like swearing."

"She changed her name," said Floyd. "But we found out what it was. Changed it to Sarah Chatham." They thought changing her name was evil and underhanded. I wanted to say, "She got married," but I held my tongue.

"Did she seem like she was out to get you?" I asked.

"She sure did," said Floyd. "But I got her. Or almost did."

"How was that?"

"Ah, it don't matter."

Conspiratorially, "But you tripped her up somehow. Made her pay a price?"

"You bet she paid a price."

"And nobody figured it out?"

"They said it was an accident. Wasn't my fault. I walked away." Then with a sideways smile and in a lower voice that I hoped the recording picked up he said, "But it weren't no accident." He gave me a wink. I could testify to the wink.

"Pretty smart," I said. Floyd looked quietly pleased with himself. His mother looked a little nervous, as though she recognized he might have said too much. And he had. I had gotten as good a confession as I was ever going to get.

"Do you have any documents from back then? Letters the BLM sent you or you sent them? Documents from the trial in federal court? Do you have the last grazing rights contract you had before they told you they wouldn't renew?"

"It's all somewhere," said Floyd. "We didn't want to get it all out until we talked with you. So how much do you think we can get from the government?" I was pretty sure the answer was *not a damned thing* but I wanted to keep my options open.

"I'll know a lot better when I can see the documents," I said. "But as I told you on the phone, it could be a half million dollars and it might be more. But let me ask you, since I'd be representing the ranch, who owned the ranch back when BLM took the grazing rights and who owns it now?"

"Mom and Dad owned it then," said Floyd. "Since Dad's gone, Mom owns it now."

"And when I'm gone," said Marilyn, "it will go to my four children. Floyd's the youngest and he says he likes ranching. So it looks like he'll be running the place. The others didn't want anything to do with ranching. There's one in Seattle, one in Portland, and one in Los Angeles. They have their own lives but they still come to visit. My grandchildren like to ride the horses."

That made me feel better. If and when Floyd went off to jail, Marilyn would still have a family left.

"I think we've done as much as we can today," I said. "Thank you for your time." I scooped up my cell phone and dropped it in my pocket. "I'll be in touch when I have some ideas about strategy." I gave them my cell number but not my business card that said Oxton on it. And I didn't ask them to sign any agreement to have me represent them, which any lawyer would naturally want at this point. We parted with handshakes and smiles out in front of the house. And cheerful Dan drove away, breathing a sigh of relief at every telephone pole he passed.

I got lunch at a little cafe in the town of Christmas Valley. They had Wi-Fi so I uploaded the recording to Oxton in Bend. Floyd's final sotto voce confession was in there, a little hard to hear but clear as day. Back on the road I called Sarah from my car to tell her the good news.

Chapter 24

Pammy's Diary

If Pammy had lived she would have been forty-eight as I read her diary. She would have had a career and probably a family. We would have known each other as adults for decades. Rajneeshpuram would have been one memory among others. But her days at Rajneeshpuram, reflected in her diary, were now the closest I was ever going to come to knowing who she was, what she thought, and what were the last and most vivid experiences of her life.

Lights were coming on in the restaurant across the pond as I settled into Ray's chair again, my cocktail for comfort this time, and picked up the diary where I left off.

August 5, 1985 – I told Shakti that I wanted to be a guide for people visiting Rajneeshpuram. I was so enthusiastic about Rancho Rajneesh I wanted to share it with outsiders. I told her I already knew where all the places were, not just Buddha Hall and the dining hall, but the dairy barn, the farm, the airport, the garage for all of Bhagwan's cars, the lake, the office building, the shopping mall, the greenhouses, and even the sewage treatment plant. I knew many of Bhagwan's sayings and was learning more all the time. The guides are called "twinkies." I think that's partly a joke but they are supposed to give visitors a sense of how wonderful the ranch is, how well it is working, and how enthusiastic everyone is about it. They are supposed to "twinkle." I said my name, Starlight, made it only natural that I should twinkle as well.

Shakti said sometimes visitors were looking for bad things to say about the ranch. They could be very hard on the twinkies and could trick them into saying things that weren't true and could make the ranch look bad. The twinkies needed to know how to handle tough questions and Skakti didn't think I was ready for that.

Then she asked if I'd like to work in Bhagwan's compound, called Lao Tzu. The job would be housekeeping, laundry, helping out in the kitchen, and attending to whatever Bhagwan needed. He already had a staff for that but they needed another person. I tried not to show how excited I was. To be that close to Bhagwan every day! I said yes as slowly and firmly as I could. But Shakti knew what I was thinking. She said I wasn't there as a student. I couldn't expect Bhagwan to pay any attention to me except when he wanted something. She said I was not to speak to him unless he spoke to me. Still, I could hardly contain myself. It was very hard to keep my mind on meditation that afternoon.

August 15, 1985 – Sometimes Bhagwan seems almost like a normal man. He sleeps. He eats. He reads. He washes. Every day after lunch he goes out for his drive-by. He gets in one of his Rolls Royces and drives very slowly on a fixed route through the ranch. Hundreds of sannyasins line up along the road to see him and wave. I used to go when I worked in the kitchen but now I see him for hours every day. Most of the time we don't talk. I could be a robot. But that is the way it should be. Bhagwan does so much good for all his followers and for all the world. It is a privilege to serve him. Sometimes he does talk to me a little, if only to ask how my meditation is progressing. But he looks at me with such understanding and compassion when he talks I think it is all I will ever need. And twice now we've had real conversations, communicating on a very deep and sincere level. Though he is being kind to me, I think he enjoys our talks as much as I do. I treasure each

*of them and relive them over and over, though Bhagwan would say
that is a mistake, that I must not cling to my memories but meet every
day as though it were entirely new.*

*My work takes me into his bedroom to clean and tidy up when he
isn't there. It is draped with fabrics and feels like being in a tent, though
some parts of the wall are solid and one wall has tall glass windows
that look out into his private courtyard. All the fabrics and walls are
shades of his colors. The curtains are pink. The carpet is orange with
abstract-like purple flowers in it. The walls are a bright shade of red.
The bed cover is a darker shade of red and the sheets are a very light
shade of pink that almost looks white in comparison. There are two
photographs on the wall that surprised me at first but I decided they
fit, in a way, with what I read in* Zorba the Buddha *about combining
the spiritual with worldly experiences. One was of an erotic carving
from a Hindu temple and the other was of a statue I'd seen in art
class called* The Ecstasy of Saint Theresa. *The statue made us giggle in
class because it was supposed to represent Theresa in an ecstatic spiritual state. But it sure looked like an orgasm. I wondered if Bhagwan
thought it was as funny as I did.*

*The person who sees the most of Bhagwan is Devya, the woman
who manages the whole ranch. I mean Rajneeshpuram is a real city,
recognized by the state of Oregon. It has a mayor and a city council.
But Devya, and the people around her, who are not part of the official government, actually run everything—the festival, city planning,
who can come to the city and who cannot, security, relationships with
the county and the state, and who does what job. Devya comes to see
Bhagwan in his private rooms every evening to get instructions about
running the ranch. I've overheard them. It is a practical business discussion, though sometimes they speak harshly to each other. I never
heard Bhagwan speak that way before and after the meeting he can
be upset and have trouble going to sleep. Devya says some people in
the city complain to each other about the police and the security. They
say the Peace Force is more threatening than reassuring and is totally*

opposite to what Bhagwan has said about how sannyasins should live. I don't know how Devya knows about all these conversations.

I sort of knew the ranch had enemies outside. But Bhagwan and Devya are much more worried about them than I ever guessed. There is a man named Turner that they think is their worst enemy. He's an attorney for the government. Bhagwan told Devya she must find a way to stop him. She said it would be risky but she and her people would find a way. It would be a catastrophe if anyone shut down Rajneeshpuram, not just for the people here but for the whole world.

August 20, 1985 – I am a lucky, lucky girl. I am very special to Bhagwan now and he is close to me. We are lovers. He has chosen me. In his bedroom this afternoon he invited me to sit down with him on a special blue rug that he sometimes uses for meditation, when he doesn't go into his private meditation room. Bhagwan said I paid close attention to keeping his rooms clean and he could tell I was making good progress in my meditation. He said that kind of attention would speed me on my way to happiness and he asked if I was ready to turn my attention to sex. I knew from my reading that sex, with the right thoughts, was an important path to becoming a whole person, to becoming a Zorba, and progressing toward becoming a Buddha as well. He said he needed sex as well, that his wisdom and his spirituality were not enough in themselves. He asked if I would go down that path with him and I said, "Yes." Then I said it louder, "YES!"

He told me to take off my clothes and fold them carefully on the floor. When he didn't tell me anything more I sat down facing him in the lotus pose. He gazed at me with his god-like eyes. I hoped he was pleased with my naked body and I waited for him to tell me what to do next. I decided to do whatever he asked.

"Turn around," Bhagwan said, "and stay in the lotus pose." I turned my back to him and waited. I could hear Bhagwan inching forward on the carpet. He rested his hands on my shoulders as though he were going to adjust my pose. After what seemed a long time he slid his *hands down my arms, then under my arms and up to cup my breasts. I couldn't help pushing my breasts out to him. I tried to keep the lotus pose but I couldn't concentrate. Bhagwan gently drew my breasts up and kissed me on the neck. I wanted to face him and wrap myself around him. He slipped his right hand down and squeezed my pubis. I wanted desperately to do something to please him. I reached behind me to grip his penis but I couldn't reach it or couldn't find it.*

"Now the downward dog," he said, "with your hands on the bed." I thought this was a version of the downward dog pose just for sex. Maybe this was why we learned the downward dog, though I'd learned it with my hands and feet on the floor and my body in an inverted V. Bhagwan released me. I stood up and bent over the bed. He cupped my breasts from behind as before and told me to spread my legs more. I tried to remember where my limbs were and what muscles I was using so I could learn this new pose. I wanted to do it right.

I felt Bhagwan pressing into my vagina and I moved my hips back to make it easier for him. I felt his body against me and his hands gripping my hips. When he first thrust into me I rocked forward, away from him, and he nearly fell out. "Push back," he said. I was clumsy at first but I learned to match the rhythm of his forward motion and the little grunts that went with them. When I heard him groan I knew I was giving him pleasure. I was so happy to be serving him this way. When he made a big thrust and held himself in me as far as he could I could feel his semen running down my leg. Bhagwan's semen. I wanted to save every drop.

Bhagwan backed away and sat on the bed. I turned to sit on the bed beside him but he said, "Don't." He placed his hand on my hip and looked up into my eyes. "You have served me well, my child," he said. "Now go in peace." I wiped myself with a dust cloth I had been using and put my clothes back on, baggy lightweight cotton pants, like they wear in India or Arabia, and a long, loose shirt. Everything orange of course. I had to dress to go to my room because there were other people in the house. I put the dust cloth in a Ziploc in a drawer in the little bureau in my room.

Bhagwan was my first real lover. I made out with boys before but I'd never let any of them touch me below the waist. I gave Bhagwan my virginity. I want to tell him that tomorrow and I hope he will be happy for both of us.

If Pammy hadn't died this would almost be farcical. She bravely sets off to seek wisdom and joy with a guru. She's totally committed. But what does she wind up doing? She's cleaning houses and giving sex to her employer. An adult Pammy would laugh at it herself.

"Can you imagine," she would say. "I was an absolute fool! And I saved his semen in a Ziploc. It's too much."

Maybe not. Maybe the memory would be too embarrassing. But it wasn't embarrassing at the time. Pammy was happy, ecstatically happy, even as she reveled in an illusion. I shouldn't judge her sixteen-year-old self from my older perspective. What was I crazy about when I was sixteen? Paul McCartney, the Rolling Stones, *Blow Up*, *Fahrenheit 451*, and the smartest boy in my high school English class. I was far less adventurous than Pammy. I didn't run away from home and I didn't have sex until my senior year in college.

Pammy, I thought, *the man's a creep.* He was selfish and self-centered and he took advantage of her. There was no mention of protection. He didn't care if he got her pregnant or if he gave her some disease. He didn't care that seducing a sixteen-year-old girl was illegal. Was this why Pammy wound up dead? Because she got pregnant or because she could testify to his crime?

And who was this Devya person? Was the "Peace Force" really necessary or were Devya and Bhagwan paranoid? I couldn't imagine the Oregon State Police coming into Rajneeshpuram firing their weapons at Bhagwan or anyone else. Even in the outback of Eastern Oregon the law moved more slowly and deliberately than that.

Did Bhagwan have other enemies? White nationalists wouldn't have liked Bhagwan and all the mixed races at Rajneeshpuram. But even by the wildest stretches of the white nationalist imagination, the Rajneeshees were far from seizing the levers of power in the United States. I thought the white nationalists would have pretty much ignored Bhagwan. It sounded like Devya was instilling fear of outside enemies to enhance her own power within the community. I'd also bet she had spies within Rajneeshpuram who told her who was grumbling about her and who might want a change in leadership. Pammy was a pawn in all of this. I knew what happened to pawns. They became the first casualties on the chessboard.

If Pammy had made it home I would have envied her a little. She had an adventure I never would have dreamed of having. I was Little Miss By-the-Book. If I had a wider range of experience, like Pammy, would I have been a wiser person? Or a more interesting person, not only to other people but to myself? Would I have been stronger, more daring, and more resilient later in life if I'd taken some risks like Pammy? If I'd survived without physical or mental injury, the risks might be worth it, I thought. But I couldn't have counted on it.

I'd had a happy life, at least until Ray died. And after months of unrelieved grief, life was still worth living. And oddly, avenging Pammy's and Ray's deaths had given my life renewed impetus, founded on anger that was scarcely less painful than grief.

I wouldn't give up the life I'd led for any youthful thrill or experience. If Pammy could see me now I think she would wish she made safer choices, though I'm sure she didn't feel that way when she was a teenager.

I made a quick dinner of fried eggs and toast, poured myself a glass of Sauvignon Blanc, and sat down again to read the rest of Pammy's diary. Now that I had some sense of her life at Rajneeshpuram I would start looking for clues to her death.

Chapter 25

Pammy's Diary

August 21, 1985 – Bhagwan is a jerk. No one could have loved him more than I did. No one could have worked harder to serve him, to give him everything he needed. Worse than a jerk he's an asshole. I trusted him. I believed in him. I believed he cared about me. Anything he wanted or needed I got it or did it for him. I tried to guess what he might need before he even asked. I thought I was special. I knew he could have sex with anyone but I thought he liked me. I was so eager to learn how to please him. I would do anything he wanted and I would learn to do it well. I would make him happy and his happiness would radiate out to the entire world.

I listened in to his talks with Devya so I would know more about what I might do for him. And tonight I overheard Bhagwan tell Devya, just so casually, that one thing he wanted, among others, was for me to be gone. He wanted Devya to reassign me out of his compound. It wasn't even a question for consideration. It was a passing thought, like a whim.

"She is cute," he said, "and she's a good worker. But she doesn't understand." What is it that I don't understand? He's my teacher. He's been right there. If there is something I don't understand why doesn't

he just tell me? I'm eager to learn. He must know that. I've worked so hard to learn. Devya almost caught me when she came out. Usually I scurry away before she gets to the door. I was so distracted I barely made it. When she came looking for me in the house I thought she must have known I was listening. But all she said was that tomorrow I would work in Confucius Compound where she lived. Quick, no explanation, that was it. As she went out the door I asked whether I could go say goodbye to Bhagwan. She answered me over her shoulder while she was walking away. One word. "No."

A rock might as well have rolled over me. I hurt so bad I couldn't even get out of bed this morning. I told Eva about Bhagwan and she said I needed to meditate, to try and find the balance between highs and lows as Bhagwan taught us. It doesn't help that Bhagwan is my inspiration for meditating in the first place. The more I try to calm my mind the angrier I get. I am in Zorba mode and I am carried away with emotions.

I need to find another man, or multiple men, to fuck. I need to show Bhagwan that he isn't that important. I need to prove that to myself. I need to dilute the memory of that time with Bhagwan, which I thought was so special, with so many other experiences that Bhagwan will be one little memory among others. I'll find another man, better-looking than Bhagwan, and I will fuck my brains out with him. I will have such deep, desperate, and satisfying sex that I won't be able to think of anything else. I will try every position known to man until the man I'm with and I are both exhausted.

August 27, 1985 – So I'm working at Devya's compound. It's cleaning and washing like at Bhagwan's but I don't love Devya the way I loved Bhagwan. Shakti says I'm still helping Bhagwan build the Buddhafield. Devya is very important to that. She is Bhagwan's right-hand person. Devya ignores me most of the time but she issues very sharp commands and gets angry if I don't do things right. She needs to meditate more, if she ever meditates at all. She works very hard from early in the morning until late at night, meeting with people, talking with people on the phone, going to meet Bhagwan in the evening, and then coming back to meet with her inner circle. Every day she goes into a secret room that I'm not allowed to go into. There are a few people who work in there and I don't know what they do. Usually she comes out looking angrier and more unhappy than when she went in.

I've found the man I need and he likes me. His sannyasin name is Samirama. He used to be called Richard. He works on Bhagwan's Rolls Royces and I met him when he brought cars to Bhagwan's compound. I saw him at the cafeteria and said hello. He's twenty-seven but he likes me. I told him I'd like to see where he lived and get to know him better. I was pretty obvious about it without outright saying I wanted to have sex with him. Every day since then we meet in his room while most other people go to Bhagwan's drive-by. Devya and Shakti think it's perfectly natural for me to leave Devya's compound for the drive-by. But that's not where I go.

Samirama is a good lover. He knows how to please a woman and I've learned things I never knew before. Bhagwan was selfish and Samirama is generous. He has to remind me not to make so much noise. I want to scream sometimes. I want to scream so loud Bhagwan will hear me and know that Samirama is bringing out the woman in me that Bhagwan never did and never could. Samirama says we should get T-shirts that say Orgasms R Us.

September 1, 1985 – Though I'm supposed to go to bed in the far end of the house, I've found a place to hide near Devya's bedroom where I can hear when she relays to the other leaders what Bhagwan has told her. If he says things about life or love or meditation or being awake, she doesn't talk about those things. All she talks about are people who want to close down Rajneeshpuram. Some are people who own ranches next to Rancho Rajneesh. Some are the old-time residents of Rajneesh City, that used to be called Antelope. Wasco County government hates that Rajneeshpuram is already the second biggest city in the county, after The Dalles, and that Bhagwan and Devya want to have more say in county government. That's democracy and I think the county is being fascist.

The state doesn't like all the homeless people who the ranch tried to help. The people had to leave Rancho Rajneesh and the state had to pay for the buses to take them away. But the worst is the US government. They want to kick Bhagwan out of the country along with many of his disciples. Most of the people on the ranch don't know anything about this but it's really serious.

This one guy named Turner who works for the US government is really out to get them. Bhagwan told Devya to consider every possible alternative to find the best way to stop him. Devya told her people that she asked Bhagwan whether that included killing Turner if necessary. Then Devya played a tape of Bhagwan talking to her about this. I could barely hear it but Bhagwan said if ten thousand had to die to save one enlightened master then so be it. That really got the whole group talking. The most excited ones were talking about killing Turner and how to do it. One man said he couldn't kill anyone but he would support whoever did.

Suddenly a woman in the room shouted out that they weren't going to kill anyone and she wasn't going to listen to any more of this. I crouched down as tight as I could behind the chair that was close to the door and she didn't see me when she stomped out of the room. She left the door open and I thought other people might be coming. So I skittered along under a table and behind another chair until I got to the door on the other side of the room and I ran as softly as I could all the way through the house to my room. I shut the door and kept the light off. Then I threw off my clothes and got into bed in my underwear. Nobody came and I tried to breathe more slowly, like I learned in meditation, so if somebody did come I could pretend I was sleeping. Actually I couldn't sleep so I got up and wrote in my diary. I picked up my clothes, put my nightgown on, and I'm going to put the diary under my mattress from now on.

September 3, 1985 – I told Samirama what I'd overheard in Devya's meeting and how worried I was about it. For Bhagwan, for Rajneeshpuram, and for all the sannyasins. I told him this in private in his room. He is very understanding and he says he will see what he can find out about the government plots. He says he talks on the phone with the companies that sell cars and parts to Bhagwan and they might be able to find things out for him. He really wants to get to the bottom of this so we both know what's going on. But he told me I shouldn't listen to Devya's meetings anymore. If they found out they might reassign me to a terrible job or make me leave the ranch.

When I thought over what Samirama said it came over me that leaving the ranch, if it were my decision and I wasn't asked to leave, might not be so bad. I still want to be near Bhagwan and I want to work with everyone else to build the Buddhafield. But everyone in my compound is tense and having secret meetings all the time. I'm okay when I'm meditating. I'm happy when I go to the drive-bys. And I feel safe and content when I'm with Samirama. But sometimes I think about going home. It wouldn't seem the same after all I've learned this summer, though I could still meditate and read Bhagwan's books. Bhagwan says we have to make our way in the world.

September 11, 1985 – I'm pregnant! Shakti told me I looked different and I should go to the clinic. I said I didn't feel sick. But Shakti made me go right away. She watched me leave from the front of Devya's house. I'd never been to the clinic before but I knew where it was. A nurse examined me and had me pee on a piece of plastic. She looked at the plastic then told me I was pregnant. She didn't act like she was excited for me or sorry for me. She was watching me to see what my reaction was. It's a good thing I was sitting down or I would have fallen over. I just sat there stunned. I didn't know how to think about it. I made a start at trying to meditate. But I couldn't stop my mind racing and I knew that meditating was not going to help me sort this all out. The nurse was calm though. She just stood there quietly. Then she took my hand and held it.

I needed Bhagwan. He would know what to think and what to do. If he knew how desperate I was he would see me, I thought, in spite of what I had heard. And then I had an inspiration. I asked the nurse how long I'd been pregnant and she said she couldn't tell. I told her it was important. I didn't tell the nurse this but if the baby is Bhagwan's I could tell him. I'm sure he would want me back at his house again. And I would be honored to have his baby. It could be the best thing in the world.

Eva came to see me in Devya's compound less than an hour after I saw the nurse. I was sitting on my bed trying to think. I tried to meditate again but I couldn't. How could I have been so stupid? How could I have thought that getting pregnant was a separate decision from deciding to have sex? I knew better but had ignored what I knew. What was the right thing to do now? What did I want to do? Thank God Eva came. At least I could talk to her, even if she didn't have the answers.

Eva said Shakti had learned I was pregnant and wanted to help me with whatever I decided to do about it. I wondered how Shakti already knew what the nurse had said. I'd barely found out myself. It's spooky the way she and Devya know everything. Eva showed me two little bottles of medicine that Shakti had given her to pass on to me. Shakti had gone over the directions three times to make sure Eva got them right. I should wait three more days to decide what I wanted to do. If I wanted to keep the baby I should drink all of the bottle labeled B+ and it would help make the baby strong and healthy. If I didn't want the baby I should drink the bottle labeled B- and the baby would go away. She said to be careful not to mix them up. Eva showed me the B+ and B- labels and put the bottles on the little table next to my bed. The liquid in the B+ bottle was clear and colorless. The liquid in the B- bottle was a faint pink but you could still see through it.

I want to talk to Bhagwan but I can't. Even if people let me see him he would ask me if I'm sure the baby is his. I couldn't lie. He would see it in my face that I'm not sure. I don't want to tell Samirama either. Although he cares about me I don't know what he'll think. Which bottle will he tell me to drink or will he leave it up to me? Or will he wash his hands of me altogether like Bhagwan did? I decided the one person I can talk to is my friend Eva. Eva's become a sannyasin too, and her new name is Pranalika. It means "channel" like a channel to enlightenment or spirituality.

September 13, 1985 – Everything is falling apart around me all at once. Devya and all her buddies, including Shakti, have just up and gone. They got in a plane and flew away. No one knows where. Samirama says we have to leave right away before the government comes to lock people up. It won't be safe here, especially for me because I worked in Devya's house. There may even be a fight between the soldiers and the Rajneesh security people. He knows a man who has a car and will drive us. I still haven't told Samirama about the baby and tomorrow I have to decide what to do about it. How did everything get so complicated and awful? I want to stay near Bhagwan. I want to be with Samirama. And part of me just wants to go home.

That was all of it. The end of the diary. There was nothing but blank pages after that. I looked at every single one of them for a word, a mark, or a scratch. Nothing.

I was so sorry for Pammy but furious at her too. She's in a nest of people who are taking advantage of her, who don't give a damn about her, and she's a sucker for every one of them. I'm mad at Bhagwan for setting up this elaborate con that pulled her in, not to mention seducing her and throwing her away like a used Kleenex. I'm mad at Eva for not being a better friend and looking after Pammy. I'm mad at Richard Winterpol, calling himself Samirama of all things. I'd like to see the look on his pompous, self-satisfied face if I called him Samirama. Poor Pammy trusted him. If he loved her at all he should have saved her. Where was he when she was drowning in the pond? And why, in all these years, did he not contact my parents and tell them what had happened to Pammy if he knew it, as he probably did. If he didn't know, then he should at least have given them and the police some facts to go on. My parents' worrying about her, feeling guilty about Pammy's leaving home, and hoping she might come back to them ruined the remaining years of their lives. Even knowing she was dead would have been better.

I'm mad at this Shakti woman, whoever and wherever the hell she is now. She clearly wanted Pammy out of the way. What was in those bottles she gave to Pammy? Nothing good. And she gave them to Pammy with a lie. I looked it up. Pammy died in 1985 and the abortion pill didn't even exist until 1987. It wasn't legal in the US until 2000, not that the Rajneeshees probably cared about the legality of it. Even then it was a pill, not a liquid in a bottle. Whatever was in those bottles, it wasn't what Shakti said it was and Shakti wanted Pammy to drink it.

Was Pammy even pregnant? Did Shakti tell the nurse to lie to her? And who was this nurse? I resolved to find her and ask her what she knew and what she did. Eva, Bruce, even Richard Winterpol must have some idea who the nurse would have been at that time. I'd track her down. And of course, Roberta Avery would know the name of the nurse or nurses who succeeded her at the medical center. I wondered, in fact, if Roberta, knowing what I was after, lied to me about leaving Rajneeshpuram in April before Pammy arrived.

Finally, I was mad at myself. If I hadn't been so wrapped up in my career, my marriage, and my first child in 1985 I might have found Pammy alive and well and brought her home. Why didn't it occur to any of us at the time that an adventurous and overconfident sixteen-year-old girl like Pammy would head for Rajneeshpuram, certainly back then the wildest and most exotic thing going on in Oregon?

I'd finished Pammy's diary lying in bed at night. I was overwrought and tired at the same time. Anger wore me out. I turned out the lamp beside my bed and said "Good night, Ray, I love you," as I always did. But I lay in the dark feeling sympathy for Pammy.

How confused and unhappy she'd been. And at the end she wanted to come home. Home where all the evil forces of Rajneeshpuram couldn't touch her. Home where her parents would have cared for her and helped her, pregnant or not. How different things would have been if she'd made it another quarter mile.

Chapter 26

Jim

Of the two suspects in the 1962 Sharon Forrester murder that Fred Karlsen thought were still living, I found out one had already died. The only one left, Joe Kuransky, owned an ice cream shop in Placerville, California, in the so-called Gold Country. I tracked him down through the National Crime Information Center file on sex offenders. He'd been convicted only once and that was fifty years ago. When I reached him on the phone from my office he sounded frail.

"No," said Kuransky, "I don't know anything about your girl. First of all I'm not really a sex offender. I was trying to make some money taking pictures. This damn thing keeps coming back to haunt me. Here you are calling me because some stupid computer won't forget my name years after they railroaded me into jail. Do you know how hard it is to find a place to live that isn't near a school? I'm seventy-nine years old. What kind of a threat do they think I am?"

"I'm not concerned with what you've done or not done," I said. "Or what you're doing now. I'm looking for ideas on who might have dumped this other girl in Mirror Pond in 1985 and why and how."

"Gee," he said, "let me check my list of attendees at the sex offender convention. Like I told you, I'm not a sex offender. And I certainly don't hang out with sex offenders."

"Were you ever at Rajneeshpuram in the early eighties?" I asked. That gave him pause. He didn't have a quick comeback for that question. Though Joe Kuransky would have been in his forties back then, if he had an inclination toward sex with young girls he might have been attracted to the place.

"You mean that crazy guru's place? No. I never went there." He paused. "Wait a minute. Early eighties? You check the record. In 1984 and most of '85 I was in prison, thanks to some whippersnapper prosecutor trying to make a name for himself." Kuransky paused again. "Now I've been as cooperative as I think you have any right to expect. I think we're done."

"We're done for now. Thank you," I said. I'd ruined his day and I didn't feel bad about it. He hadn't made my day any better either.

After my call with Kuransky I went to a meeting at the justice building with Jocelyn Nelson, the assistant district attorney, to discuss where we were on the two murders, Pammy Paulsen's and Ray Chatham's, twenty years but only a hundred yards apart.

I didn't have high hopes for this meeting. It was at nine o'clock and I was afraid it would take all morning. Jocelyn tended to want long lists of details and irrelevant facts before she prosecuted. I'd get a mountain of information for her and she'd hardly use any of it. She said she appreciated what I gave her and she did win cases, so part of my problem could be my own grumpiness.

Jocelyn, in her thirties, wore a green blouse and a narrow gray skirt, no jewelry except a watch and a wedding band, and very little makeup. She was a professional, on the job, and she was going to run the meeting. She and I were the ones getting paid to be in this meeting and she made more than I did.

Sarah Chatham and Dan Martinez were coming to the meeting, unpaid, so we could discuss the two murders they were involved in. I'd decided I liked working with Sarah. She was direct and she had a good sense of what she could and could not expect a police detective to do. And she was doing a lot of the investigation herself, though that was both good and bad. Good that she and her friends were doing the work and inveigling answers from people who probably would not have told me as much as they told Sarah's buddies. Bad that nothing the people told her could be admitted as evidence in a trial.

Working closely with a victim's family can be risky. They get overeager and spoil the case—putting suspects on their guard, muddying evidence or witness testimony, lying, or misleading the police. Worst of all, they might take justice into their own hands, wreaking revenge on a suspect and committing a crime themselves. My usual worries were minimal with Sarah Chatham. As vengeful as she might be in her heart, she would stay within the law and look for justice in court.

I wasn't so sure about Dan Martinez. I'd barely met him. I hoped he was the cooperative kind of guy he seemed to be. But he might turn into a hothead. Or a lawyer who thinks he's sharper than everyone else in the room and entitled to bully them into his way of thinking. Jocelyn wouldn't let that happen and neither would I.

The conference room Jocelyn had reserved was barely big enough for four people and it had no windows. I was going to need some bathroom breaks to keep from going bonkers. Fluorescent lights. You couldn't tell if it was day or night outside, winter or summer. I wondered if Dan Martinez, tall and athletic looking, was going to be restless like me. I wanted to move this meeting along.

"First," said Jocelyn, "Floyd Tingley and the attempted murder of Sarah Chatham." She nodded to Sarah as she said this. "We have the fact, established in the original Tingley trial for vehicular manslaughter, that Tingley did kill Raymond Chatham and narrowly missed killing Sarah Chatham. Also, though it looked like chance the first time around, we can now note that Floyd drove onto the walking path at almost the only stretch along Drake Park that doesn't have trees protecting the path from the roadway.

"What we didn't have three years ago that we have now is a motive for murder. Through court records we've established that Sarah, representing the Confederated Tribes of Fort Rock, was an advocate in a case that transferred land from the federal government to the tribes, land on which the Tingleys customarily had grazing rights.

We believe that the family harbored a long and deep resentment of this ruling and especially of Sarah's role in it. Jim will be surveying relatives and neighbors for evidence of this resentment and any intentions that Floyd or others expressed to seek revenge.

"Further, and very importantly, we have a recording of Floyd's confession, or something very close to a confession. I have a reasonable expectation that a judge will allow us to present it as evidence. The recording clearly shows he and his mother agreed to having their conversation recorded. Though Dan made the recording under false pretenses we have the whole recording, not an ambiguous excerpt from it. Floyd was not coerced in any way and Dan did not trick him into saying something he didn't mean. Dan didn't read Floyd any Miranda rights but Dan was not acting as a police officer or a district attorney and Floyd was not under arrest for any crime at the time. He was virtually bragging when he spoke of killing Mr. Chatham and nearly killing Mrs. Chatham. I have persuaded the DA to take this to the grand jury. We expect they will vote to indict."

Jocelyn was ready to end the Floyd Tingley discussion. But Sarah pushed her further.

"Obviously I want to see my husband's murderer prosecuted," Sarah said. "If there is any work or expense needed please ask me for it. If the state doesn't punish murderers like Tingley then anyone who harbors a grudge can start killing people." Sarah was right but her statement was unnecessary. Punishing criminals was the business Jocelyn and I were in. We didn't have to be talked into it.

"So, onto the death of Pamela Paulsen," said Jocelyn. "We've learned more than I might ever have imagined about events that took place over thirty years ago. Pamela's diary is the key and it is consistent with simultaneous events at Rajneeshpuram that are well documented. But we're a long way from being able to charge anybody with anything. I'm not sure we'll ever get there. We suspect that a woman called Shakti directed a nurse to tell Pammy that she was pregnant, which she may or may not have been. Shakti, using Eva as the courier, gave Pammy two bottles that may have contained a drug or a poison and passed a message to Pammy that she should choose one and drink it. It's possible that Richard Winterpol, then known as Samirama, knew about the poison and it's possible, though it looks unlikely from the diary, that Eva Keefer, also known as Pranalika, knew about the poison as well. Richard and Pammy left Henry Walters' car together, headed toward Pammy's home by a route that would have taken them over the Galveston Avenue Bridge where Pammy, poisoned or not, dead or alive, fell, jumped, or was pushed into the water."

"Pushed is most likely," said Sarah. "She was on her way home with no indication she was suicidal. If she'd fallen or jumped, Winterpol could have saved her. But he didn't."

Jocelyn asked me if the police had any updates on the case.

"We went back through everything we found at the bottom of the pond and there were no bottles near the skeleton that looked like anything but beer and soda bottles. Nothing that looked like a medicine bottle. I'm trying to get Eva Keefer's story on the record before I confront Winterpol," I said. "But we can't reach her. She hasn't been home for three days and her car is missing. The neighbors don't know where she is and her sister, who lives in Atlanta, hasn't talked with her in months. They're not close. Eva may have been more involved in Pammy's death than she let on and she skipped out on us. We put out an all-points bulletin yesterday for Oregon and the surrounding states and we've got automatic license plate readers looking for her car all over the West. We're keeping an eye on her credit card. If we don't find her by next week I'll go interview Winterpol without waiting."

"Fair enough," said Jocelyn.

Sarah straightened up a little at that. I'm sure she wanted us to move more quickly. But the case was thirty-three years old. It was hard to justify rushing.

"What about this Shakti woman?" Sarah asked.

"She can't tell us anything," I said. "She's dead. Murdered twenty-five years ago. She was easy to track down because she did federal time. The woman fled to Germany after Rajneeshpuram fell apart, was brought back here and convicted of immigration fraud.

When she got out she went to manage a spa in California owned by some Hollywood financial people, including a name you know, Henry Walters, the man who drove Eva Keefer, Richard "Samirama" Winterpol, and Pamela Paulsen out of Rajneeshpuram. An unknown man showed up at the spa one day, garroted Shakti, parked her in a restroom stall, and drove away. Nobody saw the car and all anyone could remember about the man was he wore a green hat. Given all the people who could have had a grudge against Shakti, also known as Apoorva Reddy, also known as Gisela Becker, and the lack of any description of her killer, the state attorney general down there decided to say the hell with it."

When I got back to my office after being cooped up in the conference room I took a good thirty seconds to rest my eyes on a more distant view. The city lay there beyond the window. The Cascades were there too, with snow slowly making its annual retreat up the slopes. We would have about a month when the mountains had no white on them at all. Then the first snowfall would cover the tops and we'd start the cycle all over again.

Chapter 27

Dan

I didn't think Eva had disappeared on her own. Eva didn't even know Pammy was dead until Sarah told her. What I thought was more likely, and I admitted that I was prejudiced against the guy, was that Richard Winterpol, alias Samirama, was responsible for Eva's disappearance. Winterpol would take Eva's car precisely so the police would spend their time looking for it. The car was in a barn on his property or maybe even buried in a big hole in the ground.

"Have you sent the official letter to Richard Winterpol terminating him as our client?" I asked Sarah as I stood in the doorway to her office.

"It hasn't gone out yet," said Sarah.

"Could you hold off sending it?" I asked. "He invited us to take a look at the land he wanted to put in a trust. I think I want to go see what I can find."

"Why do you want to do that?"

"Looking for Eva," I said, "without telling him about it."

"The invitation is a legal fine point, I think, given the true purpose of your visit. You could be arrested for trespassing."

"Then I won't go after all," I said, resignedly, without a wink. We left it at that. End of conversation.

I knew I shouldn't be going to Winterpol's ranch. Risking arrest or even worse was the wrong choice for a man with a wife and a job where his clients and employers depended on him.

I was right to want to help Sarah resolve her sister's death. And I was right to want Richard Winterpol, whatever his crimes, to get his comeuppance. The wrong part of what drove me out there that night was a desire to be heroic—a wish to show how clever and daring I was. It was the escapade of the unattached young man that I no longer was.

I spent the afternoon scouring satellite photos of Winterpol's land looking for signs of Eva or her car. There was an online service that took photos of most of the earth every day. It was like Google Earth with poorer resolution but with the advantage that the photos I was looking at had been taken the day before, not a year or more in the past. I could not have recognized Eva if she were there, especially not the top of her head. But I might have been able to see her car. I didn't spot the car but I did see an area, bigger than a car, where a hole had been dug and filled in again recently. The soil was dark and mounded. It was in a depression between two low hills and it looked just about the size hole you'd need to bury a green Toyota Corolla.

I took a shovel and a hoe with me. With my car lights off I drove slowly up a dirt road that ran alongside Winterpol's property. Between GPS and the moonlight I was able to pull over close to the spot of dark soil I'd seen in the photograph. On foot I used a flashlight, down low, to find my way between the sagebrush and avoid stepping off a cliff. After stubbing my boot on a rock I walked more slowly. The sandy soil crunched quietly beneath my feet but a cool night breeze hid what little sound I made. The lights of Prineville outlined the grid of streets in the distance. I was wearing dark jeans, a black T-shirt, and a black hat. Not exactly a Ninja warrior but I thought it would make me harder to see. If I found something I would take a picture of it with my cell phone.

The darker soil, when I found it, was mounded like an enormous grave, emitting a slight smell of manure. I pulled soil away from the center of the pile using the hoe, glad I could pull so much of it sideways and downhill. If whatever was under that pile was buried deep I was going to have to lift a lot of dirt. The hole I made would have to be wide as well as deep. If I made the walls too steep the sandy soil would collapse right back into the hole, burying me in the process. With my flashlight lying on the ground facing toward the hole I could barely see what I was doing. The only sounds I heard were my own soft digging and my labored but steady breathing.

I was beginning to think I might have to keep at this until first light when my shovel struck something metallic. I still had to pull a lot of dirt away before I could see what it was. It was flat and level in the six-inch wide hole I had cleared. I pointed my flashlight downward and brushed some crumbs of dirt aside. The metal was smooth and painted light green. I was sure it was the roof of Eva's Toyota. I took a photo of it with my cell phone, not sure how well it would capture the shade of green and knowing the picture by itself would not convince anyone of anything, even with the GPS location embedded in the digital photo's file. I was in the process of sending the photo to Sorenson when I was suddenly enveloped in a very bright light. It must have been the most powerful flashlight in Christendom.

"Drop the phone and stay right where you are," a man's voice said from behind the light. "I've got a shotgun trained on you. You're trespassing and I'm within my rights to shoot you. Drop the phone." I dropped it and it clinked on the metal below. I hoped the picture had made it to Sorenson's phone. I wished I'd started an audio recording on my phone but there was no time for that.

"Are you alone?" said the voice. He was an older man, I thought, at least fifty.

"Yes," I said.

"Are you packing?" he asked.

"No," I said. "No gun, no knife."

"Take your clothes off." It didn't occur to me to debate the point. If it was Winterpol, with a gun on me, and it almost certainly was, he might shoot me at any moment. My legs started to move and my feet began to dance, soundlessly on the dirt but with sharp metallic raps when they hit Eva's roof.

"Cut that out," said the voice, "and get going."

I started with my left boot and that helped. I couldn't dance on one leg. Then my right boot, my jeans, then my shirt. I thought he might tell me to keep my Jockeys on but he didn't. I stood on top of Eva's car buck naked except for my socks, squinting sideways away from the light, unable to see the man behind it. It occurred to me I might have dug my own grave. My feet itched to dance but my brain told them not to. I was facing a problem like any other problem, I told my legs. I would find a way to solve it. My lower body believed me, blind fool that it was, and my feet were still.

I wondered why the light was so high up above me, as though he were hovering in the air. I looked below the light at ground level and could barely pick out the legs of a horse. That was how he'd been able to come up on me so quietly. In between stabs with the shovel I would have heard a truck or an ATV.

"Is this your land?" I asked.

"Damn straight," he said. "And now you can tell me what you're doing on it." So it was Richard Winterpol for sure. I dismissed the hope of spinning a tale that would convince him I was somebody else and here for some purpose other than the real one. It would only piss him off to listen to a story like that.

"I'm looking for Eva Keefer," I said, neither defiantly nor as an admission of wrongdoing. A simple statement of fact. There was silence from above but the light and the gun were steady.

"And what made you think you would find her here?"

"I think you know, Mr. Winterpol. But you and I might both be better off if I tell you what the police know already. Two months ago the skeleton of a girl named Pammy Paulsen, also known as Starlight, was found in Mirror Pond, apparently dropped off the Galveston Avenue Bridge. Eva Keefer said the last person she saw with Pammy, before Pammy died, was you. I shouldn't think you'd want Eva to testify to that and I thought you might have brought Eva here. This looks like her car and my guess is she's in it."

Silence again from Winterpol. Then, "What made you come dig up this dirt pile?" I explained about finding the satellite pictures of disturbed soil on the web. He spit out a disgusted breath. I thought he was as much annoyed to learn about yet one more technology invading his privacy as he was to be reminded that I'd found the critical spot.

"Didn't occur to you it might just be dead cows or rotten hay?" he asked.

"Could have been," I said, "but I still thought this was my best shot at finding Eva."

"Who knows you're here?"

"No one right at this moment," I said. "But I described my plan in a letter that's in the mail to Detective Sorenson with the Bend Police Department."

"Sounds like you're going to make me dig up whatever's in the ground here and move it where no one will find it, satellite photographs or not. And I think I'll have to bring you with me. Who the hell are you anyway?"

"Daniel Martinez," I said. "My wife is named Amy. She's Vickie Coate's daughter." I wished I could see the expression on Winterpol's face. Instead, no sign. I waited for the shot. Or the absence of it. I was reminded of the only photo ever taken of Chief Paulina, an Indian marauder all over Central Oregon in the 1860's. When he was temporarily a prisoner the army took his picture. He didn't know anything about photography and he thought he was going to be shot. He drew himself up in the chair and put his hand over his heart. I wanted to put my hand over my heart too, though it wouldn't have done any more good than it would have done Chief Paulina.

I might not even hear the gun go off. The shot might kill me instantly or, just as likely with a shotgun, I would rapidly bleed to death. I might feel a lot of pain before I died. Winterpol would spend the night digging up the car again, probably putting me in it, and moving it to someplace out in the wilderness.

When Winterpol finally spoke he completely changed the subject. "Do you know Elizabeth Martinez?" he asked. "She was president of a bank in Bend." Anything he said was better than the report of a gun. But I certainly wasn't expecting a question like that, so far removed from Pranalika, from Pammy Paulsen, from my current position facing the wrong end of a shotgun.

"She's my mother," I said. I thought it might be the last thing I ever said.

"Shit," said Winterpol. "This whole thing has gone too far. Too damned far. I'm not doing this. Go on. Get out of here." Still, the light didn't move. I stepped slowly, beginning to climb out of the hole. I was willing to skip putting my clothes back on just to get out of there. But I would need the keys to my car.

"Can I take my keys and my wallet? They're in my pants."

"Take them out slowly and hold them up where I can see them," said Winterpol in a weary tone. He was as eager for me to be gone as I was.

"Can I get dressed?" I asked.

"Get going," he said. I thought of asking if I could put my boots on but I could tell he was impatient. He'd had a plan for killing me and he might go back to it.

Once I had my keys and wallet I scrambled up out of the hole and walked out of the end of the draw away from the light. There was a moment when I got to the farthest reaches of Winterpol's flashlight and my eyes had not yet adjusted to the dark. I kept walking. My feet hurt already from rocks lying on the ground. I slowed down to try and pick my way between the sagebrush. No boots, no flashlight. I wanted to get away before Winterpol changed his mind. But gashing my foot or falling would slow me more than anything. And no matter how fast and recklessly I ran, Winterpol could catch me up on his horse if he decided to.

I headed east in the general direction of my car, picking out what landmarks I could in the moonlight. Something made me hold my hands together, wrapped around my keys and wallet. It might have looked as if I were in prayer. But my clasped hands came more from the fear I'd kept contained while Winterpol had a gun on me. I wasn't thinking about what I was going to do about Winterpol or Eva or anything else. Being buck naked was the least of my worries. My only thought was to get in my car and go.

I came out on the dirt road about a hundred feet from my 4Runner. From the back seat I took a rain poncho that had kicked around all summer. It was scratchy on my bare skin and it quickly got too hot. The neck hole was too small for air to circulate. There would be no place to buy clothes in Prineville at this hour. I'd have to drive all the way home like this.

I stopped at the Prineville Police Department. Inside a little lobby in the building there was a window with the night dispatcher, a man in a uniform, sitting behind it. He wasn't pleased to see me at that hour, dressed in a poncho like a madman.

"My name is Daniel Martinez," I said in as calm and businesslike a voice as I could muster, "and I need to report a crime."

"Is the crime still in progress?" asked the officer. His badge said *Adair* on it.

"No," I said. "If you'll loan me a pad of paper and a pen I'll write down what happened. Then you can file it and decide whether to investigate." I didn't want to get into the details with Officer Adair and I didn't want to stay here all night answering questions. I did want to be in a place I thought was safe. And I wanted to make a record in case Winterpol changed his mind about me. I recognized, in my rational mind, that it was unlikely Winterpol would now decide to kill me, that he would come after me, or that he would even find me, at least not soon. But fear was still coursing through my veins. Officer Adair was more comfort to me than he realized.

"I'm not giving you a whole pad of paper," he said.

"I'll settle for three sheets and something sturdy to back them up while I write. And a pen." He gave me four sheets, a cheap ballpoint pen, and a day-old issue of the *Central Oregonian* newspaper. There was no furniture in the lobby so I sat on the floor to write. It took me fifteen minutes. I didn't go into much background because I figured Sorenson would eventually read it and he knew all the background already. I put his name and mine in the document. I briefly described why I'd gone onto Winterpol's land, why I went to that spot, and that I thought I'd found Eva's car there. I reported my conversation with Winterpol as well as I remembered it. All of it, in detail. I put in the GPS coordinates of the place, strictly from memory because my phone was gone, presumably destroyed and buried somewhere by now. I signed what I'd written and wrote in my contact information at Oxton.

"Thank you, Officer," I said, slipping what I'd written back under the glass with the newspaper and the pen. He put it on the right side of his desktop, not even glancing at it. That was fine with me for now. "Good night," I wished him with a smile and a wave. I'm sure he thought I was looney. Once he had the document I wanted to get out of there before he read it and started asking questions.

Amy didn't wake up until I'd taken a shower and gotten into bed with my pajamas on.

"Where have you been?" she asked, still half-asleep.

"Digging up some facts for a case," I said. "I'll tell you about it in the morning."

Chapter 28

Richard

I took some money that I hadn't earned but I took it away from crooks. And I put it to good use. I invested it in a business that served the community. I didn't blow it on good times in Las Vegas or fancy cars for myself.

The money was in a safe at Rajneeshpuram when the Rajneeshees were the biggest con in the history of Oregon. I could tell there was plenty of money around the place. They built new buildings and laid out new roads whenever it occurred to them. The Bhagwan bought Rolls Royces like candy bars. I could have had a good income making spare parts disappear from the workshop.

One day I spotted a girl at a darshan, a teaching session by the Bhagwan with thousands of sannyasins in a large hall on the ranch. She was my partner for that night. In the morning I learned she worked in the business office of the ranch, opening mail and sorting donations from around the world into a special pile for processing. I kept coming back to this girl though I couldn't stop her from having other lovers. I cultivated her, learned more about her, and more about the people and operations in the office. Her name was Eva. She was pretty and willing and eighteen years old. I began to talk with her about money. First, how important it was to the good work going on at the ranch. Then about the good the money could do in the world. Then on to the good it could do for individuals, especially young people who were pure at heart and wanted to serve the world. After a month or more I suggested that the ranch wasn't up to the task of putting all the donations they received to their best use. Perhaps some of it could be diverted to people who could see other needs in the world, or even at Rancho Rajneesh, and put that portion of the money to better purposes.

We talked about how money could be channeled to things that would be more worthwhile, like feeding the poor in India or spreading the Bhagwan's teaching to impoverished, unhappy, and misguided people right here in Oregon. We agreed that trying to persuade the higher-ups at the ranch, like Devya, would be futile. Devya was a hard, determined woman, already overloaded with her many responsibilities. We fantasized about just taking some of the donations that came in, building what the ranch really needed, and then revealing what we had done. People, even the Bhagwan, would applaud us for what we did and would put us officially in charge of good works in his name.

A few weeks more and I thought I could get Eva to start sliding a little cash to me for safekeeping, or give me some of the more illegible checks to deposit, or lift some cash straight out of the safe. She only went into the safe under the supervision of a woman named Shakti but they became so casual about it that Eva was able to learn the combination by looking over Shakti's shoulder a couple of times. Everybody trusted everybody. We were building the Buddhafield.

Eva and I were never really a couple. I'd like to say we were co-conspirators for the wiser use of cash. Any boyfriend/girlfriend relations we might have had were over before I took up with Starlight.

In September 1985, Devya and a dozen of her henchmen left Rancho Rajneesh in a hurry, along with Shakti. Got into a private plane and disappeared into the sky. They looked serious, even anxious. This was not a holiday jaunt. Eva didn't know where they were going or why but Starlight lived at Devya's compound and overheard the conversations of the higher-ups. She was only sixteen years old and I think they expected she wasn't paying attention or didn't understand what they were saying. She was cute too, still fresh, and I was more attracted to her than I had ever been to Eva.

Devya had thought the police were coming to arrest her for arranging illegal immigrations by marrying people who didn't even know each other. She was afraid police might find the wiretapping equipment she and her cohort set up so Devya could listen in on people. And she was talking about killing government officials. Bhagwan had found out what she was doing. I don't know if he told her to get out or he just told her to stop. But he was angry. Not ranting and raving and acting crazy like some people get angry. He was serious angry. And cold. I didn't think he could ever be cold like that.

Nobody was minding the store once Devya and her cronies left. I was sure Bhagwan wasn't. A perfect opportunity for an enterprising hooligan like myself.

Even easier, one of the rich Hollywood types who had his own house on a hill above the ranch called me to say he was going to leave the ranch that evening, driving to Los Angeles, and would I get his car ready. Maybe it was coincidence and maybe he'd gotten wind of what had happened with Devya. I said I sure would and asked if he could give me a lift to civilization. I reminded him that his car, a Bentley, hadn't been out for a while and it might be good to have a mechanic, such as myself, ride with him as far as Bend.

Eva and I opened the safe that afternoon. I was surprised Devya hadn't taken all the cash with her. But she could have wired millions to wherever she was going and probably didn't want to get caught with the cash. Or maybe it was just too much trouble. We took stacks of big denominations but left the smaller denominations. We put two stacks of hundred-dollar bills in the front so it might appear at first glance that no money was missing. Someone would have to consult the books to find out most of the cash was gone.

When we shut the safe we realized we'd forgotten to put back a sack of coins. Rather than open the safe again I put the sack in my backpack. It was important that Eva not have second thoughts so we went back to her room and divided up the paper money evenly between her backpack and mine. That made Eva rich and just as guilty as I was. She went back to work where she would try to act normal. I told her it would be okay if she was a little nervous. Everyone was a little wacky with Devya leaving. I found Starlight and, trying to scare her enough but not too much, told her she should leave as soon as possible. I said she should bring the things she wanted and meet me at the garage at eight o'clock. I told her not to tell anyone she was leaving. Then I took my backpack to the shop and locked it in Henry Walters' trunk. I gassed and washed his Bentley for good measure.

I was pretty sure Henry wouldn't mind bringing Eva and Starlight along. He'd bought into the Bhagwan's whole living-at-a-higher-level thing but I also knew, though he tried to keep it more discreet than many, that a big part of why he was there was all the easy, no-commitments sex. He liked to invite women up to his house for parties. Champagne, caviar, air conditioning, a taste of the luxurious life. Others thought the best party was down in the compound or thought Henry's love of wealth and possession were counter to the whole reason they were here. Sometimes he went with women to their little rooms but he clearly preferred his big bed and the view from his hot tub overlooking the ranch and looking up at the starlit sky.

Starlight was all too glad to leave Rancho Rajneesh. The talk she heard of killing people, the fear she heard in the voices of people she thought were in command, and the sudden disappearance of those same people shattered her confidence. Home must have looked awfully safe to her. Besides, it was September. Time to go back to school.

Henry kept wanting me to drive faster. The dirt road out to Antelope wasn't good and we could have easily slid off it into a ditch or even a canyon. The paved road from Antelope out to the main highway followed the twisty course of a creek and wasn't much better. Heading south on Highway 97 I wouldn't go faster than the speed limit. I didn't want to be stopped for speeding with all the money Eva and I had in our backpacks in the trunk. We hadn't counted it but it looked like at least a hundred thousand dollars apiece. Henry kept telling me to go faster, getting more and more impatient. By the time we got to Redmond he told me to pull over and give him the wheel. I said I would get out in Bend, with Starlight, and why didn't we switch then. He grumbled but he agreed. He was used to having people do what he told them.

Henry wouldn't get off the main road to take Starlight to her home. He made us stop on Third Street. Starlight had a headache and started thrashing her head around. Henry stepped on the gas and disappeared with Eva still in the back seat. Starlight and I followed Franklin Street under the railroad and came down past the little downtown. There was hardly anyone out on the streets, even though it was a Saturday night. They would have noticed Starlight if they had seen her. Every few minutes she jerked around like a spastic. I knew, the worse she got, that Eva, or someone, had poisoned her. Eva might be jealous that my attention had shifted from Eva to Starlight but this was a pretty extreme reaction. If I had spotted a payphone I might have called for help. I might have looked harder for a phone but the police would ask a lot of questions about a girl who had been poisoned and I didn't want to be in their clutches with all that cash on my back. My hope was to get Starlight to her family's house, tell them to call an ambulance, and disappear.

Starlight had told me how to go and we walked along a park for a while until we came to a bridge where we could cross the river. Starlight had been leaning on me for blocks, still thrashing, looking like a little girl I'd gotten drunk and who was struggling to get away from me. It was getting harder and harder for her to breathe. When we got to the bridge she seized up, bending backward like a bow but still jerking around. I knew it was strychnine by then. We'd used it to poison coyotes back in Burns while I was growing up. I finally admitted to myself that Starlight didn't have long to live. There was no saving her now no matter what anybody did. She wouldn't last long enough for me to carry her to her family's house. I was on the bridge and the water was there. I took the bag of coins out of my backpack and put it in hers to add weight. Then I picked her up, kissed her on the cheek, and dropped her thrashing body over the side. She sank quickly out of sight.

I walked back to Third Street and spent the night in a motel. The next day I opened accounts at three banks and put five hundred dollars in each of them. They were happy to get the cash, even though my account application form said "looking for work" where it asked me to give my employer. I did find work in the next two weeks at an auto repair shop where the previous mechanic had dropped a car on his leg and wouldn't be able to work for ten months. I was the best mechanic they'd had in a long time, though the owner wouldn't admit it. I let him underpay me for three months before I demanded a raise and got it. I didn't need the money, of course, but I needed to be doing something. Every month I put another thousand dollars in each of my accounts. And I opened new accounts with banks in Redmond and even Portland. I told myself I was in the laundry business.

After a year I spotted a small used car dealership in Prineville that was for sale. The owner was anxious to get out and didn't balk at getting checks from eight different banks and some cold cash as well. He gave me a loan to boot, secured by the cars in the inventory. I made the loan payments exactly on schedule. He didn't ask me why I made the payments in cash, he just showed up every first of the month, took the money, and signed a receipt.

The dealership had a small repair shop that I expanded. At first I just repaired the used cars I'd bought. Then I started serving people who wanted repairs on cars they wanted to keep. I always gave people fair prices on the cars they sold me and the cars they bought. I became a good, honest citizen, except for the remaining cash from Rajneeshpuram that I washed through the business. I kept the place, and myself, neat and tidy. I hired more people and joined the chamber of commerce.

I still dream of girls with gruesome, stretched-back smiles on their faces. Sometimes they dissolve in front of me. Sometimes they rage with energy and strike at me with tennis rackets or baseball bats. Sometimes we're having a friendly conversation when they change into a death's head, still continuing the conversation. Then they are pulled away by devils, with a mournful "Goodbye, goodbye," as they get smaller and smaller. Once the girl was my daughter. That really rattled me. But I didn't kill Starlight. Only Shakti or Devya would have had access to that poison and the nerve to use it. Eva didn't know she had been their accomplice.

After six years in Prineville, I met Cary, the daughter of a local rancher. I met her at church, which I joined for the sake of getting to know people and expanding my business. She had just graduated high school and didn't know what to do next. Hardly ever been out of Prineville. I treated her with respect but her father didn't want Cary to marry a used car salesman. I reminded him I owned the business, made a profit, and served the community. Two of his ranch workers had bought cars from me. Good cars.

Once we were married, Cary's parents invited us to live in the foreman's house on their ranch. Our daughters were born there. The cottage was small but the rent was free. Cary and the girls spent a lot of their time over at the big house. When the old man died we moved over there and Cary's mother moved into a smaller room so we could have the master. Cary inherited the ranch and I had no part of the ownership. But I took over the running of it. I was a proven businessman, I'd had experience with cattle, and I'd picked up a lot just shooting the breeze with her father while he was alive. We were a happy, prosperous family, pillars of the community. If I'd done anything wrong in my life it was way in the past. Unknown to anyone.

I wasn't very worried when I read in the paper about the skeleton in Mirror Pond. Especially when the police thought she was American Indian. Starlight was blond. Even if the skeleton was Starlight how would anyone figure that out? And if they did find out who she was, it would still be hard to make the connection to me. Nobody, I was certain, had actually seen me drop her into the pond. Not to worry.

But thoughts of Eva, unaccounted for, out there somewhere in the landscape like a lost calf, nagged at me.

Henry Walters I wasn't worried about. He died of a drug overdose. In Hollywood it's like dying of natural causes. I doubted
he'd told anyone that Pammy and I were with him when he left
Rajneeshpuram. I doubted he remembered any of us. He knew me
as Samirama back then and kept calling me Sammy.

But Eva might remember. She was Starlight's friend and my
fellow thief. She could tie me to Starlight's death. Where the heck
was she now? In online searches I couldn't find an Eva Keefer that
looked at all like the girl I remembered. Wrong face, wrong age. The
Eva I knew would be fifty-something now.

I tried a search for Pranalika, just to be thorough. It was a san-
yasin name, a pretend name, a temporary name for Eva while she
was at Rajneeshpuram. I found Pranalikas in India, not as many
as I imagined. I drifted through photos from the other side of the
world. Then, without a conscious recognition, my head shot up and
I sucked in my breath. There was a Pranalika in Bend. Much, much
too close. She was a spiritual advisor. There was only one picture of
her online, the same one on Facebook and on her own website. The
Eva I knew could have grown into this woman, older, of course, and
with longer graying hair. It might have been Eva and it might not. I
would have to go see what the living and breathing woman looked
like.

On a trip to Bend I swung by this Pranalika's address and parked
in front of the house next door. I knew I might be there a while so I
brought a book, a big book about the navy in World War II. I was in
the shade of a tree with my car windows partly open. Every twenty
minutes or so I'd shut the windows and run the air conditioning.
Nobody noticed me sitting there.

A woman did come out of Eva's house but it definitely wasn't Eva.
She was in her twenties, blond, attractive, athletic-looking. She saw
me as she passed by and I think I startled her, a man sitting in a car
she had assumed was empty. But her eyes snapped forward again
and she walked to a Subaru parked three cars behind mine. When
she drove past me she didn't look my way.

I saw a woman come out of the house who looked like the photo of Pranalika and I pulled up a small pair of binoculars to catch a look at her face. That was Eva, I was sure. I even thought I could see the gray eyes I remembered from Rajneeshpuram days. She got into a faded green Corolla and drove away.

I churned through my options for Eva while I took the long way home through Alfalfa. If she had forgotten me or forgotten when she last saw Pammy, I didn't want to remind her. If she hadn't forgotten our exit from Rajneeshpuram I wanted to make sure she kept quiet. I could pay her money for her silence but then she could keep coming back for more. I lay awake nights considering my alternatives.

Then Eva called me. Whatever I was going to do about Eva now was the time to do it.

Chapter 29

Jim

When I saw "Oxton, Rath" on my cell phone I figured Sarah was calling to see if I'd stopped looking for Eva and gone to talk to Winterpol. But it was Dan Martinez, calling from his office because he didn't have his cell phone. He'd sent me a photo from his cell phone the night before that made no sense—a patch of green surrounded by brown-gray dirt. No message. No explanation.

Martinez told me a wild tale of going out to Winterpol's property and finding Eva Keefer's car, or at least a recently buried square of green metal. He said Winterpol came near to shooting him and only let him leave bare naked. That's why amateurs should leave the detective business to professionals.

I got the Prineville police chief to loan me a lieutenant who knew Winterpol to go out to the ranch with me. I figured Winterpol might be difficult, maybe even start shooting, if I approached him directly. I explained the case to the Prineville chief over the phone and sent the photo Dan had sent me over his cell phone. The photo, of something green surrounded by dirt, didn't prove much of anything but the GPS coordinates embedded with the photo corroborated that Dan had been on Winterpol's property. It supported the story that Dan told me and I repeated to the chief. I told the chief about the report Dan had filed at the Prineville police station and the chief faxed me a copy of it for my records. With Dan's report and my case files I got a judge to issue a search warrant for Winterpol's property.

Winterpol's home was a rectangular one-story ranch with yellow siding and white trim—nothing fancy. The money was in the land that surrounded the house in all directions. There were spruce trees along one side of the house and two metal outbuildings across the driveway. Beyond them were fields of new-mown hay.

The lieutenant went up to Winterpol's door while I waited by the truck I'd corralled for the day from the Bend Public Works Department, along with two of their guys. I knew what the Prineville lieutenant would say—that he was sorry to bother Richard but this cop from Bend had a warrant to search a pit on Winterpol's property for a car that might have been involved in a crime. I saw the surprised look on Winterpol's face. It was a pretty convincing expression but I didn't believe for one minute that he was surprised. Then Winterpol went back in his house to get some keys and the lieutenant came over to me.

"He's going to lead us out there," said the lieutenant. I knew the lieutenant didn't know what to expect. He'd known Winterpol a long time and the man had always been a good citizen. "Lived in Prineville for decades," said the lieutenant, "local businessman, lots of friends, and no trouble with the law." Yet the lieutenant wasn't conflicted about it. He was an officer of the law and here was a search warrant. As long as Winterpol understood the man had to do his job, they could still be friends when this malarkey was over.

We got to the pit and the public works guys I'd brought from Bend started digging. Everybody knew using shovels looked silly with Winterpol's backhoe sitting eighty feet away. But we needed to look through the soil as the men dug, not take the dirt out in great gobs and dump it. They had it easy at first. The soil had been dug up recently. I wandered back down the dirt track we'd come in on while they excavated the first few feet. There were multiple tire tracks from all the cars and trucks we'd arrived in. Underneath them were the big, wide tracks of the backhoe. In one little gap, though, between all the other tracks, I spotted what I was looking for—a four-inch-long track from the edge of a different vehicle with a well-worn tread. I took pictures of it. I didn't know where we'd get sample tread from Eva Keefer's car if we couldn't find the car itself, but we might be able to match the tread to the tire model number if we could figure out what tires Keefer had bought most recently.

When the hole got chest high the men said it wasn't safe because the loose dirt could collapse on them. Winterpol offered to move the piled-up dirt away with his backhoe. I looked in the hole, now about four feet square and three feet below the surrounding ground level, a good two feet deeper than Martinez had said the car would be. No car. Just more dirt.

"Thanks but never mind," I said to him. "There's no car here." I sounded deeply disappointed, I thought, as though I had given up on any idea I had of finding Keefer's car or arresting anybody for anything. "But could you tell me why this was dug up so recently?"

"Sure," he said, "I'm raising the ground out here a bit at a time."

"Would you mind showing me where the dirt came from?" He seemed ticked off that I wasn't leaving immediately with my tail between my legs. And I could tell the lieutenant had pretty much decided I was trying to throw my weight around right after having proved I was an incompetent knucklehead with no case.

"It's back on the road we came in on," said Winterpol. "I can show you on the way out." So we all followed Winterpol out again and he stopped by a low hill where the top had been shaved off recently. I took photos of that too. It would be interesting to see if the raw earth exposed here showed up on a satellite photo of the area on the day when Dan spotted the original dirt pile. I had a feeling it wouldn't.

I thanked the public works guys and bought them lunch at a barbecue place in Prineville. They'd had a good morning—more driving than working, country they never got to see on the job, and a free lunch. I told them to not blab too much about this and not to mention the name of the owner of the ranch. "Innocent until proven guilty," I said.

One of them said, "Innocent of what?"

"Innocent of anything," I said. I didn't think Winterpol was innocent but I didn't say that.

When I called headquarters, the department secretary said the cell phone company had called back about my request to track Martinez's cell phone. It confirmed he had gone to Prineville. More than that, the last cell tower to detect the phone was on the road going east out of Prineville over an hour after Winterpol had made Martinez leave his phone on the ground with his clothes. It looked like Winterpol had dug up Keefer's car and thrown Dan's clothes and cell phone in it before he drove it off the ranch. He just never thought to turn off the phone. At least that was my theory. Beyond the last cell tower that caught that phone, though, there wasn't another tower for fifty miles. No cell service, no tracking. The road went through the Ochoco National Forest, with dozens of forest roads branching off it. Keefer's car could be anywhere in there.

Coming through Powell Butte on the way back to Bend, I grew a little more optimistic. If Winterpol dumped the car in the forest, someone would have to give him a ride back. They'd have to follow him out there or meet him at a place they both knew. With no cell he couldn't guide them to where he was. We could canvass his workers and friends until one of them fessed up. But the person he would trust to keep this strange night journey a secret, I thought, would likely be his wife. Besides, she could never be forced to testify against him if it came to that.

Still, that was a long way for him to go in the nighttime, after his talk with Martinez and after digging up Keefer's car. Maybe he didn't go that far at all. When I got back to the station I looked at the data from the cell phone company more carefully. Dan's cell phone was in range of that last tower for twenty minutes. If Winterpol had driven east for twenty minutes he would have driven out of range entirely. So he stopped. He didn't go that far. He must have stopped where the road ran alongside Ochoco Reservoir. How handy. He drove the car off the road into the water and it sank. That's what I would have done. He could have walked home from there.

If I was right, I had a new problem. The road ran alongside the reservoir for three and a half miles. I wouldn't be able to see the car from the shore and, unless it were in very shallow water, I wouldn't see it from a boat, assuming I could get hold of a boat. After the time and money I'd spent to dig up Winterpol's ranch the chief was not about to spend more money based on my speculation that the car was in the reservoir. Getting divers to search the length of the water at various depths and various distances from shore was out of the question. Getting a police helicopter up where it could see down into the water was pure fantasy.

I called a guy I knew at the Forest Service Air Center in Redmond. They were still busy fighting fires in the Cascades but they were using our department to help find out who started the fires. I asked him for a little reciprocity. When one of his planes was coming back from a fire, could the crew fly the length of the Ochoco Reservoir, down the side nearest the road, and see if they could spot a green Toyota resting on the bottom?

"It would have to be green," he said. "It couldn't be white?"

"I would have painted it DayGlo orange if I'd known this was going to happen," I told him. He said he would do what he could and I thanked him. I spent the afternoon writing up a report on what we'd done in Prineville and what we hadn't found. It wasn't fun. Late in the day, though, things turned around. Jocelyn called to tell me the district attorney had decided to prosecute Floyd Tingley for the murder of Ray Chatham. A judge told Jocelyn he would probably admit the recording of Floyd's confession into evidence.

Just before five o'clock my contact in Redmond called back. One of their planes had spotted the car, about three hundred yards above the dam and a hundred feet off the shore. I caught the chief before he left, told him what we'd found, and said I wanted divers and a tow truck.

"Get me estimates before you go ahead," he said. A reasonable request, no doubt, but we were dealing with a recent murder now, not a thirty-year-old skeleton. I'd hoped he would give me a freer hand. I called the Prineville police and got the lieutenant I'd worked with before. I said we'd found the car and I was going to pull it out the next day if I could arrange it. I think that improved his attitude toward the Bend Police Department. I didn't ask him to keep an eye on the area but I told him how far up the reservoir the car was. If he was on the ball he would send a patrol car up there periodically to make sure no one else, like Winterpol, was trying to pull the car out. It wasn't really likely. There were very few tow truck drivers anywhere near us who could do that kind of work, not to mention divers.

It took two days to get a crew together. Fortunately the Forest Service sent me a photo of the car in the water. The copilot of the plane said he clearly saw a car even though the picture wasn't completely convincing. All you could see for sure was a green rectangle about the size of a car. It was enough, anyway, to convince people I wasn't wasting their time. The tow truck driver, Byron, had to bring an extra-long cable. And he had to bring eight metal tracks so he could haul the car up over the riprap at the shore. Once we got the car up on the edge of the land and the water drained out of it I could see a woman who matched Eva Keefer's description sitting in the passenger seat. She still had her seat belt on and it was cutting deeply into her bloated body. I'd arranged transport to take her directly to the lab in a refrigerated truck. We let the transport guys get her out of her car. They were more used to dead and damaged bodies than the rest of us. Give me a fresh body with a clean bullet wound any day.

We parked the car on the wide shoulder between the road and riprap and poked around with rubber gloves on. The steering wheel was tightly tied to the brake pedal with a rope so the car would go straight. There were two cinder blocks in front of the driver's seat with another rope. It looked like Winterpol had gotten the car on the road and pointed it toward the water. He reached in and put it in gear. Then he dropped the rope so the cinder block would fall on the accelerator. By the time the car got to the rocks it was going fast enough to fly over most of them. It was still going forward when it hit the water and it was floating, or half floating, at least for a few seconds. We found the windows shut. Anyhow, the car was light enough and moving fast enough that it slid down the sloping bottom of the reservoir until it was a good forty feet down.

Byron towed the car up onto a flatbed and tied it on. He took it to the impoundment yard in Bend where the forensic guys could go over it. There was dirt several inches deep inside the car. I guessed Winterpol had left the windows open when he buried the car at his place. I told the team to check the dirt inside the car against a sample I'd put in a baggy from the pit at Winterpol's place. It took them a few days before they said the dirt in the car was "consistent" with Winterpol's pit.

"There's a lot of dirt like that in Central and Eastern Oregon," the technician said. "The best I can say is the dirt in the car doesn't rule out the car being buried at that location." Well, it helped. The chief, Jocelyn, and the district attorney all agreed we had enough to arrest Richard Winterpol and charge him with the murder of Eva Keefer. So I went to Prineville again with two Bend police officers and met the same lieutenant with two more Prineville officers. We went out to Winterpol's place together and the lieutenant, bearer of bad tidings, went to the door.

Winterpol came to the door and listened to the lieutenant. Winterpol said something brief and turned to go back in the house. The lieutenant clearly informed him he couldn't do that and he had to come out on the porch, which he did. We'd all come up to the porch by then. The lieutenant explained we had to follow procedure. We had to cuff him and frisk him before he got in the car. Winterpol asked if he could hug his wife and his daughter before he went. The lieutenant gave me a look and I nodded my head, more to show the Prineville guys we weren't badasses. And for the sake of the two women who had now come outside.

"Let us frisk you first," said the lieutenant. "Put your arms out straight and put your feet apart." Winterpol rolled his eyes but he got into the stance. I knew he hated having his family see him like this but the lieutenant was being as nice as he could be, like a friend who sympathized with him but had to follow the rules. One of the Bend officers frisked him. We were all looking at the wife and daughter checking for bulges that could hide a weapon. The daughter was thin as a rail and couldn't have hidden her car keys, much less a gun. The wife wasn't bulky and what bulges she had looked natural. And she didn't look like the type to think a shoot-out would end well. So Winterpol embraced his daughter first and then his wife.

"Call Morgan," said Winterpol to his wife. "And don't say anything to these officers or anyone else until you talk to Morgan. You don't have to say anything now at all, either of you." Tod Morgan was a criminal attorney in Bend, probably the best one. I knew him.

We put the cuffs on Winterpol and walked him to the patrol car for the ride to Bend.

"Don't worry," Winterpol shouted over his shoulder. The officers wouldn't let him turn around. "I'll be home in a couple of days."

I didn't think so.

Chapter 30

Richard

I'm rounded up, penned in, and on my way to the slaughterhouse. It's punishment already being cooped up in this cell with a man whose mind is functioning like a slow tractor with a drunk driver. He knows nothing about anything—the jail routine, who the prosecutors and judges are, who the other inmates are, or whether it's possible to get something to read. The cell is modern and clean enough, with a handicap bar next to the steel toilet. The off-white walls look like plaster but they're really concrete. I have the upper bunk which means I don't have to stare at the bottom of my companion's bed and I can forget about him. We have two very narrow windows that look at a vertical metal shield about a foot away. I get a sense of sunlight outside but there's no view of anything. I know the windows face north and I imagine I could see Mt. Jefferson in the distance if the shade weren't there. There are two windows in the door to the larger common room where we are allowed to spend some time.

There's nobody to talk to here. Some are hardened criminals. Some are mentally compromised or deeply stupid. I had a rational conversation with one man but learned he was a pedophile. Nobody, including me now, wants to go near him. There's one intelligent man awaiting trial for fraud. But he doesn't want to talk with me because I'm in for murder. I said I was a businessman too, an upstanding citizen most of my life, with a wife and two daughters. He still tries to avoid me.

Unless my lawyer is very clever I'll be convicted of Eva's death. I hid her corpse twice. I didn't think she'd be found either time. I never imagined anyone could get a current aerial photograph of my land without hiring an airplane. There's more stupid technology than a man my age can keep up with. And out of all the wilds of Oregon, how on earth did the little Bend police department know to look in the reservoir?

I'm glad I didn't shoot Dan Martinez, even though he skedaddled straight to the police to tell them about Eva and her car. I would be a free man today if I had killed him. I could have put him in Eva's car and dumped them both in the reservoir. He couldn't have told the police what he'd found on my ranch and if he'd told them where he was going they would have found nothing when they came here. Why didn't I kill him? I can think of many reasons now, with lots of time to think on my bunk in my little cell, but what was the reason that decided me at the time?

It was Dan's mother who saved his life. Elizabeth Martinez knew me as a good man, a responsible man, and an upstanding citizen. She'd been the banker for our ranch for twenty years or more. She respected me and trusted me. Even when we hadn't talked for two or three years we picked up on our business dealings as though we'd spoken the day before. In a business sense we were friends. I couldn't destroy the trust between us by killing her son, no matter what the cost to myself.

Also, I was rattled from having killed Eva, not that she was an upstanding member of society, she with her spiritual advisor act. Nobody needed her or cared about her. She had no children and no husband or boyfriend as far as I could tell. The world will not miss her. And she was a threat to me and my family. I didn't kill Starlight but a jury might not see it that way.

It was Shakti who killed Starlight. Maybe Starlight was pregnant or maybe Shakti talked the health center into telling Starlight that she was pregnant. But it was Shakti who sent Starlight the two bottles to abort the baby or "help" it in some bullshit way. The bottles that contained the strychnine that killed her.

The person I don't regret killing, not one bit, is Shakti. I killed her for killing Starlight. Justice done. I almost wouldn't mind being convicted of killing Shakti. I did a service to humanity. But I'll never be charged with it. I covered my tracks. And there are dozens of other people who had a reason to kill her.

I waited years to get Shakti. After Rajneeshpuram she fled to Germany with Devya. Changed her name to Gisela Becker. But she was extradited to the United States and served three years for immigration fraud, which the federal government could easily prove. The government also charged her with destruction of federal property and conspiracy to murder a public official. Immigration fraud was the only charge they could make stick.

When she got out I tracked her down to a spa hotel she was managing in the hills above Big Sur in California. The literature for it, which I had sent to a detective I'd hired in Portland, said the spa featured meditation and yoga. But the spa also had a swimming pool, steam baths, saunas, Pilates, massage and beauty treatments, and day hikes in the surrounding mountains. It mentioned shuttles to an ocean beach that looked beautiful in the photographs but it didn't mention swimming in the ocean. I found out the water was too cold and the surf was too rough. The brochures didn't mention Bhagwan but the spread had a sort of Rajneeshee flavor to it.

I called Gisela under an assumed name and said my wife and I were looking at spas where we could unwind and refresh ourselves for two weeks or more and could I stop by and get a tour. I asked specifically for her, as manager, to give me the tour. This was in the early nineties and I wasn't married to Cary yet. Shakti hardly knew who I was at Rajneeshpuram and she didn't recognize me at all when I showed up in a car I'd borrowed with California plates. I wore sunglasses and a sun hat with a round brim.

The spa was deep in the redwoods, up a long, curvy gravel road. The separate buildings, cabins and one building about the size of a house, were spread through the forest, connected by stone steps and narrow paths, paved unevenly with asphalt. Some of the buildings had a vaguely Japanese feel to them, with yellow grass mats partially framing the windows. But all were made of unpainted redwood planks, weathering from red to dark brown or gray. A small stream cascaded gently down past the buildings and made gurgling sounds in the windless moist air. People paid a lot of money for that gurgle.

Shakti's tour of the hotel had hardly begun when we passed a men's room and I excused myself to step inside. There was no one in the restroom and I emerged to apologize for the delay. When Shakti turned to continue the tour I cupped my hand over her mouth and dragged her, almost lifted her, back into the restroom. I snatched a short rope out of the inside pocket of my jacket with one hand and, in a move I had practiced over and over, like calf roping, I brought the cord down around the woman's neck. I took my other hand off her mouth and pulled the rope as tight as I could, leveraging myself with a knee against her back.

"This is for Starlight," I said. "Do you remember her?" The woman actually tried to shake her head no, as if denying the connection might get me to back off. God knows if she remembered Starlight in the brief moment she had left to her. I hope she did.

With the blood flow cut off to her brain, Shakti stopped struggling after ten seconds, went unconscious in fifteen, and was dead in thirty. I dragged her into a stall and sat her down, balancing her in a slumped position and pushing her feet back so they would not be visible to the next visitor to the restroom.

I walked out the front door of the spa and drove away. I hadn't met anyone face-to-face except Shakti. The two people who'd seen me at a distance had not bothered to look me over. I'd parked my car behind two redwoods and no one had seen it. Once I got down to the Pacific Coast Highway, I took a deep breath and headed north. There's a lot of thinking that goes on before and after you kill some-one, a lot of emotional back and forth. But in the actual act itself, it's not that different from drowning a rat in a pail of water.

No one has ever contacted me about Shakti's death. The newspa-per articles I read later said, as I expected, that there were thousands of ex-Rajneeshees who might have had it in for Shakti. The articles said they found my assumed name in Shakti's calendar and someone said they saw a man go into the main building around the time of her death. But they couldn't describe the man and no one saw a car.

If I am convicted of killing Eva and sentenced to die, my last act will be to tell the world I killed Shakti. Hundreds of people will nod their heads and thank me for it.

Dan

I got home early on Friday and started making dinner. I had news I needed to share with Amy and I didn't know what she would think of it. I started the hibachi to cook the salmon when Amy got home. Roasted baby potatoes. And salad with lettuce from a little place where they had lettuce grown locally and picked that same day. It was more expensive than our usual fare and we were trying to be frugal. Amy had gotten a raise the week before so the dinner was a little bit of a celebration of that.

Amy was pleased to find me home before her and kissed me in front of the kitchen counter.

"Newlyweds forever," I said.

"And you're making dinner," she said, looking a little askance with both happiness and suspicion. "What's up?"

"We're celebrating your raise. And I have good tidings, I think. Let me get dinner on the table and I'll tell you."

"So suspicious," she said.

We sat down and clinked our glasses. We were drinking cava, sort of like champagne but Spanish and softer. It was so inexpensive that if it got flat we could pour the remains of the bottle down the drain and open a new one.

"It's a little sad in a way," I began after we had a few bites. "They found Eva Keefer at the bottom of the Prineville Reservoir and arrested Winterpol for her murder."

"I am sorry about Eva. I didn't trust her but I don't think she had an easy life," said Amy. "Did Winterpol kill her?"

"Sure looks like it," I said. "Sorenson arrested him, put him in jail."

"Justice is done," said Amy. "Do you think he'll be convicted?"

"Well," I said, "wait a minute. He made bail and his wife drove him home from the courthouse. She gave him lunch. He told her he was sure they would never convict him. This is according to Sorenson. Then, after lunch, Winterpol went into Prineville for half an hour, came back, sat in his study for a few minutes, walked out into his yard, and shot himself in the head. Dead as a bug."

"Oh, the poor woman," said Amy, frozen with her fork in the air. She put it down and looked at her plate. "I thought I'd be glad if that man died. But now I'm sad." She held her paper napkin to her mouth and looked at me. "He was an evil and selfish man. But I guess I always imagined someday I'd meet him. Not because I'd like him, or really want to have anything to do with him. But out of curiosity. I wasn't curious enough to make it happen. So how big a loss can it be?"

"It's pretty clear he killed Eva Keefer," I said, "and it looks like, if he didn't intentionally kill Pammy Paulsen, he at least let her die when he might have saved her. Not a good man at all." I didn't mention that Winterpol had nearly killed me. I'd given Amy a somewhat sanitized version of my confrontation with him in the dirt overlying Eva's car. I promised myself I would tell her the full story. Later. No secrets.

"So if Winterpol didn't kill Pammy, who did?" Amy asked me.

"It looks like a whole committee," I said. "As well as Sorenson can put it together she was poisoned by the high-up muck-a-mucks at Rajneeshpuram. When Pammy got really sick or possibly once she was dead, Winterpol dumped her off the Galveston Avenue Bridge. Whether he was in on poisoning her, I don't think we'll ever know. Sorenson's trying to track down the nurse who told Pammy she was pregnant. But Pammy's diary doesn't name the nurse or provide any description. So it's pretty unlikely he can find her much less convict her of anything. He can't even prove the poison was in the bottles Shakti gave Eva to give to Pammy."

Amy pushed a potato around and cut it in two with her fork. She took another bite of the salmon.

"He left a note," I said. "Sorenson told me about it. Winterpol said he'd been a decent man, a family man, for twenty-five years and that was how he wanted his wife and daughters and his friends to remember him. He didn't want his family to sit through a trial and talk to him through bars. He didn't want them to visit him in prison. He denied that he'd murdered anyone but said that the evidence against him, circumstantial as all of it was, would probably be enough to put him away."

"Do you think he really killed Eva?" asked Amy.

"Oh, absolutely," I said, "and a jury would very likely agree."

"So my biological father was a murderer," she said.

"We are not our parents. Or our grandparents. We make our own choices." Amy looked down at her plate again and ate a little more.

"I'm lucky to be married to you," she said.

"Not as lucky as I am to be married to you." We ate slowly for a minute or two, not saying anything. Both grateful, I think, that we had each other, we had a life together, and that we weren't the kind of people who drive their lives off the rails, like their own private Amtrak accident. She was handling this pretty well, I thought. Ready for the next step.

"There is one other thing," I said.

"What is it?" said Amy warily.

"He signed the draft trust agreement Sarah sent him. Went into town and got it notarized. It leaves the land he owns next to the ranch to his children. Doesn't give their names."

"Stop it," said Amy, collapsing back in her chair with a hunted look in her eye. "You were supposed to prevent this thing, this exact thing. I told you I didn't want any part of it. None of it. I don't care how much it's worth. I don't want it. I don't want anything to do with it."

"It's your choice," I said. "I'm with you any way you want to go on this. I would point out, though, so you don't regret it later, that your share of that property is more than both of us make in a year. You sure you don't want to take the money and forget where it came from?"

"You're a selfish, greedy bastard," she said. It was the harshest thing she'd ever said to me. The worst part was she believed it, at least for the moment. I was thinking like a lawyer, looking out for his client's options. I was putting pressure on her. She had taken me seriously and she was tempted by the money herself.

"I am not going to let that man buy me off," said Amy. "He's haunted me my whole life. He's killed people."

"I understand. I agree. It should never taint our lives."

"Are we done with this subject?"

"As far as taking the money, yes we are," I said. "But you do have another choice to make."

"This thing is like a tar baby," said Amy.

"You can do nothing and assume the trustee, the bank, will never know you're his daughter and will never trouble you about it. Or you can send the bank a notarized letter saying you renounce any claim you have to the trust."

"Won't the daughters think that's strange and want to know more?"

"They may never hear about it. Or we can find twenty other people to also say they renounce any interest in the trust. You'll just be one more name on the list. The bank will think that's a little odd but since you're giving something up instead of claiming something they won't spend their time looking into it. They won't care. Winterpol's daughters won't care either and they certainly won't track down twenty people to ask them why they gave up interest in a trust that didn't even mention them."

"I want to do it," said Amy. I told her I'd set it up.

"If you ever wanted to meet your half sisters you still could," I said.

"I don't think so. And they'd be happier not knowing I exist. Certainly their mother would." We finished our dinner with marionberries we'd frozen in August. We'd practically filled the freezer with them. I washed the dishes while Amy checked her email. We snuggled in bed and read a while. We kissed good-night before we turned off the lights.

I thought Amy was more restless than usual but as far as I could tell she didn't wake up until the alarm got us up at six, early for a Saturday because we were going rock climbing at Smith Rock. If we got there early enough we might climb an east-facing area— Morning Glory if there weren't too many other climbers, Red Wall if the place was crowded. Maybe even the Lower Gorge. We had granola for breakfast and packed our bags.

We were ready to go when Amy emerged from the bathroom beaming at me steadily. She waved something at me that looked like a travel case for a toothbrush. Her smile widened as though she were advertising a new kind of toothpaste.

"We're not going rock climbing today," she said, "or for quite a while. Sorry about that. I'm pregnant." I picked her up and swung her around in a circle.

"Wow," I said, "we did it! A miracle." I was thrilled, proud, and scared to death. We had started an enormous new adventure. We and a yet-to-be-named co-conspirator. I would always remember this morning—our cheesy apartment and we two gaping at each other in our climbing clothes. We hugged each other and hung on for a very long time.

"I wish we hadn't agreed not to tell anyone," said Amy. "I want to tell everyone."

"You'll have to practice not glowing so much."

"So miracle worker," asked Amy, "what will we do today now that we're not going rock climbing?"

"We could always go for a hike," I said. "Or we could go look at houses. We're going to need one."

Chapter 32

Sarah

Jim Sorenson called to tell me that the police had found the two missing medicine bottles. They got a warrant to search Richard Winterpol's house and broke into the safe in his home office. The bottles were in there.

"The man had kept them all these years," said Jim, "one empty, one full. The empty one had a faded, hand-lettered label on it that said *B+*. The full one, labeled *B-*, contained strychnine in a solution of grain alcohol, enough to kill an NFL linebacker. We think the other bottle had strychnine in it too. Either bottle would have killed your sister."

"So was she dead or alive when she went in the water?" I asked.

"There's no way to know. We don't even know for sure that she drank the poison. But there's a limit to how far even a young Richard Winterpol could have carried her, especially through the streets of Bend, with no one questioning him. I think she must have walked most of the way from Third Street on her own two feet. She would have been in pretty poor shape when she hit the pond or she would have gotten out of her backpack and swum away."

"Was her death painful, assuming she drank the bottle?"

"It could have been worse, but, yes, it would have been painful. Strychnine doesn't put you to sleep. It makes your muscles contract, especially in response to stimuli like bright lights or a loud noise.

It starts in your arms and legs and moves to your back. That may be why her skeleton was bent backwards when we found her. After convulsing the back, the strychnine moves to the muscles you need to breathe. They clench up and you die from lack of oxygen. So it's not as bad as being burned alive or dying from pancreatic cancer without anesthetic. But the convulsions are no fun.

"But if Pammy drank the whole bottle," Jim went on, "she would have been drunk as well as poisoned. The strychnine was dissolved in alcohol. It might have dulled the pain a little."

"Poor Pammy! How long did this go on for her?"

"The lab says about twenty minutes."

"Was Eva in on it?" I asked. "Did she know the bottles were poison?"

"Probably not, I think," said Jim. "Eva and Pammy were friends according to Pammy's diary. And Eva was leaving the place. I can't see her having enough dedication to Rajneeshpuram or Shakti to help kill her friend. You've met Eva and I never did. Did she look like she could kill someone?"

"She was dishonest and manipulative," I said. "She took advantage of people. But I don't see where she set out to injure people for the sake of injuring them. And she could calculate the odds. I can't think she had a reason to help kill Pammy that would be worth the risk of getting caught. Besides, when Amy Martinez met with her, Eva believed Pammy might still be alive."

"Which leaves the question of whether Richard knew about the poison," said Jim.

"It's easier to believe he could kill someone," I said. "He killed Eva. He may have killed Shakti. But I don't see why he would participate in killing Pammy. If she told him she was pregnant he could have simply abandoned her, gone off to God knows where. As far as I can see, this was all Shakti's idea, or maybe Devya's or even Bhagwan's.

"But I still don't get," I went on, "why Winterpol kept the bottles all these years."

"If he hadn't killed Shakti himself," said Jim, "he might not know Shakti was dead. Maybe he kept the bottles to prove that Shakti had planned Pammy's murder. The bottles would be evidence. Or maybe he kept the bottles to remind himself that Pammy wanted to keep the baby, assuming she told him about it. In the midst of all this murder and mayhem it's possible he really loved her. You know, he might have been on his way to your parents' house to tell them he wanted to marry her."

"I have trouble believing that," I said. But I had to acknowledge to myself that it was a possibility. Who knew what the two of them were thinking back then? Reason and rationality were not going to get me to the answers. Richard and Pammy had not been thinking rationally themselves.

"There is not much more we could discover," said Jim. "I talked with Jocelyn in the DA's office about the nurse who told Pammy she was pregnant. Maybe your sister was pregnant and maybe she wasn't. But for Shakti's little plot to work the nurse had to tell Pammy she was bearing a child. That nurse would have been an accomplice, witting or unwitting, to the murder. The district attorney doesn't want to pursue it. We could never convict this nurse once we found her. She could say she doesn't remember Pammy. That would be the end of it. Nobody left alive knows what Shakti told this nurse or how much the nurse might have known about the poison or the murder."

It bothered me to think of leaving this person off the hook. But Jim was right. We'd never have enough evidence to charge her. And, possibly, she never knew the implications of what she told Pammy. Finally, if Pammy truly was pregnant, which we couldn't disprove from the skeleton, the nurse would have been telling Pammy the truth.

"We'll never know how to divide up the guilt for Pammy's death," I said.

"You're right," said Jim. "But whether they are guilty a little or a lot, the principals in this crime are all dead—Shakti, Eva, Richard Winterpol. None of them lived to old age. There's some justice in that. Even Bhagwan, with all his enlightenment, only lived to fifty-eight."

"Devya," I said.

"Looking over her shoulder every day," said Jim, "wondering if Shakti's killer or someone else is coming to get her."

"Case closed?" I asked.

"Case closed," said Jim. "We'll never pin this on Devya. Everyone who could testify against her is gone. There's no one else left to prosecute." Jim looked me in the eye. I nodded to show I agreed. The case was closed.

"But you and I are not done," Jim went on. "There's still Floyd Tingley and the murder of your husband. The district attorney may ask me to help. But it pretty much comes down to the confession that Dan got from Floyd. There's not a lot I can add."

"Well, thanks, Jim, for all your help with Pammy."

"Justice served," he said. "That's the business we're in." We said goodbye.

I buried Pammy in Pilot Butte cemetery, in a plot Ray and I had with four gravesites in it. Edgar Manning signed a letter from the Fort Rock Indians saying they released any and all claims they might have on the remains. Two men from the funeral home had placed Pammy's child-sized casket on a frame that would lower it into the grave and they left the moment I arrived. I hired a retired minister who had known my parents to come and say a simple service. I paid him and made a donation to First United Methodist. It was just the minister and me but he wore a black suit with a clerical collar. I wore a sleeveless black dress with a lavender pashmina to cover my arms. The minister knew how to lower Pammy's casket. When I tossed in a shovelful of dirt we said a cordial goodbye and he said what a nice day it was.

Ray and I had hoped never to need graves for our children and, now that they were grown, we wouldn't. Pammy and Ray, who had hardly known each other in life, lay near to each other with a grave left between them for me, hopefully not needed for a long time to come. I didn't imagine we'd be having afterlife conversations down there. But our bodies were part of who we were and it gave me some irrational comfort that we would be near each other. I mentally reintroduced Ray and Pammy before I walked the short distance over to my parents' graves.

"I found Pammy," I told them silently. "She was on her way home. She's lying near you." I had no illusion they could hear me but it did me good to say it. I got in my car and drove home. Back to my own life, to count myself lucky, and to make what I could of it.

As I changed into slacks and sweatshirt I realized I was tired of being the avenging angel. I'd done what I could for Pammy. Two people, Eva Keefer and Richard Winterpol, were dead thanks to me. Winterpol's death served justice, I thought, and he had chosen to shuffle off this mortal coil by himself. If he left his wife and children without a husband and a father it was his choice, not anyone else's.

I didn't exactly mourn Eva's passing either. She was a dishonest, selfish, and irresponsible person. If nothing else she could have sent Pammy's diary to my parents years ago. Yet the cause of justice did not cry out for the death of Eva Keefer. As far as I knew she hadn't killed anyone.

Floyd Tingley cried out for imprisonment, not only for his crimes but to protect others, including me, from his committing another crime. I felt certain he would be convicted of Ray's murder. He would spend all of his twenties and most of his thirties in jail. No ranch, no freedom, no wife and children. I could almost feel sorry for him. But he meant to kill me. He had killed Ray. The law, established over centuries and going back to before the Bible, decreed that people must pay for their crimes.

It was time to move on. I hadn't seen Bud Russell since we met at the concert and hadn't talked with him since we set up our dinner date. It was just as well because until we got the real story on Pammy's death I had an uneasy feeling that he might have had something to do with it. Now that I knew he hadn't I was free to anticipate seeing him again.

I felt an anxiety about him that I hadn't sensed since high school, fainter now and tempered with experience, but recognizable nonetheless. What other emotions lay dormant within me that might be reawakened?

I was nervous about how I would look and what I would wear. But I thought to myself, *Oh, come on, what would you have worn to go out to dinner with Ray?* At least my clothes still fit. The house looked neat and clean. If he didn't like my taste that was too bad.

I had coffee and ice cream ready if he came inside after dinner. I pictured us sitting in my living room, comfortable, and having a nice chat. Then maybe we'd kiss good-night with a long, richly savored hug. Sex would not be in the cards. We'd have to know each other a lot better before we exposed our old and imperfect bodies to one another.

The doorbell rang an hour ahead of the time we'd set. Bud's early arrival was annoying, I thought, though I was basically ready. It would be a bad start to our date. But I could handle this. I could show him how poised I was.

It wasn't Bud. It was a woman, my age, in jeans and a purple blouse. She'd worked on her gray hair but hadn't hired a professional.

"I need to ask you something," she said. "May I come in for a minute?" I thought she must be a neighbor. She seemed pleasant enough.

"I'm just about to go out," I said, "but if it won't take long then come on in. Pleased to meet you. I'm Sarah Chatham." The woman came through the little front hall and into the living room before she answered.

"I'm Marilyn Tingley," she said, "and I want to ask you, politely but sincerely, mother to mother, to stop persecuting my son. Floyd is a good boy. He works hard. He's going to graduate from college. And I need him to keep our ranch going. I won't be able to do it without him. And he shouldn't have to waste his life in prison."

This was the woman who had raised her son, indoctrinated him, to murder me. The idiot son who had murdered my husband by mistake. My muscles seized up in anger. I wanted to point to the door and march her out of my house, pushing her firmly to hurry her. But I stood there frozen long enough for my forty-five years of legal training to whisper in my ear there was a better way.

"This is the same good boy who murdered my husband?" I asked.

222

"That's not true," she said, trying to remain calm but with a touch of anger creeping into her voice. "It was an accident. He didn't mean to hurt anyone."

"The court will decide whether it was murder or an accident."

"Only if you push it. If you told the court that you think it was an accident, or that you think Floyd was only trying to scare you, I know it would make a difference."

"The prosecutor and the court are bound to enforce the law, no matter what I say. And they may not even have me testify."

"But you could influence them," Marilyn said in a harder voice, "and you know it."

"Tell me, Mrs. Tingley, would you forgive the person who murdered your husband?"

"My husband wasn't murdered."

"If you loved your husband as much as I loved mine, losing him was the worst thing that ever happened to you."

"It was. But—"

I interrupted her. I was still angry and knowing I was losing my cool made me even more upset. Here was this evil woman in the middle of my living room, a witch who led her son to murder my husband.

My own voice rose a notch. "How can you stand there and ask me to forgive the man who murdered my husband?"

"Floyd was only eighteen when that happened. Whether it was an accident or he was trying to scare you, it was a mistake."

My lawyer brain clicked into gear.

"Did he tell you he was planning to scare me?"

"Talking about doing something and actually doing it are two different things," she said. So maybe she knew of what Floyd was planning to do. A jury might even be persuaded she was a co-conspirator.

"Did you warn the police or anyone else about what Floyd might do?"

"I didn't know what he was going to do."

"If you even had a hint of what he was planning you could be charged as an accomplice in his crime. I don't forgive him and I don't forgive you. You brought him up to seek revenge over something that happened before he was born."

"Do you have no sympathy at all?" said Marilyn. "Not even a drop of Christian charity? How can you sleep at night? A person like you must make enemies wherever you go. It would serve you right if someday someone did kill you."

I thought her statement could be considered a threat and I wished there were someone in the house to hear it besides me. But I could remember what she said and testify to it. An imminent threat would be even more damning and I thought I might goad her into it. "Do you have a weapon in your purse?" I asked. Her purse was plenty big enough for a .45 or a hunting knife.

"It's none of your business what's in my purse."

That could sound threatening, I thought. Maybe I could get Marilyn Tingley to commit extortion as well. "Look," I said, "I don't want to worry every day that it might be the day you're going to kill me. I don't think you want to go to jail yourself. You said one problem was you needed your son to run the ranch. What if I paid you fifty thousand a year for every year your son is in jail? That would pay for a foreman with cash leftover. Would you promise not to hurt me or threaten me?"

"I don't want my son to go to jail at all," she said. Nuts, I thought to myself. No extortion. I stared straight at Marilyn and summoned up my most authoritative courtroom voice.

"I need to tell you, Mrs. Tingley, how much trouble you're in already. You've come to my house and threatened me. You can be prosecuted for four separate crimes under Oregon law—menacing me, harassing me, stalking me, and, given that I may be called to testify, for tampering with a witness. From what you've said, you might be charged with criminal liability for encouraging your son to commit this crime. If you threaten me again in any way you'll wind up in jail yourself." Marilyn glared at me for a minute before she spoke. I thought she might reach in her purse and pull out a weapon after all. I was ready to dive, as well as I could, behind the sofa.

"You are Satan's whore, Sarah Chatham, and I wish you Godspeed on your way to hell."

"Is that a new threat, Mrs. Tingley?" She turned and walked out, leaving the door wide open. I shut it firmly behind her.

I'd given Marilyn Tingley some things to worry about, though I doubted the court would really buy any of it. Menacing requires a threat of imminent, immediate danger. Harassment doesn't apply to face-to-face conversations—it has to be written or said over the phone. As for stalking—she was only here once. Tampering with a witness would be a stretch. But now that I thought of it, on Monday I would petition the court for a restraining order to keep her away from me. Even if the judge didn't grant the order the petition would be on file. And I'd tell Sorenson about Marilyn's visit and send her a letter saying that I'd spoken with the police. She'd know if anything happened to me the police would look at her and her son with a microscope before they looked at anyone else.

After that I thought Mrs. Tingley would stay as far away from me as she could get. As much as she might hate me, her first loyalties were to her ranch and to her son. And of course, her own freedom. I rested my eyes on the brass chandelier in the dining room. Ray and I had chosen it together. "I'm done with lawyer mode for now," I said to myself. "Back to trying to be a happy person with a nice dinner ahead of her." The doorbell rang and I checked the peephole before I opened up. It was Bud Russell. It was, possibly, the next chapter in my life.

Chapter 33

Jim

S ometimes hard work pays off. Sometimes it doesn't. And sometimes the solution waltzes in the door out of the blue. The answer to the Sharon Forrester case walked into police headquarters
in handcuffs. The patrolman arrested a woman named Mary Jane
Campbell for three grams of cocaine. She wanted a lawyer, a specific
lawyer, Dan Martinez. The booking officer told her he wasn't a criminal attorney and Martinez told her the same thing over the phone.
But she wanted Martinez. Mary Jane and her husband, Brad Campbell, were Martinez's next door neighbors in an apartment building and he was the lawyer she knew. Martinez brought Tod Morgan
with him, a criminal attorney who visited the jail all the time.

Mary Jane told them she had information on a very old case, a
murder, and she hoped to bargain herself down to a walk on the
drug possession. Thanks to a recent change in Oregon law, which
saved us all of lot of trouble, under two grams of cocaine was a
misdemeanor for first offenders. But Mary Jane was caught with
three grams. It was a felony. Tod told her they should at least get the
charge down to a misdemeanor and the maximum time down from
five years to one. We had a meeting in the district attorney's office
with Jocelyn about it. Jocelyn had me come with the files from the
1962 investigation.

Mary Jane brought her mother, Linda Birchel, to corroborate her story. She had to. Mary Jane wasn't even born when Sharon Forrester was killed. Linda Birchel, the mother, was an innocent-looking little gray-haired lady of about seventy-five.

"My uncle killed Sharon Forrester," said Mary Jane. "His name was Randy and he was four years older than his sister, my mom. Randy didn't set out to kill Sharon but he did. He told my grandparents about it and I guess they walked around in a daze for a week. Then Mom, who was only a girl back then, put enough pieces together and asked Randy to tell her what happened. He decided he had to tell her because she was a girl. He didn't want something like that to happen to her."

"Is this true and are you willing to testify to it under oath?" Jocelyn asked Linda.

"Yes. It's completely true," said Linda, "and I'll testify."

The story was incomplete. I asked Linda, "What were they doing in the park together on a cold night in February?"

"He told Sharon he had some marijuana to give her if she would meet him in the park," said Linda. "Then he asked for something in return, which I suppose was some kind of sex. He didn't tell me much about that part. She said no and he hit her. He said he knew he hurt her but she walked off under her own power. He didn't know until the next morning that she died. He felt terrible about it."

"What did he hit her with?" I asked.

"I don't know," said Linda. "He didn't say."

"The police found a piece of two-by-four with Sharon's hair and blood on it. Do you know where Randy would have gotten it or why he would have taken it to his meeting with Sharon?"

"No idea," said Linda, a little annoyed that, after the revelation she and her daughter had delivered, I was asking for information she didn't have. "Bend was a lumber town then, Detective," she said with a tone of condescension. "There was no shortage of two-by-fours." I let it pass but I didn't think the town or the park had been littered with scrap lumber.

"And where is your brother now?" I asked.

THE MIRROR POND MURDERS

"He died three years later. In Vietnam. Ia Drang."

I remembered reading about Ia Drang. It was the first battle with the North Vietnamese Regular Army. Though the US forces were ambushed, nine North Vietnamese died for every one American. Our generals decided we could win the war with that "kill ratio." The trouble was the North Vietnamese decided if it took nine of theirs to kill one of ours it was worth the price. The war went on for ten more years.

"I'm sorry your brother died," I said. And I was sorry. Doubly sorry. Sorry for Linda Birchel's loss and more sorry Randy wasn't around to answer for his crime.

"And your family decided not to tell the police all these years?" I asked.

"My parents didn't see any point in telling the police," said Linda. "Sharon wasn't coming back. Why ruin another young life, my brother's, for nothing? Besides, he didn't mean to kill her."

Technically, I thought, Linda could be charged as an accessory after the fact for covering up her brother's crime. But no jury would convict her and no judge would sentence her.

Jocelyn turned to me and asked whether Mary Jane and Linda had convinced me. Was I was ready to close the Sharon Forrester case? I said their statements were plausible but I wanted to run it by the detective who was on the case at the time. Mary Jane was disappointed she was going back to jail until I contacted Fred Karlsen. Actually, I thought things were looking pretty good for Mary Jane and she should be happy.

I called Fred to tell him what I'd learned.

"Never looked at Randy," said my predecessor, "but we thought it could be someone like him, someone Sharon's age who thought she was giving it away and why shouldn't he get some. I can't tell you that he's the last piece of the puzzle and it all fits together perfectly. But it makes sense. It's probably true. I can tell you this. If I'd heard about Randy in 1962, I sure would have arrested the man and I'd bet he would have been convicted." Fred thanked me for that call but his mind was still running laps. He would call me later with a critical detail.

The chief appeared in my cubicle two weeks after we found Eva in Prineville Reservoir. He wore his uniform in the office, carrying his extra weight around as though it were an easy load. He knew police work top to bottom but he spent most of his time, I knew, dealing with budgets, personnel, and most importantly, city politicians and the public.

"Eva Keefer died in Prineville," he said. He announced it as a statement of fact. I didn't ask him how he knew she died in Prineville. I was sure he didn't know. None of us knew and, with Richard Winterpol gone, I didn't expect we'd ever know for sure. So instead of asking the chief how he knew Eva died in Prineville, I asked him why. Why did it matter whether she died in Prineville?

"Statistics," he said. "The crime rate is low in Bend. Some years nobody murders anybody. The Visit Bend people want to keep it that way. Eva Keefer was not murdered in Bend."

"What about Ray Chatham and Pamela Paulsen?" I asked. "They were killed in Bend."

"Long ago," said the chief. "Let's focus on this year."

"Okay," I said, thinking the chief of police in Prineville didn't want Eva's murder on his ledger either. "My report says we don't know where Eva Keefer was killed. I'll take that out."

"She wasn't murdered in Bend," he said, "for sure and certain."

"I'll use all the best facts," I said. The chief ignored my prevarication. He knew I'd gotten his message.

"And get the medical examiner on board," he said. I nodded.

I could easily slant my report while sticking to the facts. The last time anyone had seen Eva in Bend, she'd driven away from her house in the late evening in her own car, under her own steam, and by herself. Though she was almost certainly in her car when it was buried on Winterpol's ranch, the next time anyone actually saw her was when we pulled her out of Prineville Reservoir. The reservoir was outside of the Prineville city limits, in Crook County. Even better, the reservoir belonged to the Federal Bureau of Reclamation, part of the Department of the Interior. If we all played our cards right, Eva's death would be part of a federal statistic and all of Central Oregon would be that much safer by the numbers.

As far as Bend was concerned, Eva wasn't murdered here, she disappeared from here. Her turning up dead was secondary.

By my calculation Eva was not, in fact, murdered in Bend. The day she was last seen alive, Winterpol had called her on his cell phone. We got the call record. They talked for three minutes, enough time to set up a meeting but not enough to hash out all they might have to talk about. Winterpol would want to avoid killing Eva in her own house, getting the body out to her car, and then driving all the way to his ranch with the risks of being pulled over, getting in an accident, or having Eva's old car break down. He would want Eva to drive over to see him, probably at the used car lot he still owned. Maybe he promised her money.

The Crook County medical examiner said no one could tell from Eva's body where and when she had been killed. Eva was dead at least five days before she was hauled out of the reservoir. She'd been buried for part of that time and been underwater for at least a day. She'd been garroted but not assaulted, sexually or otherwise. No poisons, drugs, or alcohol. That was all the ME could say.

Once I finished making my final changes to the report on Eva, I stretched back my arms and took a minute to look out the window and admire the mountains, one of the perks of the job. I could see tops of maples starting to turn red above the downtown buildings. The phone interrupted my reverie. It was Fred Karlsen.

"I have a surprise for you," he said in his rough and rumbling voice. "I tracked down Sharon Forrester's brother. He left here years ago to be a fishing guide in Wyoming. Now he sells real estate in Pinedale. He's still a country boy, he says, has a little place on the Green River where he runs a handful of cattle. He can walk out his door and go fishing in the river. Wife and grown children. His daughter is some kind of banker in Hollywood. When the winters get rough, he and his wife go visit the daughter, name is Caitlin, and sit by the pool."

I hoped Fred would get to the point and, after his admiration of life in Wyoming and California, he did.

"I told Larry, that's his name, Larry Forrester, what Linda Birchel told you. That Linda Birchel's brother, Randy, was the one who killed Sharon. And you know what he said?"

I waited.

"He said Linda Birchel told him that forty years ago. Called him up. Wanted him to know. Why the hell didn't Linda tell the police? I was still working then. It would have been nice to find out. For that matter, why didn't Larry tell the police?"

"Did you ask him?"

"Sure did. He said he thought we already knew. And in any case, he said, it didn't matter. Sharon wasn't going to come back from the dead. And her killer, Linda Birchel's brother, was dead too, killed in Vietnam."

"You've seen this kind of thing before," I said, "and so have I. Sometimes the public cares and sometimes they don't. You've got the police and the courts trying to do the right thing and people don't even notice if the wheels come off."

"We keep trying," said Fred.

"We do," I said.

Fred's story made me thankful for Sarah Chatham. She wanted justice. She worked for it. Sarah cared a lot if the wheels came off.

~~~

Mirror Pond Extras

We hope you enjoyed *The Mirror Pond* Murders. You can find photos of settings used in the book and thirteen poems by selected characters at www.tedhaynes.com/mpx.html

Acknowledgments

I am greatly indebted to my editor, Caroline Tolley, and to my brother, Jared Haynes, whose clear and insightful counsels contributed immensely to making this a better and more exciting book. Major credits go to my copy editor, Amy Knupp, who did so much to make *Mirror Pond* a pleasure to read (I think) and a book I can be proud of.

My early readers waded through typos to recommend numerous excellent improvements. I am deeply grateful to Deon Stonehouse, Joann Holder, Trish Smith, Barb Tate, and to my first reader and number one fan, my wife, Joan Stafford Haynes.

Thanks to Jim Crowell, Bend historian, who alerted me to the true story on which the fictional murder of Sharon Forrester is based and to Andrea Dupree, who added to the story.

Sources

The following books and one documentary were essential to the writing of *The Mirror Pond Murders*.

Dreisbach, Robert H. *Handbook of Poisoning, Diagnosis & Treatment.* Ninth Edition. Los Altos, CA: Lange Medical Publications 1977

Franklin, Satya Bharti. *The Promise of Paradise, A Woman's Intimate Story of the Perils of Life with Rajneesh.* Barrytown, NY: Station Hill Literary Editions 1992

Gordon, James S. *The Golden Guru.* Lexington, MA: The Stephen Green Press 1987

Osho. *Zorba the Buddha.* New Delhi, India: Niyogi Books 2013 (originally published in 1982. Bhagwan Shree Rajneesh adopted the name Osho after leaving Rajneeshpuram)

Stork, Jane. *Breaking the Spell, My life as a Rajneeshee and the long journey back to freedom.* Sydney, Australia: Pan MacMillan Australia Pty Limited 2009

Watts, Alan. *Rock Climbing Smith Rock State Park.* Lanham, MD: Rowman & Littlefield 2010

Wild Wild Country. Directed by Chapman Way and Maclain Way. Los Angeles, CA: Duplass Brothers Productions (a documentary on Rajneeshpuram for Netflix), 2018

Notes – Fact and Fiction

Bend, Oregon is a very real, growing, and beautiful place. Many Bend settings appear in this book—Mirror Pond, the Deschutes River, Drake Park, downtown Bend, the Bend Police Department Headquarters, the Les Schwab Amphitheater, Pilot Butte, Pilot Butte Cemetery, and Awbrey Butte.

The eclipse that Dan and Amy watch from Sean and Grace Wray's house took place as described on August 21, 2017, as did the Symbiosis Gathering in the Ochoco Forest.

The book's representation of Rajneeshpuram and the sudden departure of its top management does not stray far from historical fact, though all of the book's characters at Rancho Rajneesh and elsewhere (except Bhagwan Shree Rajneesh who is used fictionally) are fictional.

Upriver Ranch is an imaginary community that combines features of Crosswater, Vandevert Ranch, and Sunriver.

Fort Rock and Christmas Valley are actual locations. But the Confederated Tribes of Fort Rock, their reservation, and their casino are imaginary.

The ingestible sensor technology ascribed to Amy's employer, Greenwood Biomedical, derives from products developed by Proteus Digital Health (www.proteus.com)

About the Author

Ted Haynes is the author of *Suspects* and other works of both fiction and non-fiction. He has studied creative writing at Dartmouth College, UC Berkeley, and Stanford University. He and his wife spend their summers on the Little Deschutes River, near Bend, and their winters near San Francisco. Ted is a member of the Deschutes County Historical Society, the Central Oregon Writers Guild, and Mystery Writers of America. He is a founding board member of the Waterston Prize for Desert Writing, located in Bend.

CPSIA information can be obtained
at www.ICGtesting.com
Printed in the USA
LVHW020055180722
723713LV00002B/148